A Future of Her Own

SAMANTHA QUAMMA

Black Rose Writing | Texas

First printing

ISBN: 978-1-68513-547-8
LIBRARY OF CONGRESS CONTROL NUMBER: 2024943553
PUBLISHED BY BLACK ROSE WRITING
www.blackrosewriting.com

Printed in the United States of America
Suggested Retail Price (SRP) $23.95

A Future of Her Own is printed in Minion Pro

Cover photo by Berezko/iStock

*As a planet-friendly publisher, Black Rose Writing does its best to eliminate unnecessary waste to reduce paper usage and energy costs, while never compromising the reading experience. As a result, the final word count vs. page count may not meet common expectations.

PRAISE FOR *A FUTURE OF HER OWN*

"Ramona steps into college life bright-eyed and hopeful, but she soon discovers the outrageous restrictions of 1960s' society and collegiate life limit women like her, and she decides to fight back. We watch Ramona grow into a brave, moraled young woman who won't let anyone use her gender to hold her down."
–Kerry Chaput, award-winning author of the *Defying the Crown* series

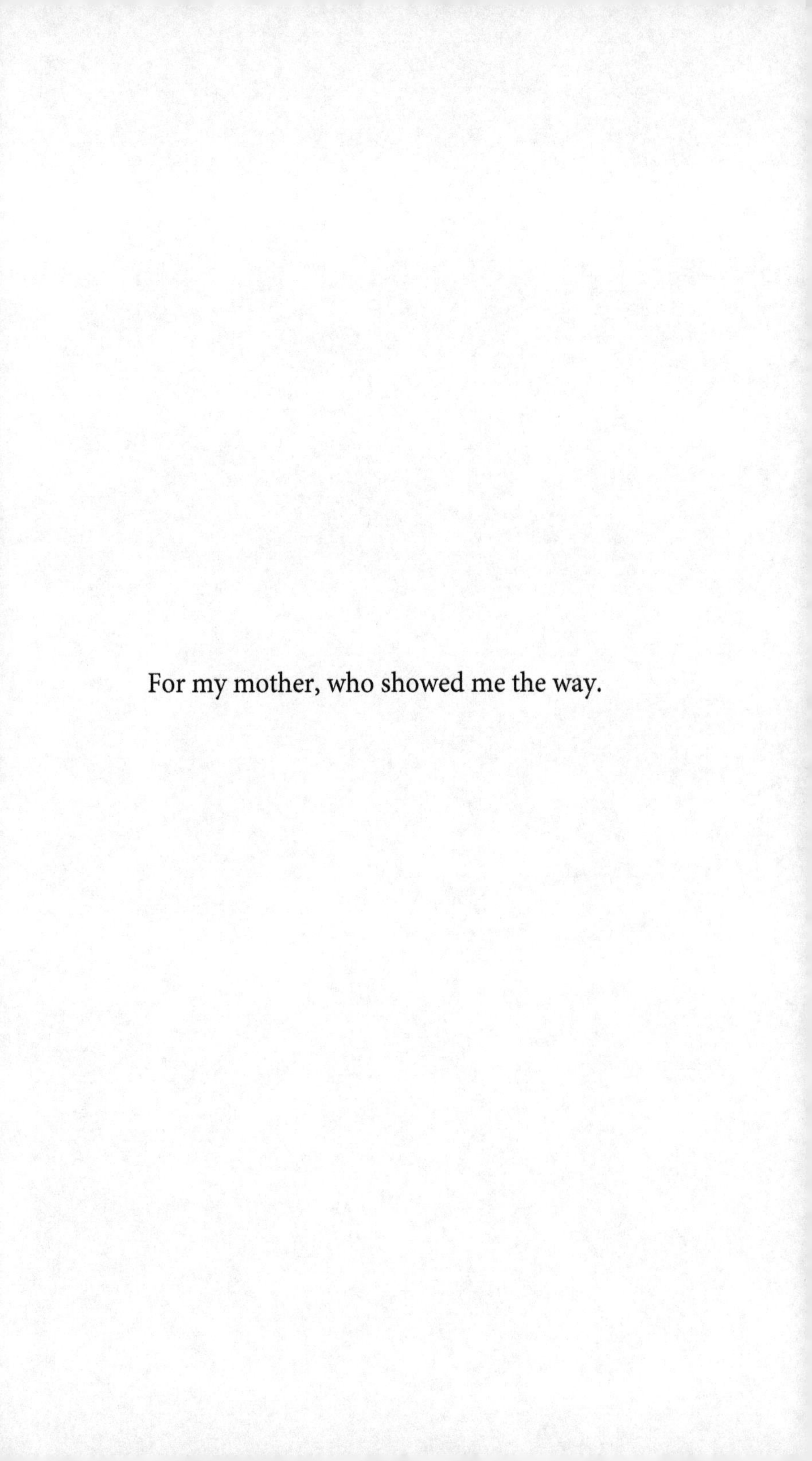

For my mother, who showed me the way.

A Future of Her Own

CHAPTER 1

During a rare free moment, Ramona peeked into her apron pocket. She set a goal for every shift and frowned as she counted two one-dollar bills and a handful of change. She was short … by a lot. It had been an unusually slow afternoon at Dusty's Drive-In, and it showed in the tips.

Time seemed to pass at half speed without the usual chaos to distract her. She rubbed her thumb across a nickel, trying not to think of tomorrow. She'd been looking forward to her first day of university for so long that it had become the anchor point against which she categorized all other events. Before university. After university.

"Stop counting your tips."

Her boss's voice penetrated the quiet back hallway and Ramona jumped.

"Randy." Ramona held a hand to her heart. "You scared me."

"Yeah, well, it doesn't look right to count your tips with customers around. What if someone comes back here for the bathroom? Wait until your break like the rest of us."

Ramona sighed and dropped the coins back into her pocket, knowing that Randy was right. Dusty's, a diner housed in a round building just off Interstate 5, was a local favorite with lots of regulars who tipped well. Mostly, at least. That's what made this gig so good.

The bell rang from the kitchen and Bobby, a line cook sporting the thickest mustache Ramona had ever seen, shouted, "Number 58."

"That's mine," Ramona said before smoothing out the wrinkles in her blouse and slipping past Randy.

She scooped up the order, and as she'd done thousands of times before, Ramona carried the plastic tray from the kitchen to a car of hungry customers. Above, a large, fluorescent-orange sign advertised the best burgers in town. That neon glow starred in her dreams.

As Ramona moved between cars, taking orders and dropping off seemingly endless burgers dripping with greasy cheese, she appreciated the breeze against her legs. For now, they enjoyed the tail end of summer on this warm September night that refused to cool. Only during weather like this did Ramona feel grateful for the uniform. More often though, she considered arguing with Randy about the white-collared, short-sleeve blouse and skirt combination. It was a ridiculous uniform during three out of the four seasons in western Washington. While she was quite certain that Randy wouldn't fire her over something as trivial as an opinion, she didn't dare raise the matter, just in case.

Roy Orbison crooned about a pretty woman from the speakers just as Ramona took an order from one of her regulars, Jeff. He scanned her legs as he muttered, "And speak of the devil herself."

It took a herculean effort to keep her face neutral as Ramona wrote down his request for chili fries.

"Are you going to accept my offer one of these days?" Jeff stretched to rest a meaty forearm on the car's windowsill.

Ramona scoffed, as she did every time he brought up this line of questioning.

"Are you referring to your offer of marriage?" Ramona asked before adopting a teasing tone. "Because I'm still half your age, and the answer is still no."

Jeff, just like the many other men who thought these remarks were compliments, was old enough to be the father she didn't know. He raised a hand to his chest as though she'd shot him, and honestly, she'd imagined doing so more than once. Although Jeff framed it as a joke, she had the sense that his tune would change if she said yes. Still, she didn't want to offend a customer or come off as a spoilsport.

"Hey miss?" A young voice pulled her attention, and she gratefully left Jeff behind.

A kid leaned halfway out of the backseat window of a powder-blue Ford Mustang and waved to her. Amused, Ramona walked over. She rested a hand on her hip and waited.

"Can I have a strawberry milkshake?" The kid grinned from ear to ear. "Please!"

Ramona looked at his parents for confirmation. Plenty of kids made orders that their parents didn't want to pay for. When the woman in the front seat nodded, Ramona said, "Sure thing, kid. I'll be right back."

When Ramona dropped off the milkshake a few minutes later, after she'd put an extra cherry atop the whipped cream, she chuckled at the kid's eager expression. He swallowed a mouthful of French fries and grabbed for the cup, guzzling the milkshake as though someone threatened to take it. As he neared the halfway point, quicker than Ramona thought possible, the kid slowed and then stopped drinking.

His eyebrows fixed together before his eyes widened in alarm.

"I don't feel so good."

A split second later, the kid vomited strawberry milkshake, and Ramona stood in range. She felt the wet impact across her stomach with a thwack before the smell hit.

"Oh God," Ramona yelped, covering her nose with her hands to keep from gagging.

In the front seat, the parents stared as if they'd been hypnotized before the woman blurted, "Jimmy!" and then, "I'm so sorry, he's so sorry."

Ramona tried to shrug, adding a muffled, "It's okay."

But it wasn't. A wave of nausea rolled through her, and she ran straight for the bathroom, locking herself inside. Grabbing a wad of paper towels, she spent the next few minutes scrubbing her blouse and gagging until all that remained was a pale-pink stain that smelled like hand soap. *Goddamn kids.*

As clean as she could be without a shower, Ramona watched her shoulders droop in the mirror. Things like this happened a lot. Customers spilled on her as though she were a part of the background. She washed her hands once more, taking care to scrub her fingernails, before facing Dusty's again.

When Ramona went back outside with a handful of napkins and their bill, the kid slumped on the back seat, and the parents looked guiltier than sinners as they paid.

"Thank you for these," the mother said as she accepted the napkins. "I'm terribly sorry."

Ramona forced a closed-mouth smile as she watched the Mustang pull out of the parking lot. Ignoring Randy's warning, she counted her tip. It was generous. Maybe the money was worth the gross experience. At least now, she had another excuse to object to the uniforms if Randy ever asked.

During the remaining hour of her shift, Ramona pictured herself working a better job. A life of steady paychecks rather than unpredictable tips from temperamental customers. A life where she could take care of herself and help her mother too. A college degree unlocked that possibility. A wave of anxiety rolled through her. Anticipation and nerves were two sides of the same coin, weren't they? High stakes and all that come with them.

Her shift now over, Ramona cleaned out her apron pocket, depositing her tips in her purse and a clump of napkins in the trash, before hanging it up behind the counter. She couldn't wait to take off her uniform the minute she got home.

Randy looked up from the cash register where he tinkered with the tray. "Hey Ramona, hang on a minute, will you?"

"Sure," Ramona said as she adjusted her purse strap more securely on her shoulder, her feet aimed toward the door.

As he concentrated, Randy's forehead bunched in such defined rolls that his skin resembled a row of pale worms. He didn't look up as he said, "I need to switch you back to the night shift starting tomorrow."

"What?" Ramona stiffened.

"Mary-Sue just quit. Apparently, she's getting *married.*" His eyes fluttered on the last word.

Ramona's stomach sank. She'd begged all the day-shift waitresses to switch with her, and Mary-Sue had been the only one to agree after more pleading than Ramona would like to recall.

"You know I can't work the night shift anymore, Randy. I start at university tomorrow, and the curfew's midnight."

Dusty's closed at midnight, and that didn't include the cleaning needed to close up or the half-hour drive to campus. Ramona typically worked three shifts a week, usually Wednesdays, Fridays, and Sundays. When she'd been admitted to the university, she'd received a partial academic scholarship, and from then on, all of her earnings went toward the rest of her tuition and living expenses. Even so, they were still short, and her mother helped by picking up extra shifts at the hospital where she worked at the front desk. Her mother already worked hard enough, alone in providing for her, and Ramona refused to ask for anything more.

"I don't know what to tell you, kid." He shrugged. "Nights are busier than days, and that's when I need a waitress. You want to work? You're working nights."

Without this job, and the tips, they couldn't afford her tuition. She would be the first person in her family to go to college … Ramona Bronson, a freshman at one of the most prestigious universities in Washington. And in four years, or earlier if she pushed herself hard enough, she'd graduate with a degree. From there, Ramona would have her pick of careers and the financial freedom that eluded her mother since she'd gotten pregnant at seventeen. The security glimmered like a mirage. She couldn't remember wanting anything more. Now Randy, and Mary-Sue in her engagement glory, threatened to ruin it.

"Fine," Ramona muttered through clenched lips. "Put me back on the night shift. I'll be here tomorrow."

"Glad to hear it."

Randy's attention returned to the register. Ramona tightened her fists as she left the diner. She hurried to her car, a beat-up VW Beetle she'd bought from her neighbor for cheap when she'd saved up enough tips that summer.

"Shit!" Ramona gripped the frame of the car. "Shit, shit, shit."

She held on until her fingers turned white and forced in a deep breath. She needed to think.

Ramona got into her car and pressed on the gas pedal, speeding out of the parking lot and rolling down the windows to welcome the cool air in. Her dark curls whipped around her head. How strictly would the curfew be enforced anyway? She'd find out soon enough.

***

A banner hung above the entryway of Wolden Hall, welcoming students to the fall term of '65. The dormitory was an impressive brick building, the stuff of collegiate dreams, and Ramona's spirits lifted at the sight of it. Students and their families hustled in and out, carrying suitcases and boxes full of clothes, books, and bedding—anything and everything needed to achieve academic success. Her chest swelled with pride to be among them.

She watched her new neighbors until a bead of sweat formed between her breasts and reminded her that she may not be finished herself. Moving into her room on the second floor had required more trips up and down the flights of stairs than she'd anticipated, and her back ached. Ramona strode past a neat row of tables lining the path, each advertising one club or another, craning her neck for a glimpse of her mother.

If they finished within the next hour, and it took her another to get ready and drive to her waitressing shift, Ramona could squeeze in a twelve-minute break … a break to rest her would-be-sore-tomorrow body. But more likely, sitting still would allow the dread that had robbed her of sleep the night before to re-emerge. Ten hours remained until the female-only campus curfew, at which point she would still be miles away at work. No, she wouldn't rest. Better to keep moving.

"Hello there!" A voice singsonged so close that Ramona couldn't ignore it.

A girl wearing a pastel-pink, collared blouse wiggled her fingers at Ramona to come closer. She stood behind a table filled with neat stacks of red handbooks, each the size of a Nancy Drew novel.

"What's your name?"

Confused and curious, Ramona answered. The girl consulted her list before making a note and handing over one of the handbooks.

Ramona stilled. There, on the cover, printed in swooping letters, was her name. *How strange.* She considered the handbook as though it might bite.

"Gee, thanks," Ramona said, knowing that she couldn't possibly leave it at that. "This looks cool."

The sun glared, and Ramona pulled her sunglasses, an old pair of her mother's, down from her head. She lifted her damp T-shirt from where it clung to her skin.

"It's your handbook! As a member of the Associated Women Students, you get your very own copy," the girl gushed.

"But I didn't sign up for anything."

The girl giggled, making Ramona feel entirely out of place. "Silly you. You don't have to sign up! All female students are automatically part of AWS. Isn't that great?"

Her grin didn't falter, so Ramona smiled back and hoped that hers didn't look half as forced. She bristled at the notion that she'd been enrolled in something without her permission. It sounded awfully official. It better not cost anything.

"You're all set."

The girl's gaze shifted away from Ramona just as her mother appeared.

"The car's clear. We got everything," her mother said.

"Thank goodness. I'm not sure I could've stomached carrying another box up those stairs." Ramona wiped a finger across her sweaty forehead. "Did you get lost? You were gone for a while."

Her mother waved her hand as though to brush off the concern. "I stopped by to see an old friend."

Ramona frowned. As far as she knew, her mother didn't know anyone on campus.

"Who?"

"Someone I used to know." Her mother pointed at the handbook and asked, "What's that?"

"A *Women's Handbook*, whatever that is. I guess we all get one."

"Hmm." Her mother made a noncommittal sound, but frowned.

Mother and daughter drifted away from the crowded tables toward the shade of a wide-trunked maple tree. Ramona looked around, expecting the judgmental gaze that trailed her mother everywhere she went in their small town, but only saw uninterested eyes. She relaxed, but the relief was quickly replaced by dread for her looming shift. She hadn't thought of a solution yet.

"Hell no, we won't go! Hell no, we won't go!"

Ramona looked toward the shouting.

A dozen or so students carried picket signs that read "Get out of Vietnam" in bold, angry lettering. She shouldn't be surprised, considering that Walter Cronkite reported the body count in Vietnam to Americans in their living rooms at night while anti-war protests spanned the country. Still, she hadn't expected to see it so soon. Ramona wished she could peek inside their heads, unable to imagine doing something so bold.

"We live in wild times, don't we?" Her mother gestured toward the protestors, and Ramona nodded.

Then her mother reached for her hand and squeezed.

"This will be such an adventure, sweetie. Enjoy it."

Tears gleamed at the corners of her mother's eyes and she blinked them away, forcing a smile through the goodbye.

Ramona couldn't bear to see her mother upset. It was the one thing that would make her reconsider their well-crafted plan.

"Are you sure you want me to do this now?" Ramona hedged, hardly believing what she said next. "I can defer for a year and work full time until I can cover my tuition on my own."

This suggestion had been rejected more than once already, but one that Ramona continued to offer no matter how much she hated the idea.

"No," her mother answered. "And don't ask again. You are going to college now and will get a degree if I have to work the night shift for the next four years."

No way, Ramona thought, but she stayed quiet, knowing that her mother's stubbornness hadn't lessened on the matter during their many, many conversations. The same ones where her mother declared that she would help Ramona pay for college, and that was that.

Ramona sighed. "You know I will."

"I do," her mother said softly, and Ramona could feel pride wrap around her like a blanket.

Ramona hugged her mother just like she'd done as a child at school drop-off. They held each other for a long moment before Ramona let go.

"Write. And call when you can."

"I will," Ramona promised.

Her mother reached into her handbag and fished around for her wallet. She removed two crisp five-dollar bills and extended them toward Ramona.

"Mom, I can't take this." Ramona shook her head and stepped back. "It's too much."

Her mother's brow furrowed, her hand still extended. "You will. You're eighteen years old and work like a middle-aged woman. I want you to have this."

Ramona opened her mouth to object but came up short when she saw the determination in her mother's eyes. She tucked the bills into her pocket.

"Thank you. You know I wouldn't be here without you."

Her mother wrapped her in another hug and squeezed before releasing.

"How could I forget?" She winked. "Now don't run off and get pregnant before you graduate."

Ramona cringed at the teasing on a subject so tender. Dating was the last thing on her mind.

"Mom ..." Ramona groaned.

"All right, I'll stop embarrassing you. But you know I want better for you."

"I know."

Her mother looked at her for another long moment and smiled before wading through the stream of people toward the parking lot. Ramona's throat tightened until she could no longer see her mother's curly, dark hair. She touched her own matching strands pulled back in a ponytail. It had always been the two of them, even though they lived with Ramona's grandparents, and she hadn't realized how absolute the separation would feel.

Ramona huffed a deep breath, frustrated with herself for feeling lonely already, and pushed back her shoulders. This was why getting her degree was so important. She would figure out the curfew, and it would all be fine. It had to be.

She wound her way through the packed entryway of Wolden Hall and up to her room on the second floor. Ramona gripped the doorknob to let herself inside, but paused. Her stomach clenched at the thought of meeting her roommate. Slowly, she opened the door and relaxed when she saw the empty space. Similar in size to her room in her grandparents' home, she would now have half the space. A pair of twin beds rested against opposite walls, along with matching wood desks. A wide window on the far wall overlooked a crowded pathway below. While her boxes sat on the floor beside a bare mattress, the other bed was made up with a pink blanket tucked in just right.

Ramona opened the flaps of the closest box to reveal her uniform, folded on top of the brand-new tennis shoes she'd worked a double on Labor Day for. Normally, she wouldn't buy new. But once she'd seen the photo in the catalog, she couldn't stop imagining herself wearing them at college. Ramona Bronson, college student in sparkling-white, new shoes. She wanted to look her best, and for once, she felt she deserved the indulgence.

Beneath her uniform was her mother's antique hand mirror. It was beautiful with a gilded frame and intricate handle. It had been given to her grandmother by a wealthy friend back in Italy and had been passed down to her mother on her eighteenth birthday. She could hardly believe her mother had let her take it from their home, as treasured as it was, but she'd insisted that Ramona should have it with her.

Picking up the mirror, Ramona surveyed her flushed cheeks and the flecks of mascara covering her eyelids. She wiped away the black smudges. There, that was better. With one last look at herself, her hazel eyes bright with excitement, she put the mirror back.

Ramona twisted her hair over her shoulder and considered unpacking but couldn't summon the energy. Instead, curiosity struck, and she had extra time before needing to get ready for her shift. She grabbed the handbook and sat down cross-legged on the mattress, the stretch of her high-waisted pants giving just enough room to allow the movement.

The table of contents outlined over fifteen sections. She flipped through the pages. The first section explained the mission of the Associated Women Students—"to unite and guide female students through shared experiences"—and introduced the AWS council. Each square, black-and-white photo showed a girl who looked much older than Ramona felt.

The next sections dug into student life and activities to get involved in on campus, as well as academic programs to consider. As Ramona read, she considered what the next four years would hold. In another universe, she might have studied art history, but that wasn't in store for her in this life. She'd decided years ago to earn a degree that would lead to high-paying careers, or as high-paying as a woman could get these days. Maybe a nurse. She didn't mind blood.

Ramona read on in a haze until the word "dating" jumped off the page and she refocused.

As women students at one of the finest universities in the country, if we do say so ourselves, we must hold ourselves to high standards when it comes to socializing. Whether you're in the market for a boyfriend or not, it's important to treat our male counterparts with polite respect and never speak out of turn. As a member of AWS, you should strive to be companionable, pleasant, and presentable at all times. No one likes a hysterical woman—least of all the male students. Believe us. You'll find more success if you're enjoyable to be around, and it never hurts to look your best. For example, consider the way your voice sounds. Is it soft and agreeable?

Ramona laughed so hard, she almost choked. She'd never considered such a thing.

"What does my voice sound like?" Ramona said aloud, grimacing.

Definitely not soft. Instead, it sounded scratchy. The cooks at Dusty's kept the radio so loud, the waitresses had to bark orders so they could be heard. Surely, no one expected them to change their voices for the men.

Curiosity shifted to apprehension as Ramona read the headline on the next page, "Curfew."

Her stomach soured. She skimmed the page. All female students living on campus had a curfew of 12:00 a.m. Ramona groaned and pulled at the collar of her shirt, which suddenly felt suffocating.

"What the fuck am I going to do?" she said at the exact moment that the door opened.

A tall, thin girl stood in the doorframe wearing a matching set that Ramona recognized from the JCPenney catalog. She held a basket in one arm, and her eyes immediately went to Ramona. The girl frowned, looking as stern as a school principal.

"Well, that was crass," the girl said in a high-pitched voice. She strode to her side of the room and set down the basket on her desk. "My name is Patsy Connell. Looks like you're my roommate."

Ramona felt her cheeks redden and set down the handbook. She stood up, extended her hand, and said, "I'm Ramona Bronson. It's nice to meet you."

As the girls shook hands, Ramona's gaze caught on the steam rising from the basket.

"Muffins." Patsy smiled. "My boyfriend loves my baking."

The scent of cinnamon wafted through the room.

"That's nice." Ramona tucked a strand of curls behind her ear. "Look, I'm sorry about that. I don't normally curse." Lie. "It's just that I got some bad news."

Patsy nodded as though forgiving her. Then she eyed Ramona's hands. "I see you got your copy. That's great," she said sweetly. "I'm the vice president of Associated Women

Students. I'm a junior, by the way, and soon to be president if all goes according to plan."

Ramona recalled the black-and-white pictures of the AWS council in the handbook.

"So what's the problem?" Patsy asked.

"It's the curfew." Ramona pulled at the ends of her curls. "I work at a diner a few nights a week, and my shift doesn't end until midnight. I don't know what to do."

"A diner?" Patsy echoed. "Why on earth would you work there?"

Ramona answered sarcastically without a second thought, her voice as sweet as an apple in autumn. "Because it's a real swell time."

"I'm sure," Patsy replied with a raised eyebrow.

"I work to pay for college," Ramona said, her voice returning to its normal rasp.

Patsy considered her. Ramona's limbs loosened as she forced herself to calm down. There would surely be a solution, some sort of exemption made.

"What do you think?" Ramona couldn't keep the hope from her voice.

The quiet hung heavy until finally, Patsy shrugged. "Looks like you'll have to quit your job."

CHAPTER 2

Green leaves fluttered on the other side of the window. Ramona stared at the tree, unwilling to look at Patsy as she rattled on about the importance of the curfew. Apparently, the Dean of Student Affairs ensured that the curfew remained enforced. Ramona's eyes narrowed as she tried to keep her rising anger off her face—both about the curfew and at the way Patsy talked down to her.

"Are you listening?"

Ramona had stopped paying attention sometime after Patsy had explained the punishment for breaking curfew—written citations for the first three violations, and then a review by the advisory board for any further violations. Now that Patsy had finally shut her mouth for more than five seconds, Ramona faced her.

"You don't expect special treatment, do you?" Patsy's pale-blonde hair threatened to burst from the hairband holding it in place with all the vigorous scolding she'd done in the last few minutes.

"No," Ramona said.

But that's exactly what she thought. This wasn't some frivolous matter. This was essential. Surely, an exemption could be made. And she would find out. Ramona filed away the dean's name for later.

"Good." Patsy sat on the edge of her bed with stick-straight posture and studied Ramona.

Uncomfortable with the attention and desperate for an escape, Ramona mumbled, "I have to shower." After all, she'd been moving boxes all day.

Ramona rifled through her belongings for a towel and soap while Patsy watched and fled to the communal bathroom down the hall. Seconds after turning on the shower, steam filled the stall. Ramona closed her eyes and stepped under the hot water, submerging her head until the heat consumed her.

She replayed their one-sided conversation as she scrubbed her body, taking extra care under her arms and around her breasts. She scowled. How had she ended up with such an uptight person for a roommate?

Ramona couldn't catch a break, but she didn't have time to sulk. Her shift started soon. She could try calling out, but she knew Randy would see through the attempt, especially after their conversation yesterday. Randy liked her well enough, but unless you were on your sickbed, he didn't put up with canceled shifts. Ramona gripped the wall, her fingernails catching in the grout, and pressed her forehead against the tile. She couldn't think of another option, so she'd have to go and hope that the curfew wasn't as strictly enforced as Patsy had described. It's possible Patsy had been trying to intimidate her as an upperclassman.

"Excuse me," a voice called from outside the stall. "Are you almost done in there?"

Ramona startled and wiped off the last remnants of soap. She dried herself as best she could in the tiny stall and nodded at the girl waiting as she stepped out.

A flock of girls crowded in front of the mirrors with tubes of lipstick and cans of hairspray. By the way they gossiped, the group had big plans. Of course there would be parties on the first day, and Ramona felt a pang in her chest at the sight of them chatting and joking like merry friends. She imagined introducing herself and joining them. Another time. Maybe even tomorrow. She'd be lying if she didn't begrudge them for having a social life that she could only dream about. The biggest problem these girls had was meeting the right people at a party, while she had to work to pay for college and figure out what to do about the curfew.

A girl chomping bubblegum noticed Ramona and called out, "Need a spot in front of the mirror?"

Ramona shook her head. "Thank you, though."

"Are you going to the barbeque on the quad?" the girl asked before popping a bubble.

"No. I have work, but I wish I could." She really did.

"Bummer," the girl said as she fluffed up her already impressively voluminous hair.

Ramona agreed, but she didn't have a choice. If she'd learned anything from her mother, she couldn't squander the opportunity for a college degree, and that didn't come freely. Ramona adjusted the towel wrapped around her and wound through the girls to get ready for her shift.

***

A red pickup truck idled in front of Ramona's Beetle, blocking the entrance to employee parking at Dusty's. Ramona honked until the truck moved enough for her to pass and pull into the closest spot. She may not have had much of a choice in the type, but she'd grown fond of her little car and how fast it could speed down the highway. Rush-hour traffic had turned the thirty-minute drive into forty-five minutes, and her shift started right now. Ramona raced toward the front door, only hesitating long enough to smooth out the wrinkles in her blouse before heading inside.

"There she is," Randy called from behind the register. He looked toward the clock. "Don't you think you're cutting it a little close?"

"Someone's got to keep things interesting around here," Ramona said as she pulled an apron out from behind the counter.

Randy rolled his eyes. "I wasn't sure you'd make it."

"I'm here, aren't I?" Ramona snapped, sharper than she'd intended, and Randy raised his hands in surrender before directing her toward her usual section.

Ramona tied the apron to grip her waist, grabbed an order pad, and went outside, only to see the red truck parked in her section. Great. Hopefully, they wouldn't recognize her. Honking at a customer didn't usually bring in a big tip.

Customers arrived in a steady stream, and Ramona hustled to stay ahead. The quicker she moved, the more customers she'd serve and the more tips she'd get. At least, that's what she told herself as sweat formed in her armpits. Her only break came in the form of a tuna melt dinner, which she ate in the parking lot out back with a view of the employee cars. She cleared out the remaining customers with a polite smile as soon as the fluorescent "open" sign turned off at midnight and locked the door behind them.

The diner looked strange when empty. Sticky plastic the color of a Creamsicle, the type that clung to bare skin, upholstered every seat from the bartop to the booths. The orange shade popped against the bright-turquoise walls that Randy insisted the customers loved. Ramona had yet to hear that feedback herself.

Ramona chuckled at the thought of her boss picking out paint swatches and began wiping the counter with a gray rag that had once been white. She grimaced as she swept crumbs into her palm and swayed to the music booming from the kitchen. She could never keep still when "The Twist" came on the radio.

"He's great live."

Ramona jumped, dropping the rag and crumbs on the floor. Dimitri appeared beside her and crouched down to scoop up the mess. After spending many late shifts cleaning up together, they'd become friends.

"What's with everyone sneaking around?" Ramona snapped. "You scared the bejesus outta me."

"Sorry, promise I didn't mean to." Dimitri stood up. "Do you like Chubby Checker?"

"Of course. Who doesn't?"

"I saw him play when he came to Seattle last spring. Fantastic show."

Ramona softened as she regained her breath. "You're lucky. I'd kill to see him live."

"I bet he'll come back on tour. Maybe we could go?"

Dimitri wiped the counter for her with the freshly rinsed rag. He stood tall, taller than anyone else at Dusty's, and appeared even longer as he extended his arm across the counter. Despite his height, or maybe because of it, he appeared lanky in the way that teenagers do before filling out. He looked up from the counter when she hadn't answered, and a strand of his dark, slicked back hair fell across his forehead. She realized what a nice face he had. A kind face.

"Sure."

Dimitri nodded before switching subjects. "How did moving in go?"

An image of the handbook came immediately to mind, and Ramona grimaced.

"That bad?" Dimitri laughed.

"I guess you could say it's been a long day." Ramona tried to smile, but only managed something halfway there.

Also a freshman at the university, Dimitri was living on campus in a male dormitory. Ramona glanced around, and when she saw no sign of Randy, she sat on a barstool and relaxed. She filled Dimitri in, from moving the seemingly endless number of boxes with her mother, to her disastrous conversation about the curfew with Patsy, to Randy switching her back to the night shift.

"Seriously? Do you want me to talk to him?" Dimitri offered.

"Don't bother."

While she appreciated the offer, Ramona didn't want someone fighting her battles for her. She could handle it. Besides, Randy listened to her more than he did to Dimitri.

Dimitri scratched the back of his neck. "What are you going to do?"

Ramona shrugged. "I had this all planned out, you know? I switched my shifts and everything, but of course, something had to ruin it." She should've seen it coming and cursed herself now for thinking it might just work out for once.

"You know what I'm not doing? Quitting like my lovely roommate suggested."

Dusty's sat smack-dab in the middle between campus and her hometown, so she could work while at school and at home during breaks. Practically perfect. Not to mention the tips she earned and the relationships she'd built with her regulars at Dusty's.

"You shouldn't have to," Dimitri said. "I'm sorry."

"You didn't do anything wrong."

"Yeah, but I could've tried to think of a backup plan. I forgot about the curfew for girls."

Dimitri's older brother was a junior, and as such, he knew a lot about the way things worked on campus.

"That's not your responsibility." Ramona sighed. "I appreciate it, though."

"How can I help?" Dimitri asked.

There Dimitri went, lending a hand as usual. Ramona liked Dimitri, a nice, harmless guy for a change, but not in the same way he liked her. He hadn't told her how he felt, but she couldn't mistake the way his eyes lingered on her. So she encouraged his friendship while turning down multiple offers to hang out, just the two of them.

"Actually, yes. Can you cover my next two shifts on Friday and Sunday?"

Ramona had made enough money working seemingly endless shifts over the summer to cover her first quarter of tuition and living expenses. She could afford to miss two shifts worth of pay while she figured out what to do.

Dimitri agreed, and she sighed in relief. That would give her a week until her next shift.

"Do you have a party to go to this weekend or something?" Dimitri teased, his voice a touch tighter than natural.

"Definitely not," Ramona answered before adding wistfully, "but it seems like everyone else does."

"What do you mean?"

"All these girls were getting ready to go out earlier. Parties. Dates. You know."

Dimitri studied her. "Do you want that? To go on dates?"

"No," Ramona scoffed. "I can't afford to date right now. I need to stay focused on school and work, and now dealing with this curfew."

It might be the truth, but that didn't mean she didn't wish for different circumstances.

They were quiet for a few minutes as Ramona sat and Dimitri wiped. In the background, the radio played on in the kitchen, alongside the sound of sloshing water from the sink filled with dishes.

Then Dimitri brightened. "You know what you could do?"

Ramona waited, eyebrows raised.

"A petition."

"What are you talking about?"

"No, really. A petition to push back the curfew is perfect! My brother and his friends petitioned to move the ROTC recruiting tent last year, and it actually worked."

"But I'm not trying to push back the curfew. I just need an exemption for the nights I work. I don't want to make a big deal out of it." Ramona frowned at the idea of putting her problems out there so publicly. The last thing she needed to do was draw attention to herself as some sort of rebel.

"Besides, maybe the curfew isn't actually enforced." She looked at the clock on the wall, reading 12:08 a.m., and her chest squeezed. She'd find out soon.

"Yeah, maybe," Dimitri agreed, if not with much confidence. "Let me know if you change your mind. You could help a lot of people."

"That would be good, I guess."

But honestly, she didn't care about helping others. She cared about helping her mother and her grandparents. She cared about helping herself. Ramona knew what happened when you put others first—you came last.

Dimitri seemed to think so highly of her, and she didn't want him to realize how selfish she could be. Ramona pivoted.

"Your brother's name is Theo, right?" Ramona asked, enjoying the feel of the name on her tongue.

Something like jealousy flashed across Dimitri's eyes before he shrugged and turned back to the counter. He wiped up a lone squirt of ketchup. Ramona waited. Once the counter gleamed and all abandoned crumbs were long gone, Dimitri sighed.

"You don't want to get mixed up with Theo's group."

"Why?"

More curious than before, Ramona examined Dimitri.

Dimitri looked as if he'd swallowed too big a bite and choked it down anyway. "The Foes have a reputation on campus."

"The Foes?" Her voice rose.

"It's weird, I know. Everyone calls them The Foes. They're an activist group against the war in Vietnam and are a part of the Free Speech Movement."

And there went her curiosity, growing again.

"What does that mean? What do they do?"

"They protest, host demonstrations, and carry around a bunch of signs mostly. But they're hardcore. You don't want to get involved."

This didn't surprise her. Students across the country were organizing like never before. One particularly well-known group Ramona had heard mentioned in the news was the Students for a Democratic Society, a leftist movement largely against the war and for free speech.

Before Ramona could respond, headlights lit up the diner as a car pulled into the parking lot. Theo's Chevy.

"He's here," Dimitri said, taking his apron off. "Do you mind finishing up? You know how impatient he gets."

Ramona nodded. Cleaning the counters was technically part of her job, so she grabbed the rag without looking away from the car.

The first time Ramona had seen Theo was in profile. Last winter, he'd driven up in his beat-up, gray Chevy with his arm hanging out the open window despite the chill. Since then, she'd grown used to seeing his car at the end of the shifts that Dimitri worked. She only caught small glimpses of him, but she couldn't help looking at the way his muscled forearm gripped the metal and how sharp his jaw looked in the shadows of the car. She didn't know him, but she sure liked pretending she did.

Dimitri smiled, the whiskers of his thin mustache spreading out, and thanked her before hurrying toward the door. He paused in the doorway.

"Look, they're trouble. I know how much school means to you. You don't want to be a part of their shit."

And with that, Dimitri left before Ramona could respond. Her eyes tracked him as he made his way to the Chevy. The car rolled forward, and Ramona's breath caught in her throat when Theo leaned out the open window to say something to Dimitri, his face fully illuminated in the orange glow. Something about Theo captivated Ramona, and she couldn't look away. A straight nose, striking eyes, and a jaw that starred in her dreams. As the Chevy shifted gears and peeled out of the parking lot, Ramona thought The Foes sounded anything but weird.

Once the Chevy disappeared, Ramona came back to the moment and glanced at the clock. She swore. She finished wiping the counter and carried the rest of the dishes back to the large industrial sink. She'd be late, but that didn't mean she wouldn't hurry. She dropped off her apron, pocketed her tips for the night—better than yesterday's—and drove back to campus.

The parking lot closest to Wolden Hall was empty of people, all the good girls surely snug in their beds before curfew, and Ramona easily found a spot. A group of guys stood in a circle a hundred yards away with a silver keg between them. No girls in sight. Ramona grabbed her purse and locked the Beetle before hurrying toward the dormitory.

She went up the front steps and reached for the handle. For a moment, she worried it would be locked, and then she'd surely be out of luck, but it opened beneath her grip. Ramona held her purse to her chest as she tiptoed through the dim entryway toward the staircase.

"Excuse me. Where have you been?"

Ramona froze. A lamp illuminated the plump cheeks of a woman sitting in the front room with a small book perched on her lap like a cat. Ramona recognized her from earlier that day. It was Mrs. Garth, the housemother of Wolden Hall.

"Did you hear me, young lady?" Mrs. Garth asked as she sat up straighter and dug her low heels into the maroon carpet. "Where have you been?"

Her heart beat furiously in her chest, and Ramona immediately knew it had been a mistake to downplay the curfew. She could feel herself on the brink of big trouble, and on her first day too. What a terrible first impression she was making.

"Hello, Mrs. Garth," Ramona said in as respectful a tone as she could manage. "I'm a waitress at Dusty's Drive-In, and I had a shift tonight." She pointed at the name tag pinned to her blouse as proof.

Still seated, Mrs. Garth snapped the book shut in her lap and considered Ramona's answer. An unwrapped bar of chocolate rested on the side table within arm's reach.

"What's your name?"

After Ramona told her, Mrs. Garth said, "Miss Bronson, this is a serious matter. You've broken curfew by forty-two minutes. Not to mention that it's the first night of term."

They both looked at the clock on the wall. Ramona gulped to hold off the panic closing in. Then an idea struck.

"What curfew?" Ramona asked as innocently as she could muster.

"What curfew?" Mrs. Garth echoed like an incredulous parrot. "Miss Bronson, there is a curfew for all female students living on campus. Surely you were informed."

Ramona shook her head and did her best to make her voice sound small. "I'm so sorry, Mrs. Garth. I had no idea. I'm new and the first person in my family to attend college. Today has been awfully overwhelming."

Something in her expression must have convinced Mrs. Garth because she softened ever so slightly. "Well, there is a lot to learn on your first day, so it's possible that something was missed in this case. I'll let you off without a citation this time, but you are to review your *Women's Handbook* immediately and familiarize yourself with the rules. This behavior will not do."

Mrs. Garth turned up her nose as though she smelled something bad. Then she sent Ramona to bed with a stern look.

With shaky hands, Ramona gripped the railing as she tiptoed up the stairs to her room. She had been wrong. Very wrong. The curfew was enforced more strictly than she could have imagined. She didn't realize that the housemother, who was no doubt harsher the later she had to wait up, would be monitoring the ins and outs of the dormitory so closely. Thinking of this level of supervision made Ramona's skin itch. If she got into trouble, could she lose her scholarship or get kicked out of school? If that happened, everything she'd worked for would be for nothing. She would end up in the same situation as her mother—no degree and no options.

Ramona reached her dorm room and opened the door. The only light came from the moon. Patsy slept with a silk mask covering her eyes. Ramona sighed in relief. She couldn't handle another confrontation today. As quietly as she could, she changed into her pajamas and slipped beneath the covers.

Taking a deep breath, she tried to calm the racing thoughts in her head. Only two days ago, her biggest challenge had been balancing work and school. Now, that didn't seem like a challenge at all. Packing their cars this morning with her mother seemed like ages ago, and despite being exhausted, her mind wouldn't settle.

Fall classes started tomorrow, and Ramona decided that as soon as they were over, she would see the dean whom Patsy had mentioned. She would ask for an exemption. She forced her eyes shut and counted her breaths.

In for one, two, three and out for one, two, three.

Repeat.

Repeat.

It would work. It had to. Ramona didn't fall asleep for a long time, and all the while, the dull roar of men laughing could be heard from outside as they enjoyed a beer with friends.

CHAPTER 3

The large chalkboard at the front of the classroom read "Professor Scott." Said professor stood before the students wearing a dark-brown blazer and cream-colored pants. She had tucked her brown hair, threaded with silver, into a low bun, and she gestured at the board with a pair of glasses in hand. Impressed, Ramona watched closely.

"Welcome to Public Speaking 101."

The class responded with inaudible murmurings of hello.

"Now that's the bright-eyed eagerness I look forward to every quarter," Professor Scott said. At this, the students glanced around sheepishly.

Professor Scott drifted from one side of the room to the other. There were about forty students in total, not many more than Ramona's high school classes. In fact, this classroom looked very similar to her high school classes from the individual desks to the wide windows. The professor turned on her heels to face the students. Her eyes swept over the classroom before quickly doubling back to Ramona. Professor Scott stared at her for a beat longer than felt comfortable and Ramona looked back, confused at being singled out. She'd never met the professor before, but it felt like recognition. Another moment, and Professor Scott looked away.

"I'm sure that for some of you, this is your first college class."

The students buzzed, and Professor Scott continued drifting from one side of the room to the other as she spoke.

"As a teacher, my goal is that each of you learn something you weren't expecting during this course. Public speaking is so much more than giving speeches. It's about communication, confidence, and persuasion. By the end of the quarter, I hope that every one of you can exhibit these qualities."

Professor Scott paused now, turning forward to face the class, and smiled. "Let's get started."

The next hour sped by, and Ramona scribbled as many notes as she could manage before fumbling her way to her next two classes, clear across campus. After her third and final class of the day, Ramona made her way toward Gauld Square, the location of the administration building. Her professors had assigned more reading and homework than she'd expected on day one, but she couldn't study just yet. She had to meet with the Dean of Student Affairs first.

As she walked, Ramona's arms ached beneath the weight of her books. She made a note to herself to find a bigger bag, like the ones she saw other students carrying. Maybe there would be something at the thrift shop near the pharmacy. She'd expected the first day of classes to be a rush, but the flurry of activity on campus surprised her. Dozens of tables lined walkways promoting this club or that, and the sun warranted games of Frisbee and picnic lunches on the great, green lawns.

Despite enjoying her classes, especially Public Speaking, Ramona's attention returned to the curfew throughout the day. Her restless night of sleep hadn't helped her focus either. This morning, she'd woken up to find Patsy heading out the door and wishing Ramona luck on her first day.

Now, Ramona narrowly avoided colliding with a guy carrying a picket sign that read "Leave our trees be" by jumping out of the way. He didn't acknowledge her, and Ramona restrained herself from confronting him, continuing on her way into Gauld Square with her eyes on the administration building ahead.

A circle of people stood twenty yards away, and Ramona recognized Dimitri's tall form. The group laughed, and Ramona felt a small jolt in her chest when her eyes latched on to Theo, standing in the center. Were these The Foes? Gosh, she wished she could hear him. Then he turned, catching her eye, and her stomach dipped. They stared at one another, and everything else slipped away. Ramona could've sworn she saw a flicker of recognition in his eyes … as though he'd been looking for her. Then her toe collided with a step, and Ramona caught herself on the railing to keep from falling.

"Shit," Ramona mumbled at the sight of a scuff on the top of her black, leather loafers.

When Ramona looked back, Theo still watched her, and her stomach flipped again. Unsure what to make of his stare, she looked away and entered the administration building. Wood doors and crowded bulletin boards lined the hallway. She found the dean's office and straightened her shoulders before greeting the secretary.

"Hello, dear," the woman said as she looked up from her typewriter. "What can I do for you?"

Ramona glanced at the nameplate on her desk. "Hi, Mrs. Davis. I'm here to see the Dean of Student Affairs."

"Do you have an appointment?" Mrs. Davis asked, checking what Ramona assumed to be a scheduling book that lay beside a copy of *Ladies' Home Journal.*

"No," Ramona answered. "Is that a problem? I'm sure the dean is busy, but this is urgent."

"Not a problem, my dear, not a problem," Mrs. Davis said. "What would you like to see him about?"

Ramona glanced around the crowded sitting room before lowering her voice a touch. "I'm looking for an exemption to the curfew."

Mrs. Davis's expression flattened as though she'd been told the cake ran out at her birthday party. Ramona gulped. Surely, the dean received requests like this all the time. No one could expect thousands of students to all have the same circumstances.

Recovering slightly, Mrs. Davis answered, "I'll see what I can do" before disappearing down the hall.

Ramona sat down beside a pair of students who looked as though they were about to go before a jury serving a guilty verdict. She felt just as nervous. She squeezed her hands to stop the shaking. Finally, Mrs. Davis reappeared and called her forward before showing her into the dean's office.

Inside, the Dean of Student Affairs stood up from his desk and invited her in. He was a tall man, who also happened to be quite wide. His thick hair swooped to the side, and he had a mustache just shy of red. Not a gray hair in sight, but so many wrinkles lined his skin that Ramona couldn't tell his age.

"Please come in." He gestured toward a set of chairs. "Have a seat. I'm Dean Redley, the head of student affairs here on campus."

Ramona thanked him and perched on the edge of the chair. The large office had three tall windows that overlooked Gauld

Square, and matching wood furniture decorated the space. Most prominently, a glass case rested behind the desk, filled with shelves of golden awards and plaques that were just a tad too far away to read. Ramona squinted toward one in the center that appeared brighter than the rest.

He smiled as he caught Ramona looking at the awards.

"Impressive, isn't it?" Dean Redley gestured toward the gleaming display case. "This university has won many awards over the past few decades. In fact, we're in the running for the Top 10 universities on the West Coast."

Ramona nodded. "That's very nice."

"But that isn't what you're here for," the dean said, chuckling. "Now, what is this I hear about you seeking an exemption to the curfew?" A single eyebrow rose in disbelief.

Ramona sat up straight and tried to swallow the thick spit that had accumulated in her throat. Adopting her most polite, and dare she say pleasant, voice, she began, "Dean Redley, thank you for seeing me on such short notice. My name is Ramona Bronson. I'm a freshman this year and have been assigned to Wolden Hall.

"You see, I work as a waitress three nights a week to pay for college, and my shifts don't end until after the curfew. I tried to change my shift, really I did, but it didn't work out." To Ramona's dismay, her voice rose. "And I'm hoping that you will approve an exemption for me to miss curfew—by only forty-five minutes—on the nights I work."

While his smile remained, Dean Redley's face hardened like stale bread the longer she spoke. His pause before answering told her everything she needed to know, and yet a glimmer of hope lingered until he said, "Miss Bronson, we don't offer exemptions to the curfew."

"But what about in extreme circumstances like this?"

Ramona felt ashamed to hear herself plead, and yet, she had to try.

"To be frank, this doesn't sound like an extreme circumstance to me," Dean Redley said so condescendingly that Ramona wondered if she'd heard him correctly. "The answer is no, Miss Bronson. You will meet the curfew like every other student."

No warmth lingered in the dean's demeanor. Instead, the room froze over. Ramona's gaze caught on a pair of picture frames on the desk. Three children smiled in the first photo, and in the second, they sat with the dean and a woman with the same wide-set eyes. Proof of another family's wholeness that made her feel like something was missing in her own.

She swallowed the lump in her throat and made a decision.

"You mean, the female students."

As soon as the words left her mouth, Dean Redley's expression soured. That made Ramona want to smile, even though she'd lost hope of winning him over.

"Thousands of students manage to attend this university without issue with the curfew. This sounds like a personal problem. I suggest that you follow their example and put this behind you."

No way. Ramona didn't believe, for a second, that she was the only one who wanted an exemption to the curfew.

"We didn't get into the running for the Top 10 universities by letting girls out all night. It just isn't done. President Howard would never allow it," Dean Redley continued.

The idea of kicking him in the shin crossed her mind.

"I'm glad that I've gotten a chance to meet you, Miss Bronson, but I'm afraid I have another meeting to get to." Dean Redley stood from his seat and gestured for her to follow him to the exit.

"Good day." He closed the door behind her.

Ramona's dread over facing the curfew had turned to mild panic last night when Mrs. Garth caught her. Now, that panic grew like the mold that filled the crawlspace at home every summer. She tried to reorient herself in the hallway. Her hands shook, and as she turned around, her hip collided with a table, causing her to yelp at the biting pain. People stared and Ramona ducked her head, embarrassed, and hurried outside.

The fresh air relieved her, or maybe the open space did. Ramona found the nearest bench. She could hardly believe what had just happened. She'd really thought the dean would grant her an exemption. Thank goodness Dimitri had agreed to cover her next shifts to give her more time.

Then she remembered Dimitri's suggestion.

A petition.

If Dean Redley thought the curfew wasn't a widespread issue, she'd prove him wrong. He may be able to ignore her, but he couldn't ignore students en masse. She just needed to figure out how to petition.

As the idea took root, Ramona knew she would see it through. Not only had Dean Redley been unreasonable, but he'd made her feel small, and for that, she wanted to prove him wrong. A strand of her hair blew across her face, and the image of Dean Redley's smug expression lingered like a curse. One she wouldn't soon forget. And for the first time, ever the rule-follower, Ramona understood the urge to protest.

CHAPTER 4

The next day, Ramona wound her way up the spiral, stone staircase of Zuccaro Library. The railing felt cool beneath her palm. At the top, she smoothed out the wrinkles that had formed in her skirt after sitting through three classes.

The entrance to the university's infamous reading room faced her. Before heading to the meeting spot, she couldn't help peeking inside. Her breath caught at the sight. High, wood-paneled ceilings arched to a point in the center overhead, and stained-glass windows lined the walls. Students eager to start the term on the right foot filled every seat. She should join them and study, but she had a more pressing matter at hand. Ramona turned around.

After a few minutes of searching the stacks, she found Dimitri at a lone desk, just where he said he'd be. His back rounded forward as he concentrated on the open book before him. Surprised, Ramona realized that she'd never seen him in regular clothes as she took in his collared shirt and navy trousers. She stepped lightly, but despite how gently she pulled out the chair opposite him, Dimitri noticed the movement.

"You found me." He looked up with a smile spread across his face.

"Am I interrupting?" Ramona asked, but he shook his head before she'd gotten the question out.

She dropped her book bag on the floor, sat, and clapped her hands together.

"I need you to tell me more about petitioning."

Dimitri's eyes narrowed. "You changed your mind?"

"Dean Redley wouldn't grant me an exemption."

Dimitri sighed and closed the book, giving her his full attention.

"It's easy," Dimitri assured her. "Really, all you need is a notebook, a pen, and some confidence. The Foes will stand in popular areas on campus, especially between classes, and will ask everyone who passes by whether they'll sign."

Ramona could do that. Confidence came to her like donning a mask—easy to slip on when she needed it. But she wondered whether petitioning could get her into trouble. There's no way Dean Redley would approve, but could he do anything? The last thing she needed was to hurt her reputation on campus. The whole situation threatened to intimidate her into submission. But how important was her reputation if she couldn't pay to attend college? Besides, she liked the idea of proving Dean Redley wrong. She'd bet her Friday night tips that his face would turn an angry shade of maroon at seeing a signed petition.

"If you'd told me two days ago that I would be considering asking strangers to sign a petition to push back the curfew, I wouldn't have believed you." Ramona sighed and covered her face with her hands. "I hope I don't look ridiculous."

"Never." Dimitri's eyes bore into hers. "I'll help, okay?"

She studied the jagged edge of the nail she'd picked throughout her classes. "Okay."

Ramona pulled out her notebook, half-filled with notes from her high school classes last spring, and opened it to the next blank page. She gritted her teeth and wrote:

PETITION TO EXTEND THE CAMPUS CURFEW
The students listed below request to extend the curfew for female students to 1:00 a.m. Monday–Sunday.

She paused, wanting to replace 'extend' with 'remove,' but it felt unlikely, impossible, that the curfew would be lifted entirely for female students. Besides, she didn't need that.

Ramona added columns for name, signature, and date and signed her name in the first row.

"How's this?"

Dimitri took the notebook from her and skimmed before signing his name in the second row. When he handed it back, he nodded. "It's perfect."

He may not be the toughest critic, but she appreciated his encouragement.

"How many signatures do we need for the administration to take us seriously?" she asked.

Dimitri ran his hands over his knees and considered. "There's no hard-and-fast number. It really depends on the issue and the dean's mood. I'd say you need at least a few hundred, though. That's what Theo and The Foes had."

Ramona groaned. That was far more than she'd anticipated, and she frowned at her own naivety. It would take a long time.

"Don't worry," Dimitri said. "You'll get that many. People have been pissed about the curfew forever."

That wasn't as reassuring as Dimitri probably meant it to be.

"All right, what's next?" Ramona asked.

Dimitri stood up and shoved his books into his bag. "Come on."

Ramona followed Dimitri toward the library exit, hurrying to keep up with his long strides as they moved across the bustling campus. The sun shone brightly from high in the sky, and Ramona appreciated her short-sleeved blouse. A few minutes later, Dimitri stopped on the path in front of a familiar building.

Crane Hall looked almost identical to Wolden Hall. Both of the brick buildings had a wide, front staircase leading up to imperial-looking doors. Ramona counted three stories, just like Wolden, and recognized the windows spaced every few feet. Again, a match.

"Are you going to tell me what we're doing here?" Ramona asked.

"This is my dorm," Dimitri explained, confirming her assumption.

"You don't say," Ramona quipped as she eyed the droves of male students coming and going from the entrance. During moments like this, the size of the university felt overwhelming.

Dimitri chuckled before responding, "You might not believe this, but I think the guys will be just as on board to remove the curfew as the girls."

"I believe it, all right." It didn't take a genius to see why the boys would want the girls out for an extra hour every night. It's not how she planned to use her hour of freedom, but she wouldn't judge.

Ramona gripped the petition and scanned for the kindest-looking person to approach first when a lanky guy in need of a haircut rushed toward Dimitri. He wrapped his arms around Dimitri's shoulders and grinned widely.

"Well, if it isn't lil' Rhodes, my best friend's kid brother!" the guy said with an English accent. "It's such a trip seeing you here."

"Hey, Olly," Dimitri said as Olly rubbed his head as though petting a dog. "You don't need to call me that."

"I know." Olly's grin widened.

Dimitri shook his head as though there was no point arguing before looking at Ramona and then back at Olly. It took three rounds of this before Ramona got the hint.

"Hi there," Ramona started, immediately wishing she'd practiced what to say, but pushed forward. "I'm starting a petition to extend the curfew for female students. Do you want to sign?"

"So the girls can stay out later? I want to sign it so much, I'll do it twice," Olly teased with a wink that caught Ramona off guard. He practically pulled the petition from her hand along with her pen.

Three signatures.

Ramona unsuccessfully tried to suppress a smile as Olly handed them back.

"See? Easy," Dimitri said.

"Fine, you were right," Ramona agreed. In fact, she hadn't expected it to be so easy.

Dimitri cocked his head to the side. "I have an idea."

Then he startled her by jumping on top of a nearby bench.

"Listen up!" Dimitri announced to the droves of male students who filled the path, and everyone within earshot turned toward him. "We're collecting signatures to extend the curfew for female students!"

Ramona's cheeks heated as Dimitri pointed at her, unused to so many eyes on her. A few students whooped, which caused a ricochet of laughter through the small crowd. Dimitri held his peers' attention, and Ramona couldn't help feeling impressed. That was one way to get the word out.

"If you lot don't sign it right now, I'm egging every one of your windows, yeah?" Olly teased the crowd, but with an edge to his voice, and his chest puffed out more than before.

That did it. The floodgates opened, and guys swarmed around Ramona. The petition passed from hand to hand, and Ramona lost sight of it more than once. By the time the crowd thinned and moved on, they had thirty-eight signatures.

Olly told Dimitri to take it easy, and called to Ramona, "Good luck, petition girl!"

Ramona rolled her eyes to hide her smile.

"Thank you for doing that. I'm not sure what I'd do without you." Then, upon seeing the hopeful look on his face, she quickly amended, "You're such a good friend."

"It's my pleasure," Dimitri said, his eyes lingering on her long enough to make her shift.

"I should probably keep petitioning," Ramona said as she raised the notebook. "Keep up the momentum, you know?"

With more than an hour before the dining halls served dinner, she had plenty of time to collect signatures.

"Sure," Dimitri answered. "I'll see you around?"

Ramona nodded. She turned from Dimitri and Crane Hall, walking toward the quad where she'd seen a steady stream of students earlier, and wondered whether there may be a real chance of changing the curfew.

Construction consumed the campus. From every direction, Ramona saw construction crews, industrial-grade building materials, and partially formed structures. As she neared the quad, she saw a construction site to her right that looked bigger than all the rest. Curious, she approached the fence surrounding the site and read the attached sign. Apparently, this would be the student union building. The illustration showed a large, commanding building surrounded by more green lawns. Estimated completion date was spring '66. She pictured herself attending the opening … as long as she wasn't working.

Ramona reached the quad to find it just as crowded as it had been earlier. She paused beneath the cover of a wide-trunked tree. Six matching buildings circled the quad, all brick with intricate lattice work and paths that crisscrossed the green lawn. She gripped the notebook tightly against her chest, and if it wasn't for her pounding heart, she might have convinced herself that these weren't nerves she felt. She couldn't rely on Dimitri, or Olly, for that matter. She needed to do this herself.

You can do it. Ramona recited her personal pep talk. She pushed back her shoulders in a show of confidence she didn't feel before stepping out of the shade.

Students passed without a word. She sighed and pursed her lips. Okay, clearly they weren't going to just come up to her, so she would have to make the first move.

Up ahead, a couple strode down the path and Ramona waited. She held the petition in one hand and twisted her hair over shoulder with the other to give her hands something to do.

"I'm telling you, you've gotta try it before you say no. It's the best around." Ramona overheard a guy saying to the girl whose shoulder he leaned on.

They headed straight for Ramona, and if no one moved, they would collide. The girl looked up in surprise, and Ramona seized the opportunity.

"Excuse me," Ramona called to get the pair's attention. "I'm collecting signatures to petition the curfew for female students."

They stared at her like the stranger she was.

"Do you want to sign it?"

Without slowing, the guy shook his head and the girl mumbled, "No thank you," paired with a raised eyebrow.

Ramona stared at the back of their heads as they walked away. Her stomach dipped at the rejection. She'd really thought they would sign. All those guys had signed so easily when Dimitri and Olly had asked. Ramona scowled. So that's how it would be on her own.

Ramona rolled her shoulders to shake off the hurt and kept on, just as her mother would do.

Plastering on a smile, Ramona called out to everyone who passed, differing her approach each time to see what got her the most attention.

"Excuse me, will you sign my petition?"

"Do you have a minute to sign my curfew petition?"

"Hello there, can I speak to you for a minute about this petition?"

"I'm collecting signatures to remove the curfew for female students ..."

"Will you help me keep my job?" Ramona mumbled under her breath as another student passed her by without stopping. She considered banging her head against the closest tree when she noticed a girl coming her way. Might as well give it another go.

"Hi there, do you want to extend the curfew for female students?" Ramona asked weakly.

To her shock, the girl stopped.

"Yeah," the girl said, like it was obvious.

"Really?"

"Yeah," the girl repeated. "I just moved into Wolden, and it's ridiculous."

"Exactly!" Ramona exclaimed, feeling renewed hope. "I'm collecting signatures for this petition. Do you want to sign?"

"Absolutely."

The girl reached for the notebook and signed. Ramona thanked her before introducing herself.

"It's very nice to meet you, Ramona. I'm Mable."

Mable had short, pale-blonde hair that she wore in a ponytail so small, Ramona wondered how it didn't fall out. Her bangs covered her eyebrows, and she had delicate, pixie-like features.

Mable smiled and returned the notebook. "Good luck! I certainly hope it works. I'll see you around?"

"Definitely." Ramona nodded. "I heard they're playing the new episode of *Bewitched* in the lounge later."

Ramona had heard talk of it in the bathroom earlier.

Agreeing to meet, Mable said goodbye and continued on the path. Ramona looked down at the petition and smiled. The second signature from a female student. She started to feel the confidence that she wore just a bit.

The next half hour passed slowly, and she lost track of how many times she'd been ignored. But she collected a few more signatures, and that was better than none.

Ramona's stomach grumbled, and her legs were tired from standing in place when she decided to wrap up. She still had five days to collect signatures and present to Dean Redley before her next shift. Ramona reached for her book bag when she felt someone come up beside her. Turning, she saw Patsy in the same bright-pink sweater she'd been wearing that morning that looked far too warm for the weather. A guy stood slightly behind Patsy with cropped, sandy-colored hair.

"Oh, hi, Patsy and …" Ramona paused, turning toward the guy. "I'm Ramona, Patsy's roommate."

Before he could speak, Patsy spoke for him. "This is Archer, my boyfriend. He's the president of the university's student body council."

Archer smiled stiffly and muttered, "For the next few months at least."

To that, Patsy swatted his chest. "No way! You'll get reelected in November. We both will."

Patsy beamed as though they were campus royalty, while Archer's gaze shifted beyond Ramona's shoulder.

"How was your second day?" Patsy asked as she turned back to Ramona.

Surprised by the thoughtfulness, Ramona answered, "Great. Tiring, but really great. I like my professors."

"That's wonderful," Patsy said before her focus shifted toward the open notebook, which Ramona hadn't finished shoving into her book bag yet. "What's that?"

Shit. Her heartbeat sped up. Ramona had hoped to keep the petition a secret from Patsy, not wanting to further tighten the tension that had formed between them.

"It's a petition," Ramona said as casually as she could muster, like it was simply nothing at all.

"A petition?" Patsy's eyes widened. "What on earth are you petitioning?"

"The curfew," Ramona said, resisting looking down as she wanted to.

Patsy's eyes blazed and Ramona's fists tightened. The air hung heavy between them.

"You know your little petition makes you look like a slut, right? Nothing good happens after midnight."

The air left Ramona's chest in a woosh. That word. That sharp word cut through her now just as it had when she'd overheard those awful women talking about her mother all those years ago.

On a grocery trip, when Ramona was seven years old, her mother had sent her for a jar of marmalade while waiting her turn at the meat counter. Ramona had been about to turn down an aisle when she heard laughter that made her pause. Mean laughter.

"And do you know who's here? Diane."

"Really? I would've thought she'd be working. She always seems to be."

"I feel sad every Sunday, seeing her at church alone with only her daughter and parents. I imagine it must be so lonely."

"Well, that's what happens when you're a slut." The three women cackled.

Ramona had had to bite her tongue to keep from crying. She hadn't known what that word meant at the time, but she sensed the judgment and disapproval. Ramona had shrunk back so the women wouldn't see her and returned to her mother, explaining that the marmalade was out of stock.

That word had made her realize how people had judged her mother, and Ramona hated them for it. She'd never forgotten, and her anger blazed stronger now. She glared at Patsy.

Behind Patsy, Archer groaned like a fed-up parent. "Jesus Christ, you can't keep your mouth shut, can you?"

The tension hardened like bread left out overnight.

Ramona gritted her teeth and looked Patsy straight in the eye. She hadn't said a thing to those women, not in the grocery store and not every time she'd seen them afterward, and had always regretted it. She wouldn't make that mistake again.

"Just because you need rules to stay out of trouble"—Ramona's eyes flickered to Archer tauntingly—"doesn't mean the rest of us do. I can take care of myself just fine."

Ramona let the implication hang heavy between them.

Before Patsy could respond, and Ramona could tell that she wanted to, Archer gripped her shoulder and said, "Let's go, Pats. We don't want to be late."

Ramona fled in the opposite direction. She ran across campus, not caring who saw, until she reached Wolden and climbed the stairs to the bathroom. Tears welled at the corners of her eyes, so she bit her tongue, promising herself that they could be free once she was in the privacy of a toilet stall.

She flung the bathroom door open, startling a girl putting on lipstick in front of the mirror, and hurried for the closest stall before letting the full weight of what had just happened settle. Ramona sat down on the lid of the toilet and bent her forehead to her knees, wrapping her arms around herself into a tight ball. She gripped the sides of her neck until the sharpness of her nails bit into her skin.

Patsy had called her a slut.

Patsy had called her a slut in front of her boyfriend.

Patsy had called her a slut in the middle of campus.

How dare she?

The last forty-eight hours replayed in Ramona's mind, leaving her more exhausted than before. She'd been here for two days, and she already felt broken. Her mask slipped, and a small part of her wondered whether Patsy was right. Snot ran down Ramona's nose, and she grabbed a wad of toilet paper when she saw the shadow of feet in front of the stall door.

Please, Ramona thought, *go away*.

"Ramona, is that you?" a soft, familiar voice asked just outside the door. It took a moment to place.

Sniffling, Ramona answered, "Yeah."

Ramona pulled herself up and took a deep breath before opening the stall.

Mable stood a few feet away, leaning against the white sink. She shrugged when Ramona tipped her head in question, saying simply, "I saw you running."

Ramona nodded and felt a glimmer of appreciation. Stepping up to the sink, Ramona washed her hands before splashing cold water on her face. The mirror showed black streaks of mascara running down her cheeks, and red, half circles on her neck from her nails.

A paper towel appeared and Ramona accepted it, wiping the ruined makeup from her face.

"My roommate called me a slut because of the petition."

A sharp inhale of breath was quickly followed by, "You're kidding." Mable's eyes were wide with shock.

"I'm not. Didn't even flinch when she said it either."

The color drained from Mable's already very pale skin. Momentarily, Ramona wondered why she'd opened up to this girl, who, although very nice, was basically a stranger. Mable patted her shoulder. Something about her manner made her easy to talk to.

"That's terrible," Mable said before her eyes shifted from concern to determination. "We're going to need another copy of that petition."

"Why?"

"Because I'm going to help you." Mable winked. "There were plenty of bullies at my high school, and I won't put up with them here."

CHAPTER 5

By Tuesday morning, 448 students had signed the petition. Ramona and Mable walked in unison toward the administration building, their Mary Janes clicking in sync. Despite the warmth, Ramona wore her nicest blouse and the same high-waisted skirt she'd worn on the first day of classes the week before. Beside her, Mable wore a similar outfit. They had a meeting with the dean, after all. And the timing couldn't have been better. Ramona's next shift was the following day.

Out of the corner of her eye, Ramona noticed Mable leaning heavily on her right leg.

"Why are you walking funny?"

Mable huffed. "I've got a terrible blister. I shouldn't have worn those loafers yesterday. They're too stiff."

They had spent every free minute of the weekend petitioning, and their hard work had paid off in the form of more signatures than they'd hoped for, but their feet ached as a result.

"I've got a bandage back in my room if you want one," Ramona offered, but Mable shook her head, saying that she wore one already.

"I'm fine, really." Mable continued, "But I do think we've walked more in the last two days than I have in the last year. My mother would be thrilled at all the exercise."

They must've walked a dozen miles and talked to a thousand students. A petition turned out to be the ideal icebreaker. The warm weather had continued over the weekend, and the sun drew students outside to eat and play and laugh and flirt. Students shed their khakis, button-down shirts, and skirts for weekend wear—T-shirts and jeans all around.

Ramona and Mable had taken advantage of the good spirits to discuss the petition with anyone they encountered at the football game, library, drive-in movie, and across campus. Most hadn't signed and instead turned their noses up in judgment, some even glaring with downright hostility, like Patsy. It had become excruciatingly tense each time Ramona and Patsy were in their room together, but it only fueled Ramona's resolve.

Although the curfew had been in place for as long as anyone could remember, many students deeply detested the limitation. The unfairness of a curfew for only female students stung the most.

One story stood out to Ramona. She and Mable had gone to the boathouse, where students could rent canoes to take out on Lake Washington. There had been a long line of students waiting, and "Help!" by the Beatles, which seemed to play on the radio constantly since it had hit number one, echoed across the water.

"We could use a little help ourselves," Ramona had muttered as they'd approached the line, and Mable laughed.

"If we have a theme song, that would be it." Mable hummed along.

The girls had greeted a handful of students before meeting Donna, a sophomore. When they gave her their now well-practiced pitch, Donna had looked from side to side before nodding and gripping the paper so tightly, it bunched.

After signing, Donna asked, "So you've got about three hundred signatures so far?"

Ramona had nodded.

"It's about time someone did something about the curfew," Donna whispered harshly. "I'm sick of seeing guys do whatever they want, while we're treated like porcelain dolls."

"It's so unfair," Mable agreed.

"You want to hear unfair?" Donna asked, and the girls leaned in closer. Absolutely, they did.

"Last year, I'd dated this guy for a few weeks. I thought he was nice. He'd taken me to the drive-in and wouldn't so much as put his arm around me without asking. That is, until he thought it would be a good idea to surprise me on my birthday by pelting my window with rocks in the middle of the night. It was well after curfew, and the idiot broke the window, scaring me and my roommate. Somehow, the housemother found out, and I got into trouble for apparently luring him to visit me after curfew and had to go in front of the council. It was ridiculous."

Ramona's mouth dropped open with shock as Mable blurted, "Did you keep seeing him?"

Donna had leveled a stare at Mable that could've put out a candle and said, "Not a chance."

She returned the petition and said, "Give them hell."

The more stories Ramona heard, the more their actions felt justified. At some point over the weekend, this had become a cause rather than her personal problem, and she didn't know how to feel about the expanding responsibility. And now, just minutes away from presenting the petition to Dean Redley, Ramona braced herself for round two.

Ramona looked over at Mable. "I'm surprised we haven't lost our voices at this point."

"True. Do you think I can add this to my resume?" Mable adopted a formal tone, "It could say, 'Top-notch collector of signatures and advocate of equal rights for women.'"

"Mine would say, 'Curfew-breaker and rule-smasher," said Ramona.

"That's better. I'll go with that as well."

They turned a corner, and the administration building came into sight. "I can hardly believe we got so many signatures, can you?" Ramona asked.

"Yes," Mable answered without hesitation. "Because it's a ridiculous rule."

"This has to work," Ramona said.

They both refused to say the alternative out loud. How could it not work? They had hundreds of signatures. Dimitri said that they had just as many as the petitions that The Foes had won. Ramona was beginning to feel strange about referring to Theo and The Foes so regularly, even though they'd never met.

Ever the optimist, Mable asked, "So what will we do to celebrate? I think I'll run across campus barefoot at midnight and jump into the fountain."

Ramona laughed and pictured Mable, running until her feet were covered in dirt. "Well, we'd need champagne, of course."

"Of course," Mable agreed.

When they reached the front doors of the administration building, Ramona led the way to the dean's office following the same route she'd taken last week. Mrs. Davis sat behind her desk, and Ramona approached her with a touch more confidence than the first time.

"Hi, Mrs. Davis," Ramona greeted Dean Redley's secretary. "We have an appointment to see the dean."

The frown lines around Mrs. Davis's mouth deepened upon seeing Ramona. She steeled herself for the judgmental gaze that was becoming commonplace the more she talked about the curfew.

"I'll let him know that you're here."

Mrs. Davis disappeared around the corner, and when she re-emerged a few minutes later, gestured for Ramona and Mable to follow. This time, Dean Redley stood in the doorway, waiting.

"Miss Bronson, I have to admit, I'm surprised to see you again so soon." His voice carried a touch of scorn that made Ramona's skin itch. Still, he showed them to the chairs before his desk and waited until they were all seated before asking, "What is it you'd like to discuss?"

"Thank you for agreeing to see us, Dean Redley. As you know, I'm Ramona Bronson, and this is my friend Mable Mooney." Beside her, Mable waved at the dean. "After our discussion last week, we got to talking with other students, and it turns out that many feel similarly about the curfew."

Ramona pulled the petition out of her bag and laid it on the desk between them.

"There are 448 to be exact," Mable chimed in.

"We're very grateful to be students at this great university." Ramona and Mable had agreed that laying it on thick would be a good approach. "And we're hoping that you will reconsider your stance on the curfew by accepting our request to push back the curfew by just one hour."

This time, Dean Redley's smile fell. His cheeks turned red, just as Ramona had predicted, and for a moment, she felt gratified as he studied the petition. He flipped through the many pages of signatures.

"Ladies, I must admit that I'm impressed that you've done so much within your first week as students here. Your effort and coordination are admirable."

"Thank you, sir," Ramona answered. She gripped her hands together in her lap to keep them from shaking with anticipation.

"However, I'm afraid that what you're asking for simply isn't possible."

The second the words left his mouth and reached her ears, the ball of nerves in Ramona's stomach morphed into panic. Dean Redley continued, explaining that the curfew had been in place for decades, as long as female students were living on campus, and that the curfew was for their safety. Ramona only heard bits and pieces of his words, like an unformed papier-mâché, as her thoughts raced around what to do next to keep her job and keep her place as a student. It hadn't worked. Again.

It was only when Dean Redley set down the petition that she snapped out of it. Ramona stared at him as he smoothed out the lapels of his tweed blazer.

"But why?" Mable asked.

The dean's expression hardened as did his voice. "It's for your own protection. There are dangers for women at night. In fact, you should really be grateful for the curfew."

Instead of looking at him, Ramona watched Mable's mouth fall open for a half second before snapping shut like a nutcracker.

Men.

Men were the danger. So why weren't they shut in at night?

"I think I'll hold on to this for safekeeping." Dean Redley reached toward the petition, but Ramona snatched it off the desk without thinking twice and stuffed it into her bag.

Dean Redley looked as if he smelled something foul, and Ramona had no doubt her expression mirrored his. She forced herself to soften. This was the dean, after all, and she knew they toed a thin line. Ramona said, "No, thank you. We'll take care of it."

She felt absolutely certain that they needed to keep hold of the petition and all those names of supporters.

Dean Redley seemed as though he might object, but he merely clapped his hands together. "Thank you for scheduling an appointment to see me. I'm glad that we were able to discuss this *again*."

Ramona opened her mouth to say something. Surely, this couldn't be over, but Dean Redley continued, "I have to prepare for my next appointment. You ladies have a nice day."

They were being dismissed, and the rejection felt worse than the time in high school when Roger Stan had changed his mind and took Wanda to the homecoming dance instead of Ramona.

The girls stood and smoothed their skirts before walking toward the door to leave.

Dean Redley called out, "And ladies, I would advise that you stop this effort of yours. The curfew is a serious matter, and it wouldn't serve you well to go on causing trouble. It will remain in place as long as we feel the need to protect our female students."

Without a word, Ramona and Mable walked out, retracing the route back out of the building marked by the clicks of their shoes echoing down the crowded hallway.

Mable whispered under her breath so only Ramona could hear, "We should be grateful? What a toad."

Ramona bit her tongue, frustration and desperation threatening to surface as tears. Dean Redley hadn't taken them seriously at all, and to be patronized by the dean was humiliating. Now he would surely keep an eye on her.

As they reentered Gauld Square, Ramona felt completely deflated, like a discarded balloon after a birthday party.

Beside her, Mable fumed. "I can't believe it! I really can't. Something's seriously wrong with that man."

Only fifteen minutes ago, they had been as hopeful as can be. But the petition didn't work, the curfew was still in place, and Ramona had a shift tomorrow night.

"What do we do now?" Mable had such hope in her eyes.

"I need a minute to think." Ramona's brain swirled, seeking a solution.

"We have to do something," Mable insisted.

"Don't you think I know that?" Ramona snapped, her hands extending outward. "Shit. I can't believe it didn't work."

Not only did she feel the pressure of her own problems, but she also felt the weight of every person who'd signed. Ramona didn't want to be the face of some anti-curfew movement, especially if that came with the scorn of the school administration. Anything that threatened her degree wasn't an option. Her chest felt as hollow as a Russian stacking doll. She had nothing to give.

As her chest heaved, Ramona watched Mable's eyes widen. She knew she was acting unfairly, her anger not meant for Mable. Taking a deep breath, Ramona twisted her hair back out of her face and forced herself to calm down.

"Shit, I'm sorry. I shouldn't have snapped like that."

"I get it," Mable said. "I'm mad too. We'll figure something out."

Ramona wasn't so sure, but Mable looked certain.

"I have to go to class, but we'll talk later, okay?" Mable asked and Ramona nodded.

The girls said goodbye, and Ramona hurried to Wolden. She needed advice.

The lounge was empty when she arrived, not a single seat filled among the couches, chairs, and tables for girls to gather. A phone booth stood off the lounge, and Ramona slipped inside and dialed her home telephone number.

"Please pick up," she whispered into the receiver.

After four droning rings, her grandfather's familiar voice answered, "Hullo? Bob speaking."

"Hi, Grandpa, it's me."

"Well, if it isn't our college girl." His voice softened like butter left out overnight. "How's school?"

Ramona's throat tightened at the simple kindness of a question. If she could snap her fingers and be in the living room with him, she would in a heartbeat.

"It's been good," she lied, unable to tell him the truth. "Is Mom there?"

Soon, her mother's voice came on the line.

"Hi, sweetie."

"Hi, Mom." Ramona crumpled into a heap in the phone booth. "Stupid Mary went and got engaged and quit, so Randy moved me back to the night shift, and I won't get back in time to make curfew." Hiccup. "So I made a petition, and we got a lot of signatures, I made a friend by the way." Hiccup. "But stupid Dean Redley rejected our request, and now I don't know what I'm going to doooo," Ramona wailed.

"Ramona, oh, sweetie," her mother soothed. "Take a breath."

Tears pooled at the edges of her eyes, and Ramona wiped them away.

"Breathe in with me." There was an inhalation on the line.

Ramona sucked in a wet breath that barely relieved her.

"Good. Now breathe out slowly." A whooshing sound came across the line, and Ramona followed her mother's lead.

"Do it again," her mother directed once more, and then another time after that until Ramona's breathing steadied. On the other end of the telephone, her mother waited.

When she could speak again, Ramona asked, "Mom, what am I going to do? You know I need this job."

Her mom clicked her tongue, something she did when concentrating, before answering, "Yes, I know you do, sweetie. Now let's see. You have a few options here. You can ask for a new, earlier shift at Dusty's—"

Ramona cut in, "That won't work. Randy specifically said he needs a waitress on the night shift."

"Well, in that case," her mother continued, as though she hadn't been interrupted, "you may need to get creative."

"What do you mean?" Ramona hiccupped and wiped her eyes dry.

"Sweetie, sometimes you have to work around the system."

If anyone was in a position to give this advice, it was Ramona's mother. As a single parent, she'd had to live in a system made for traditional families and married couples with a mother and a father. That's why they'd lived with Ramona's grandparents since she was born. It had lightened the financial strain, and her grandparents watched her when her mother worked. Ramona couldn't wait to graduate and use her degree for a better job, a higher-paying job, to help them all.

"If you can't change your shift and you can't change the rules," her mother continued, "then you'd better find a way to work and get back inside unnoticed."

Ramona considered the idea. The prospect of sneaking in after curfew three nights a week, especially considering Mrs. Garth standing guard, filled her with dread, but she didn't see any other way.

"All right, I get it."

"I knew you would," her mom answered. "I have to run … I have a shift tonight. Are you going to be okay?" her mother asked. Ramona felt guilty for making her worry, but she couldn't keep something so big from her.

"You know I will be," Ramona assured. "Thank you."

"Always."

Ramona sniffled once more and said goodbye. Two girls waited in line for the phone, and she hoped they hadn't heard her conversation. She had a day to figure out how to sneak in after curfew. Wolden Hall housed hundreds of female students, and she needed to get to know the building better if she planned to slip in unnoticed.

A smattering of clouds filled the previously blue sky when Ramona got outside. She walked the path encircling the building, surveying the windows, entrances, dark-green bushes, and thick-trunked trees that stood every few paces. Then she did it again. There were five entrances—the main entryway in front, two doors in the back leading to the kitchen that looked like a docking zone for deliveries, and two emergency exits on either side of the building. Maybe she could—

"Hey! Ramona, right?"

Ramona didn't recognize the voice, and it was only when she saw who'd called to her that she realized why. Theo Rhodes stood a few yards away. Her stomach dipped delightfully, and her pulse thudded in her ears. He stood before her as though she'd wished him there.

His grin showed dazzling, white teeth and a dimple that could break a heart. Surely, it had already done the job many times over.

He extended his hand. "I'm Theo."

Ramona nodded, and Theo looked amused when she didn't respond right away.

"Ramona," she said and held out her hand to meet his. His warm palm encompassed hers. "But you knew that."

"Ramona," he echoed, as though learning a new language. "My brother told me you work together at Dusty's."

Again, she nodded. Words felt just out of reach. Even so, she couldn't look away. His eyes were a dark shade of blue that reminded her of the chilling Pacific Ocean where she'd spent summer weekends with her family. He wasn't as tall as Dimitri, but still far taller than herself, and she could see the flex of muscles beneath his black T-shirt as he held one hand in his pocket and the other gripped a copy of *The Making of the President, 1964*. The scent of soap and musk wafted from him, and she resisted leaning in.

"He mentioned your petition protesting the curfew. That's far out, really good stuff."

The surprise of his sudden appearance had made her forget the curfew for a moment. Now the memory of Dean Redley's smug face came flooding back, and she couldn't stop the bitterness that filled her voice when she said, "Not really. It didn't work."

Theo waited for her to continue, looking curious.

"My friend Mable and I met with Dean Redley today and showed him the petition. We got 448 signatures, but he rejected it."

Theo frowned and his jaw clenched. "I'll bet he barely looked at the petition, right? Said no before even really considering the stance of the students?"

"Exactly," Ramona said. Theo seemed to get it.

"This damn administration." Theo sighed. "They're so set in their old ways, even if it's against the will of the students."

Theo pushed back his dark, wavy hair, which had fallen across his forehead. His voice softened. "Still, it's impressive. What you did. You should hang out with me and my friends sometime." He cracked a smile that lit a fire in her stomach. "We've got a lot planned this year. You know, petitioning, protesting"—he paused—"and stuff."

"Hang out with The Foes?" Ramona blurted.

Surprise flashed across Theo's eyes. "So you've heard of us." Theo grinned and took a step closer, and Ramona lifted her eyes to meet his. "We're not as bad as people say. Maybe we can find a way to remove the curfew together. You know, join forces and all that."

"Why would you do that?" Ramona asked.

"Everyone needs help sometimes," Theo answered. "What do you say?"

Ramona had the sense that there was more he wasn't saying, and curiosity bloomed within her. His attention was fully focused on her, and even though it made her nervous, she liked it even more. She ignored Dimitri's warning in the back of her mind. "Okay."

Theo nodded with a satisfied quirk of his mouth. "We're meeting at Earl's tonight at 8 if you're free. You could bring your friend too."

Earl's was on a popular street filled with restaurants and shops just off campus.

"Sure. That sounds fun," Ramona agreed, feeling like she may go into shock at the unexpectedness of his invitation. Had he really sought her out to meet her and invite her to hang out?

His eyes brightened. "I'll see you tonight, Ramona."

He was about to turn away when Ramona blurted, "What does 'The Foes' mean?"

Theo laughed and cocked a dark eyebrow in challenge. "You'll have to show up to find out."

He swaggered away like someone who knew exactly what he was doing.

Ramona collapsed on the nearest bench to give her mind a moment to catch up with her racing heart. She'd thought of Theo so often that she could hardly believe what just happened. And what had he meant by *protesting and stuff*? Ramona saw protests on the television, of course, and a few small rallies on campus in the last week, but Theo's vagueness intrigued her. She intended to find out, especially if it meant extending the curfew.

CHAPTER 6

With low ceilings, dim lighting, and cheap beer, Earl's was a dive bar in every sense. And that meant students loved it there. With course loads still light during the second week of term, students crammed inside the joint. Some played pool, some played darts, and some danced next to the jukebox. Most simply pressed up against one another with a drink in hand, shouting to be heard over the noise.

As soon as Ramona stepped inside, she knew she'd overdressed. It felt as muggy as a sauna, and her skin itched in a turtleneck as she searched for a familiar face. Mable had stayed in to study and grumbled about the unfairness of having a quiz during the second week until Ramona promised to bring her the next time. Actually, Ramona had changed her mind about going multiple times. She didn't have time to hang out at a bar, even if Theo had been the one to invite her. She felt drawn to him in a way she couldn't explain, as though an invisible thread connected them. But he had offered to help them with the curfew, so really, this was like a business meeting. And if she had fun, that wouldn't be the worst thing in the world.

Ramona squinted in the dark until she saw Theo sitting in the far corner at a crowded, round table. Dimitri was there too. Ramona's body hummed with anticipation.

From the moment Theo invited her, butterflies had taken flight within her. And it didn't help that she planned to sneak in past curfew for the first time the following night with Mable's help. Once Mable had returned to Wolden that afternoon, they'd started planning over a dinner of beef stew in the cafeteria. They'd figured out that as long as Ramona left for her shift before students were required to sign out for the night, she wouldn't be on the list that Mrs. Garth would be waiting up for. For all Mrs. Garth knew, Ramona would be in her room, studying the whole night. At least, that's what they hoped.

Ramona took a deep breath and pushed thoughts of tomorrow night—of anything other than this moment—away. Steeling herself, she walked toward The Foes.

"Hey," Ramona said as she arrived in front of Theo.

Everyone looked up, and surprise flashed across Dimitri's face, who spoke first. "Ramona, what are you doing here?"

"I invited her," Theo replied.

Ramona looked at Theo, and as soon as their eyes met, she felt it again. Whatever it was that connected them. He stood up and held his arms out toward the rest of the group. "You made it. Come sit down."

Beside her, Dimitri blanched like he'd kissed a slug. His eyes widened, and he stared between her and his brother. Theo moved to offer her his chair, but Dimitri cut in.

"Here." Dimitri gestured to his chair. "You can have my seat."

A look of amusement crossed Theo's face as Dimitri stood up and switched places with Ramona. Dimitri looked shaken, but he quickly regained his composure. Ramona observed the exchange, unsure what to make of it.

"Ramona, let me introduce you to the group," Dimitri said.

"You've met Olly." Dimitri clapped him on the shoulder, and Ramona recognized him from their meeting outside Crane Hall. He looked cramped in the wooden chair, his knees high and shoulders slightly slouched. A cloud of smoke bloomed from the cigarette between his fingers.

Olly smiled widely. "Petition girl! Nice to see you again." Once more, his English accent delighted her.

"That's Don," Dimitri said, moving on to the next guy sitting in the circle. He was so thick-chested, he looked as though he could lift the table without breaking a sweat. Freckles covered most of his visible skin, and his thick, brown eyebrows stood out. Don raised a hand in greeting before gulping his beer without a word. He went back to shuffling a deck of cards.

Next, Dimitri introduced the two girls who sat side by side. "This is Cat. She's an English major and the smartest of the bunch." Cat had long, auburn hair, fair skin, and managed to look both engaged and completely uninterested all at once. She wore an oversized jacket that Ramona immediately envied.

"This is Betsy—" Dimitri said, before the second girl cut him off.

"And if we're assigning roles, I'm the coolest. Ask anyone." She smiled confidently, and while there were multiple eye rolls, everyone looked fondly at the petite girl with coiffed, blonde hair, chewing on a piece of gum.

Finally, Dimitri came to the last person in the circle. "And this is my brother, Theo."

Theo leaned back and hooked his right arm over the back of his chair. "Ramona and I met earlier," Theo explained.

Ramona added, "Theo was walking by Wolden and asked about the petition."

They all looked at her with interest, and Ramona squirmed under the attention. They seemed so much older than her, even if the age gap was only two years.

"Great," Dimitri mumbled before recovering some of his brightness. "Ramona, can I get you a beer?"

She nodded and thanked him before he left her alone with the group. When she turned toward him, Theo stared at her as though she was the only person there. A tingle ran down her spine under his gaze.

"So, Ramona," Olly said, before wiping his mouth with the back of his hand. "How many signatures did you get?"

Ramona shook off thoughts of Theo's eyes to answer, "Almost 450. But Dean Redley denied our request."

Across the table, Don grunted, and the rest made a range of frustrated noises as though they were on her side. When no one spoke, she continued, "Dean Redley"—she drew out his name—"said that extending the curfew was impossible. Actually, he said it was to protect female students." She choked out a bitter laugh. "He said it's for our own good and that we should be grateful."

"He didn't!" Betsy shrieked and leaned forward to slap a palm against the sticky table filled with empty cups.

Ramona nodded and Betsy shouted, "I hate him!" As loud as she'd shouted, the chaos of the bar swallowed the noise.

"Hate who?" Dimitri asked, reappearing with two beers in hand. Ramona accepted hers and recognized the familiar taste of Pabst, her grandfather's favorite. He'd always kept their fridge stocked, and every so often, Ramona would sneak a can and enjoy it from the vantage point of her windowsill. Now she appreciated having something to hold besides her own hands.

"Dean Redley," Cat snapped, "is a grade-A asshole."

The group laughed, and everyone chimed in.

"You all know the dean?" Ramona asked, looking around.

Noise erupted around her as they all spoke. Finally, Theo cut through the chaos. "Hey! One at a time. She can't hear you when you're all talking at once."

They quieted, and Theo looked at Ramona. "We've had a lot of interactions with the dean over the last couple years. He seems to have a particular interest in us. Just last week, he called campus security on one of our rallies. We weren't doing anything wrong. Well, not much anyway …" Beside him, Don snickered.

"Do you remember the letter he wrote to all students during our freshman year?" Cat asked. "Saying we should focus on our studies and ignore what's happening on campuses across the country. Yeah, that would be convenient for him, wouldn't it? So manipulative."

"And he's fake nice! Like he acts polite, but it's all a cover. He's a jerk. It would be better if he was just straight about it," Betsy added.

Ramona watched the group go back and forth, trying to keep up with everything they shared. She didn't want to miss anything. The fact that they'd faced off against the dean made her feel less alone.

Betsy turned to Ramona. "So what are you doing next?"

Ramona shrugged. "I haven't figured that out yet."

She sensed that she could trust them, and yet, she didn't want to tell them about her and Mable's plan.

"Well, you've gotten people to start talking about the curfew again at least," Betsy complimented.

Ramona raised her eyebrows in acknowledgment and lifted her glass to drink rather than reply that it didn't feel like enough.

"What do you say, Foes?" Theo leaned forward until his elbows rested on the table. "I think we should join forces with

Ramona and Mable to see what we can do about the curfew while we fight for free speech."

"You can't be serious," Cat snapped from across the table. "What gives?"

They all turned in her direction, but Theo was the one who answered. "Gee, Cat, tell us how you really feel. What do you mean?"

"Her," Cat declared, pointing at Ramona with a long fingernail. "We're not exactly giving out invitations to join us."

Ramona's stomach flipped as embarrassment coursed through her.

"That might be true, but she isn't just anyone," Theo remarked. "Ramona and Mable got hundreds of signatures in less than a week. During their *first* week. It's fucking impressive, and honestly? It reminds me of us." Then Theo turned to Ramona as he said, "Whatever they're doing is working, and we'd be lucky to have them."

Admiration shone through his eyes, and Ramona felt it from her fingers to her toes.

"Besides, we're all juniors, other than Dimitri," Theo continued. "If we want to leave a legacy of activism on campus, we need to bring in underclassmen."

Cat seemed to consider this, and to her left, Betsy nodded like she agreed, but she didn't let go just yet.

She cocked her head to the side and claimed, "She could blab on us."

"I promise," Ramona said, shaking her head, "I won't say anything."

Cat looked unconvinced but a touch less hostile. Ramona turned to Theo again, who held her gaze as he said, "I trust her."

The tension stretched until Cat snapped, "Fine" and got up from the table. She strode toward the bar, her long hair swishing across her back.

Silence hung for a beat longer than comfortable until Don spoke.

"Sure," he answered in response to Theo's original question. "Anything to piss off Dean Redley."

"Hear! Hear!" Olly cheered, and Betsy echoed with claps. Everyone smiled besides Dimitri, who looked as if the hot water had run out halfway through his shower.

"Dean Redley won't know what hit 'im!" Olly bellowed, clinking glasses with everyone around the table.

When they'd calmed down some, Theo leaned toward Don. "Speaking of, has the administration responded yet about the rally?"

It turned out that The Foes had hosted a rally in Gauld Square to protest the war in Vietnam, and the campus police shut it down, despite it being largely peaceful. As she listened, it sounded like the school administration had recently implemented a policy limiting political activities on campus.

"And I want to know why," Theo practically growled with a white-knuckled grip on his beer glass.

Ramona sat back to listen and finished her beer before pouring another from the pitcher that had appeared. Suddenly, the heat hit her, and she peeled off her turtleneck, leaving her in a tank top. When she looked up, Theo's eyes seemed to spark on her. Surprising herself, Ramona held his gaze as she smoothed her hair until his smile widened and he turned back to Don.

"It's against our right to free speech is what it is," Theo responded to something Don had said.

In the background, the tinny whine of a guitar blared from the speakers. And had someone turned down the lights? Ramona could've sworn it had gotten darker in there.

"Why would they stop you from protesting?" Ramona didn't realize she'd spoken aloud until Cat, who had reappeared at some point in the last few minutes, whipped around to face her.

"Because," Cat said, drawing out the word like it was obvious, "the Man doesn't want their pretty-as-a-picture campus to turn into chaos."

Cat reached down and pulled a tube of lipstick from her purse. She uncapped the lid and puckered. Olly whistled and started fake-panting as she coated her lips in a shade somewhere between red and orange that matched her hair.

"Down boy," she said to Olly before continuing, "they want to control us."

Ramona scanned the room, worried what other students in the bar might think. In fact, lots of students looked their way, but none seemed upset. They looked at The Foes with a mixture of admiration and longing, like every kid who'd ever been left out during recess. And somehow, she sat with them.

"Have you seen their plans for the student union building?" Betsy asked. "It's going to be massive."

"Wouldn't you like that?" Cat teased, causing Betsy to turn bright pink from ear to ear and erupt in giggles. "You're not wrong." She covered her mouth with her hand.

"We don't want a fancy building ... we want free speech," Cat answered seriously now.

"Speak for yourself," Olly chimed in. "I'd take both."

"My buddy Archer, an old friend from growing up"—Theo turned toward Ramona to clarify before continuing—"told me they're planning to use the new student building to host President Johnson when he visits in the spring. He also told me they've added faculty to the student body government, claiming that it gives them 'more opportunities,' but we see right through that. It's about administration oversight. And I'll tell you what it all means. What we're doing is working. We're getting to them. And I have a plan to make sure it works," Theo said.

Surprisingly, the group stilled as they waited for more, but Theo remained quiet.

Betsy was the one to burst out, "Tell us the plan!"

"Later." Theo raised his eyebrows playfully as he leaned back.

Don slammed his glass against the top of the table in salute, and Olly howled, his arm snaking behind Cat's neck.

"How high do you think that sign is?" Olly asked out of the blue, nodding toward the neon outline of a woman's body on the wall. Ramona hadn't noticed it until now.

Don shrugged. "Ten feet?"

"Bet you can't touch it," Olly taunted with a mischievous glint in his eyes.

Don's face shifted to a look of determination as he studied the sign. Beside him, Dimitri sighed and shook his head. "You two are menaces."

"And a pair of chickens," Theo chimed in wickedly. "Do it."

Don finished his beer and walked toward the sign, while Olly's eyes gleamed with delight. When Don stood a few feet away, he shifted his weight back before launching forward and running one, two, three steps to jump with his arm outstretched. As he crashed into the wall, his fingers just barely grazed the lit sign.

Olly and Theo roared in delight, and Cat rolled her eyes. Groups around the bar were staring at them, and the bartender looked none too happy, but Don walked back to their table like he'd won a battle.

"Next round is on you," Don said to Olly.

"You know, I think it's been a while since Bets paid." Olly turned to Betsy.

"I paid last week, you doofus," Betsy snapped.

Olly raised his hands and stood up before heading to the bar.

By the time Olly returned with more drinks, they'd all moved to one of the pool tables. As Olly handed her a drink, Ramona noticed the clock over his shoulder and stiffened. Fifteen minutes to midnight. Shit. It felt as if she woke up from a dream as she remembered the curfew. Wolden was clear across campus, so she'd have to hustle to make it in time. She couldn't get a citation.

Ramona waded through bodies to scoop up her turtleneck from the table. Theo appeared before her. She looked up, her face only inches from his neck, and gulped.

"You're leaving?" he asked.

"The curfew."

Theo set down his not-yet-finished glass. "Let's go."

Warmth spread through her and she nodded. As they made their way toward the exit, at least five people called out to Theo in greeting, and she felt curious eyes on her. Then they passed Dimitri.

"Ramona, are you leaving? I can take you," Dimitri said.

Before she could respond, Theo cut in. "I've got her. I invited her, so it's only right that I get her home safely."

Dimitri's face drooped, but Ramona didn't have time to linger. Soon they were outside, and the cool night air felt as good as aloe vera on a sunburn. There were others hurrying back toward campus, indebted to the same curfew as she.

As Ramona and Theo walked in companionable silence, he seemed content, but she wanted to hear his voice.

"Thank you for offering to help with the curfew."

"Of course."

"But why would you? What's in it for you?"

Theo chuckled beside her before answering, "It's just like I said. We'd be lucky to have you in our group."

"I feel like there's something else," Ramona teased, feeling bold enough to push him.

"You do, huh?"

"Yeah, I do."

"All right, fine," Theo hedged. "I might have one other reason."

"I knew it." Ramona grinned.

She hadn't realized they'd reached Wolden, in the very spot where they'd met a few hours earlier, until Theo stopped walking.

"So what is it?" Ramona asked.

Theo sighed, and then his face grew earnest as he answered, "I want to know you."

Her breath caught in her chest at the admission, and Ramona couldn't ever remember hearing anything more wonderful. His attention overwhelmed her in the best way, but once she'd finished committing the look on his face and the words he spoke into her memory, she pushed against the feelings he brought out in her. Otherwise, these feelings, this crush, could become something real.

"But why?" she asked again. Who was she to him?

"Now that," Theo chided, "I won't say."

She opened her mouth to protest, but then she noticed a couple girls run by and toward the front steps of Wolden and hesitated. Seeing that Theo wore a watch, she asked him for the time.

"11:58."

Soon she would be inside and he would be gone, probably back to the bar with all the students who could be out at any hour. She deflated, picturing the dozens of girls at Earl's, and then immediately scolded herself for thinking such a thing. She looked up at him and reluctantly took a step back. It had been such a good night, practically perfect, and she already mourned its passing. This could all just be a dream, and tomorrow she'd wake up with Theo a stranger once more.

"Hey," Theo said softly, "what is it?"

He reached out to touch her, but hesitated when the tips of his fingers were only a few inches from her cheek. Ramona's heart pounded, and she restrained herself from closing the gap. His jaw clenched before he sighed, and looking resigned, he slipped his hands in his pockets instead.

"I have to go."

Theo nodded. "I'm glad you came tonight."

"Me too. Thank you for inviting me."

"You know, we're making a leaflet to call out the campus police for shutting down our rally last week. You should help us."

Ramona agreed, wanting to see him again. Only a foot away, Theo's mouth cracked into a smile, and that dimple appeared again.

Then he leaned forward to whisper at the edge of her ear, "Sleep well, Ramona."

His voice, like a lullaby, sent chills down her spine.

"Almost midnight!" a girl shrieked from the front door.

Ramona turned away and ran up the front steps without looking back. As soon as she stepped inside, she pressed her hand against her fluttering heart and hurried upstairs. For the first time in a week, she didn't think about the curfew as she drifted off to sleep.

***

On the one hand, Ramona had made more in tips tonight than she usually did on weekdays. On the other, she'd mixed up three orders, which meant that Randy barked at her more than usual, making her barely held control that much more fragile. But she'd made it through her shift, and the drive back to campus had been uneventful.

Now Ramona saw the top of Wolden over the trees as she pulled into the closest parking lot and turned off her car. The absence of the radio and engine running meant that she could practically hear her heart beating rapidly. She felt so nervous, she was having trouble breathing. Was any air getting to her lungs? Pulling at the collar of her blouse gave little relief.

Suddenly, a loud, clattering noise startled Ramona. Heart racing, she looked out the front windshield expecting the worst, but laughed when she saw the cause of the disruption—a raccoon perched on top of a tipped-over garbage can with trash spilling out.

"Well aren't you trouble," Ramona mumbled under her breath.

She looked at her watch and gulped. Just after 12:30 a.m. Ramona steeled herself and got out of the car. It was time to see if their plan would work. If it did, Mable would be waiting beside the back door, listening for the signal.

Ramona clutched her purse to her chest and tiptoed toward Wolden. No one was out, besides the raccoon, and she felt slightly more confident. It had been a wet, overcast day, and the weather kept students inside. A good thing, too, because she knew she looked guilty as she crept across campus past curfew.

Ramona went to the unmarked emergency exit at the back of the building and tried the handle. Locked. Ramona grimaced. She released the handle, and her hands trembled. Taking a deep breath, she knocked three times.

Amazingly, the door cracked open an inch.

"Ramona?"

"It's me," Ramona confirmed.

The door opened to reveal Mable standing in a darkened hallway. She gestured for Ramona to come inside and closed the door behind her with a barely audible click of the latch.

Standing in the dark space together, they looked at one another until they broke out giggling.

"Shh," Mable hushed before pointing a finger toward the stairs.

Slowly, slowly they snuck up the stairs and went to the second-floor bathroom where Ramona had stashed a pair of pajamas. If anyone saw them, they would say they'd woken up to pee. As soon as they were inside the bathroom and checked that they were alone, they jumped up and down in delight.

"You're amazing!" Ramona whispered. "The door was locked. I would have been stuck outside."

"Don't mention it." Mable shrugged. "I've always been a rebel at heart."

Ramona dropped her purse on the tile floor and changed into her pajamas.

"Really, thank you. I don't know what I'd do without you."

"You can make it up to me by telling me how Earl's was." Mable reached for a paper towel and began splashing water from the sink across her face. "I've been dying to know."

There hadn't been time to fill her in yet.

Ramona shoved her uniform into her purse and began the painstaking process of washing her own face and wiping her black mascara off. Side by side, they leaned over the white, ceramic sinks, leaving makeup stains on the sides of the bowls.

"You know, I'm not sure how to describe it."

"Well, that sure paints the picture." Mable scowled. "Go on, tell me what happened."

Ramona sighed and took a moment to dry her face. Sensing that Mable wouldn't let this go, she started at the beginning from the moment she'd walked into Earl's, embarrassed to be by herself, to Theo walking her home.

"Theo Rhodes walked you home?" Mable's eyes were wide and red from all the rubbing.

"Well, he did invite me …"

"Wow," Mable said in hushed reverence.

"It doesn't mean anything," Ramona insisted.

"What are you talking about?" Mable snapped. "Of course it means something! How exciting."

"Now, why'd you say his name like that?" Ramona asked.

"This is just the grooviest thing I've ever heard! We've only been on campus for a week, and I've already heard Theo's name mentioned by ten different people. He's a legend around here. And he likes you!" Mable beamed as if she'd gotten the last slice of cherry pie in the cafeteria.

"No, he doesn't."

Ramona shook her head before tying her hair into a braid to sleep in. She wouldn't allow herself to go down that path of thinking.

"Whatever you say," Mable muttered, unconvinced before giving her a quick hug and saying good night. When she was halfway out of the bathroom, she paused and turned back. "I can't wait to go with you next time."

Ramona smiled and agreed before grabbing her things to go to her own room. Inside, Patsy slept with a silk mask over her eyes and ear plugs wedged deep. Ramona's limbs loosened.

That part had been tricky. Just that morning, Patsy had commented on Ramona's sleeping habits.

"You sure stay up late, don't you?" Patsy had asked.

Over the past week, Ramona studied late into the night to make up for all the time she'd spent petitioning during the day. But Patsy didn't need to know the why, so Ramona told her, "I've been studying."

Patsy had nodded. "The coursework is more than you expected? That's what everyone says. Well, don't forget the importance of beauty sleep." Then she'd given her a once-over so thorough that Ramona felt stripped bare.

"I didn't realize you were so aware of my sleeping schedule," Ramona said.

"Speaking of," Patsy said, "you shouldn't sleep on your side, you know."

"Yeah? Why's that?"

"You'll get wrinkles on your chest."

They had both looked down at Ramona's décolletage, and Ramona scowled. "Anyway, can you study in the lounge at night?" Patsy asked. "I'm turning the lights off at 10 p.m. I read an article saying that the best night's sleep starts then."

"Sure, no problem," Ramona agreed, not believing her luck. From then on, she wouldn't have to explain her absence to Patsy, who believed her to be a night owl, studying away in the lounge.

Ramona beamed as she tiptoed toward her bed and slid beneath the covers. It had worked. Seeing Mable on the other side of the door had sparked a glimmer of hope. They could do this.

Ramona closed her eyes, but sleep didn't come easily. Somewhere underneath the hope and excitement was an uncomfortable feeling—guilt. She couldn't help thinking of Donna and all the girls who had signed the petition. What would they do with the curfew in place? She burrowed deeper beneath the covers and thought about the others until exhaustion overtook her.

CHAPTER 7

Ramona didn't think she'd ever felt grateful for a Coke bottle before, and yet, here she was holding one to her left eye. The cold seeped into her skin as she rolled it back and forth. At home, her mother kept a stockpile of spoons in the freezer to depuff their eyes each morning. The soda bottle made for a nice substitute. Ramona repeated the movement before looking at Mable across the cafeteria table.

"Any better?"

"Honestly?" Mable asked and Ramona nodded. "Not much. Maybe if you did it longer."

Ramona sighed and uncapped the bottle. She drank greedily and savored the sharp, sweet taste. Across from her, Mable looked amused.

"If it makes you feel better, mine don't look much better."

"It doesn't." Ramona scowled. "I don't think I've ever been this tired before."

Her reflection in the mirror that morning had startled her. Ramona looked awful. Between school, work, and sneaking in after curfew three times in the last week, she always felt on the go. And then sleep eluded her when she'd slipped into bed each night.

"You and me both," Mable said between bites of soup. She gestured to the table. "I think I may just lie down right here and take a little nap."

"Thanks for letting me in last night," Ramona said as she twirled a strand of her hair. "Seriously, you say the word and we stop."

"I told you already, we'll keep going as long as the curfew's in place. I'm fine. I'm just not much of a morning person."

"It's noon," Ramona remarked, and Mable waved her hand as if that didn't make any difference.

Ramona forced down a bite of grilled cheese as anxiety clawed its way up her throat. So far, Mable had been able to sneak Ramona in without difficulty, but they could get caught any time. They needed a backup plan, one that would help other girls too. Theo's offer last week had given Ramona hope for the first time since leaving Dean Redley's office.

About twenty yards away, Patsy entered the cafeteria and strode toward the food counter. Ramona sank in her seat.

Mable frowned. "What are you doing? Oh." She caught sight of Patsy too.

Patsy wore a long, pale-green skirt, the color of the mints at her doctor's office, and clutched a bundle of books. The *Women's Handbook* was on top. Ramona rolled her eyes.

Once they'd finished eating, Ramona and Mable cleared their trays before leaving for their remaining classes of the day.

"Hang on," Ramona called as she went to the beverage cart looking for coffee.

Only a layer of thick, brown sludge remained at the bottom of the coffeepot. Ramona sighed before looking for tea, only to find that out of stock from the breakfast and lunch rush. The only option appeared to be a jug of juice. Ramona sniffed it.

"Apple cider?" Ramona mumbled to herself. "I just want some caffeine." But without the option, she opted for sugar instead of nothing and filled the canister she'd brought before returning to Mable.

As soon as they left the cafeteria, wind whipped against Ramona's body, and she tightened her scarf around her neck. She wished she could be back in bed huddled beneath the blankets, but there wasn't a chance she'd skip class and hurt her grades.

A few minutes later, Ramona took a seat in her Public Speaking class by the generator as the bell rang and Professor Scott stood at the front of the room.

"Good afternoon. I hope you all enjoyed a filling lunch and are able to keep your eyes open because I have two speeches to share with you today."

Ramona sat up straighter and blinked a few times. She wasn't the only one.

"Before we get started, I want to remind you all of the upcoming assignment due in two weeks before we're consumed by today's lesson. Does anyone need a refresher?"

Multiple heads nodded around the classroom.

"I thought so," Professor Scott remarked. "For your next assignment, you are each to attend a live speech and write a report on it. It can be on any *appropriate* topic given by anyone, as long as it's presented live. I look forward to reading your reports and hearing your thoughts on how hearing a speech in person differs from reading about them. Now, let's begin today's lecture."

Professor Scott wrote two names on the blackboard. The first was a famous politician whose speeches and interviews were regularly aired on the radio. Ramona hadn't heard of the second.

"Today, we're going to dissect two political speeches, the first of which by this gentleman"— Professor Scott indicated toward the first name—"inspired the second."

"Let's start with the first," the professor said before reading the following snippet of the speech aloud:

For those of you asking me for my stance on the war, I have this to say: You're damn right that we need to be in Vietnam. When our French allies needed our help, America wasn't going to stand back. We were needed, and we're still needed. America is founded on freedom, and that freedom is at risk by communism. Look toward China and the Soviet Union and tell me that the threat of global communism isn't there. It is. The foundation of freedom is democracy, and America will do everything possible to uphold the power of democracy around the world.

Our boys are fighting as hard and as fast as they can to get the job done. No one likes to see such violence and death, but it's the price we pay for our freedom, and I commend those boys for their service. While there's more to be done, America is making progress, and I have no doubt that we'll come out victorious and bring our boys home soon.

Professor Scott's voice echoed around the room as the students shifted in their seats. The choice of speech surprised Ramona. While Vietnam was a constant in the news and in protests on campus, it hadn't been discussed so directly in any of her classes yet. Earlier in the year in March, President Johnson made the move that he'd been long avoiding—he put ground troops in Vietnam. And ever since, the pressure to send more increased. Ramona didn't know what her stance on the war was, only that it made her sad.

"Now before we shift to the second speech, does anyone want to share their thoughts on the first?" Professor Scott wore the hopeful and expectant look common to teachers, just a shade toward vulnerable.

A brave student in the first row raised his hand.

"The speech is passionate," he ventured. "It's clear by their use of 'I' and 'We' statements that they feel a personal stake in the war, and that came through clearly."

Professor Scott nodded. "Good observation."

A second student, a tall guy to Ramona's left, chimed in. "The politician is clearly in President Johnson's pocket."

"Elaborate," Professor Scott prodded.

"Well, it's obvious. The speech is very pro-war and glosses over all the reasons we shouldn't be there."

"Another good observation. Now we know where you stand, Jeff," Professor Scott remarked not unkindly. "That's a good transition to the next speech."

Professor Scott picked up a second piece of paper and read aloud:

You're not asking for my opinion on the war, but you can bet your bottom dollar I'm going to say it anyway: I think we need to be in Vietnam because my ego is too fragile to have a single original thought. For example, rather than holding our French allies accountable for mistakes made in Vietnam, America blindly went in to support them at harm to our own people and the innocent Vietnamese civilians. America is founded on the notion of freedom, and we don't care what the destruction left behind looks like. Rather than coming up with a modern solution to combating global communism—see China and the Soviet

Union here—we've resorted to what we know best: Firearms and men on the ground to show our power and the power of so-called democracy around the world.

Our boys are fighting and dying until the government says that the job is done. No one likes to see such violence and death, but it's not my life, so I'm willing to put their lives on the line for our freedom. I commend those boys for their service, but America is not making progress. We will not come out victorious and should bring our boys home. What's the definition of victory when it comes to death anyway?

Somehow, the room was even quieter than before.

Professor Scott spoke through the silence. "Now this isn't intended to become a discussion on political stances. You can save those debates for your political science courses. But I would like to hear your opinion on the speech structure and the juxtaposition between the two."

The clock ticked on the wall, and playful shouts floated in from the window, made all the louder by the quiet within. Professor Scott paced at the front of the room as the students reflected.

Ramona realized she had something to say and raised her hand. Professor Scott nodded.

"The second speech is structured in exact parallel to the first. It seems as though the second speaker intended to do this to leave no doubt that they oppose this politician's position. I've never heard of the second speaker, so I have to assume that they may not be as well-known as the politician, and they used this direct approach to get more attention on their own speech. In fact, the parallel makes the second speech more original than if it had been written completely separately." Ramona's heartbeat quickened as her classmates surveyed her. But Professor Scott looked at her warmly, and she appreciated the encouragement. When no one spoke, Ramona added, "In my opinion."

"You'll tire of hearing me say this phrase, but here it comes. Good observation, Ramona." Professor Scott smiled. "Who else?"

The class carried on, and a few more students shared their opinions as raised hands turned into blurted comments that bounced around the space like popcorn. She couldn't remember a more interesting conversation. As she listened to her classmates discuss the symmetry between the two speeches, an idea popped into her head completely unbidden … an idea to bring the issue of the curfew to the forefront on campus by leveraging existing materials, just as the second speech had done. As the idea took shape, Ramona smiled, knowing that it was good. Really good. And it would infuriate Patsy.

***

Pages spread out before her on the desk, each filled with rows of crossed-out sentences. Ramona glared at the words as though they would reformulate before her eyes if only she stared hard enough. They didn't. Ramona groaned.

The idea that had formed from the pair of speeches in Professor Scott's lecture had only grown clearer over the past two days, and she'd spent all her free time working on it. If the *Women's Handbook* was treated as the ideal by all the good girls on campus—Ramona was quickly learning that she didn't fall into that category—there should be a version for everyone else. For the girls like her.

A *Women's Anti-Handbook.*

"Should we go?"

Mable leaned against the doorframe. "You said we're meeting Dimitri in fifteen minutes."

"Oh yeah." Ramona rubbed a hand across her cheek. "I guess so."

"Good, because I'm dying to know what he's showing us. Who's Dimitri again?"

Ramona stood up and grabbed the jacket resting on the back of her chair. She followed Mable out of the room and locked the door behind her.

"He's my friend from Dusty's. Theo's little brother."

Mable danced down the stairs on the balls of her feet and looked back at Ramona with a glint in her eye.

"Interesting."

"If you say so," Ramona mumbled and shifted to lead them toward the meeting spot.

When they arrived, Dimitri stood up from the bench and greeted them. Ramona introduced the pair, and Dimitri stuck out a hand toward Mable.

"It's nice to meet you, Mable."

"Same to you," she answered, before turning to business. "Where are we going?"

Dimitri chuckled and waved for them to follow.

After meeting The Foes at Earl's last week, Dimitri had offered to bring Ramona to discuss the leaflets. And she'd invited Mable.

They walked across campus in silence until Dimitri scoffed at a makeshift stand recruiting for the military. Ramona followed Dimitri's gaze to a poster hanging from the table. A good-looking man smiled at passersby with the claim 'Go navy and travel' above his sailor's cap. Dimitri quickened his pace as he led the girls past the recruiters.

A few minutes later, impatience overtook Mable. "C'mon. Won't you tell us where we're going yet?"

"We're almost there," Dimitri said, gesturing to the building ahead. "You see, Theo's good at making friends. He knows almost everyone from the custodians to the cooks, and that means he knows about everything that happens on campus. That's how he found out about this spot."

"Which is ...?"

"The old, abandoned pool." Dimitri beamed with amusement, and Ramona felt the excitement exuding from him.

Mable stopped in the middle of the path, and Ramona bumped into her.

"Seriously?" Mable asked.

"Seriously," Dimitri confirmed.

"Cool!" Mable cheered before jolting forward to catch up with Dimitri, and Ramona did the same.

"The pool's been empty ever since the swimming program lost funding. Now, it's where The Foes plan their demonstrations. Technically, they broke in when Don smashed the lock on the chain with a hammer," Dimitri explained. "But no one uses the pool, so it's no big deal."

Ramona looked toward Mable and saw her own anticipation mirrored on her friend's face.

Once they reached a dilapidated building, Dimitri led them toward the side entrance. The door went down to the basement, and they slipped inside a dimly lit hallway filled with spider webs and footprints in dust. At the end of the hallway, a chain dangled off one handle of a set of double doors. Dimitri raised his hands to push the doors open but paused to look back at the girls.

"You can't tell anyone about this, all right?" Dimitri asked, looking at Mable specifically. "They'd be pissed if they lost their spot."

Mable scowled and Ramona assured him, "We won't." She shifted forward on her toes, eager to see inside.

Dimitri nodded, pressed both palms to the doors, and pushed. They revealed a cavernous space with high ceilings. The sound of laughter echoed and hit them squarely in the face as they walked inside. Sure enough, there was a large, empty pool that clearly hadn't seen any care recently. Rust stained the edges of the blue paint, and the '57 and '59 swim championship flags hung limply.

A group sat on the floor of the deep end in chairs with trailing scuff marks. Ramona recognized each of them from Earl's. Ramona's eyes went straight to Theo, who sat backward in a chair, his forearms resting atop the backrest, and her heart fluttered at the sight of him.

"Hey!" Olly called out from his seat on the floor, leaning against Cat's legs, the noise echoing off the walls. "It's petition girl! 'Bout time you got here."

Ramona said, "Hi, Olly."

Cat pressed her lips together and looked away just as Olly noticed Mable. "And who's this?"

Ramona introduced them, and it didn't escape her that Mable's cheeks pinkened at his attention.

Olly greeted her, "Welcome, Mable."

Dimitri, Ramona, and Mable lowered themselves, one at a time, down the railing to join the others in the empty pool. Theo stood up and patted his brother on the arm before reaching out a hand to introduce himself to Mable. Then he shifted his full attention to Ramona, as though he'd been waiting for her.

"Hey."

He stepped forward as if to hug her, and although she wanted him to, he hesitated and waved instead. Eager to hide her disappointment, she asked, "So this is your hideout?"

Theo nodded. "The administration would have a fit if they knew we were here planning demonstrations, but that's what makes it fun." He winked.

"Here," Theo said, dragging his chair toward them, "get comfortable." Ramona offered it to Mable and sat down beside her with legs crossed.

Once they'd settled in, Theo continued on with what he'd been saying. "Now, about these leaflets. We agree that they should bring attention to two things. First, the new limitations on political activity on campus—"

"Fucking free speech restrictions is what it is," Don interrupted.

"Couldn't agree more." Theo clapped his hands together. "Second, the addition of faculty to the school's student body government. The whole point of a student body government is to elevate the voice of students, but Dean Redley and his idiot team are only elevating their own."

Ramona nudged Mable and rolled her eyes at the mention of the dean.

"Does that cover it?" Theo asked, and everyone nodded. He surveyed the group, checking in with each person before moving on. Ramona's breath caught when his eyes met her own. "All right, then, we're in agreement. Cat, do you want to take it from here?"

Cat unwound her legs from Olly to pull out a notebook, and he frowned as though he'd been kicked out in the cold without a jacket. Over the next hour, she outlined the content for the leaflet with the helpful, and sometimes unhelpful, input from the group. Ramona had barely spoken during the brainstorm, had only answered a question directed to her, and Mable hadn't said a thing.

When they'd finished, Cat ripped out a piece of paper and handed it to Don, who was tasked with getting the leaflet printed using the school's newspaper printer. Apparently, Theo had befriended the editor of *The Daily*.

Theo leaned against the wall of the pool looking pleased until he noticed Ramona's expression.

As Betsy talked about the benefits of colored paper, Theo mouthed to Ramona, "Are you okay?"

Ramona nodded just as Betsy whined, "Can I tell them yet?"

"Tell us what?" Cat snapped.

"Tell you how we're going to pass out the leaflets," she said with a waggle of her eyebrows.

"Let's keep it a secret." When Betsy pouted, Theo reassured her, "It will be more fun."

To the group, Theo said, "Let's meet here on Monday at 11:30. Don, print a thousand copies, more if there's time. And Ramona and Mable, that goes for you too. I want you here."

The excitement bloomed among the group, and Ramona couldn't stand to wait through the weekend.

Done for now, the group shifted and stood up. They grabbed their bags and headed out to join the rest of the campus, their shoes squeaking against the pool floor.

"I almost forgot," Theo called out with a devious look, bumping into Olly's shoulder. "Bring your sneakers."

CHAPTER 8

Three days later, with a bundle of papers tucked beneath her arm, Ramona found Mable lounging in her room. Upon her arrival, Mable lifted her eyebrows in a silent question and Ramona nodded. Mable jumped off the bed and switched off the radio from which Dusty Springfield crooned about wishing and hoping. Ever since Ramona had worked up the courage to share the idea for a *Women's Anti-Handbook*, Mable had provided the encouragement and push Ramona needed to finish writing it.

"It's about time." Mable extended her hand. "Give it here."

Ramona passed her the pages of the drafted *Women's Anti-Handbook* and sat down at the desk. "You're the first person reading it, so go easy on me, all right?"

Mable hushed her and held the paper inches from her nose.

"I think you might need glasses," Ramona teased.

"Can you imagine? I got picked on enough as a kid. Now let me read."

Nerves rolled through Ramona while she did her best to be patient. After spending every waking hour thinking about, writing, and editing the *Women's Anti-Handbook*, she'd finished it. When she'd delivered a cheeseburger and fries to one of her regulars, she planned. When she should've been looking for speeches for her Public Speaking assignment, she wrote. When she ate, she edited. She didn't know what surprised her more—the fact that she'd done it or that she'd enjoyed it.

Another plus was that she'd found a favorite spot in the library. She'd stumbled upon one of the elusive, cushioned chairs and set up a private spot to work. On Friday, when students swapped their books for beer and welcomed the weekend like a good friend, she'd dragged a chair to the back of the stacks without another person in sight. On her way to Zuccaro Library, Theo had spotted her.

"Ramona!" he'd called out, and when she turned, he was leaning against a tree across the quad.

Somehow, she wasn't surprised. Every interaction felt preordained, like her body expected him before her mind caught up.

"Where are you going?"

Without slowing, she'd yelled back, "Zuccaro!"

"What's the rush?"

"I'm working on something."

"What is it?" He had shifted toward her, but Ramona waved him off. She didn't want to be distracted.

"You'll see!"

Even now, she couldn't get the image of his reaction out of her mind. As she'd waved goodbye, she caught a glimpse of Theo's eyes crinkling at the edges in amusement.

Now, Ramona picked up the wooden bird carving that lived on Mable's desk. A cardinal, specifically. When Ramona had asked about it the first time she'd seen it, Mable had explained that her dad made it. The Mooney family enjoyed bird-watching. Ramona rubbed her thumb over the smooth wood to distract herself and read over Mable's shoulder:

Female students receive a Women's Handbook *at the start of term with a set of rules that are only applied to half of the student body. While all students are adults, only men are treated as such. We women don't have the freedom to choose what's best for us—we don't have control over where we go, how we spend our time, and when. Every student deserves the freedom of adulthood.*

The school administration thinks that we're sheep that all look, sound, and think the same. Sheep that they can control.

If you want to be seen as a student, this Women's Anti-Handbook *is for you! And you know what it says? Do whatever the hell you want.*

She'd written it with firm and direct language. Written that they should ignore the advice on dating, socializing, making friends, and dressing from the AWS-sponsored *Women's Handbook*. There were also tips for sneaking in past curfew that she and Mable had picked up over the past couple weeks of doing it themselves. That's where the biggest risk came in. The more people snuck in after curfew, the more likely someone would get caught, and security would tighten for everyone.

Mable ran her pointer finger along the lines of text before announcing, "Done."

"So? Be honest."

"It's really good," Mable said, her eyes shiny like a proud parent. "It's readable, the tone is spot-on, and it has detailed advice for what we in the business like to call 'navigating' the curfew. I have some edits for that last section, though, if that's all right?"

Ramona nodded, and her chest warmed at the positive feedback, just as it had when she'd received an A for her last Public Speaking essay.

"We should add a note about the housemothers," Mable suggested.

The pair spent the next hour or so editing the section concerning the curfew before they called it complete.

"Do you want to show it to The Foes next?"

Ramona sighed, the vulnerability making her uncomfortable. "I think we've got to, don't we?"

The Foes had sway on campus, not to mention the access to printers. Besides, they were partnering now, weren't they?

"After the leaflets?" Mable asked.

"After the leaflets," Ramona confirmed.

The girls made their way to the abandoned pool.

***

Ramona wore her old sneakers, which carried her through countless shifts at Dusty's, and she hoped they'd do the same this afternoon. She stood at the top floor of the staircase in Cobble Hall, only a foot away from Theo. She drummed her fingers across the banister. Class was about to let out.

Beside her, Theo bent at the waist and leaned his elbows on the railing. Her eyes tracked from his own sneakers, up his tight blue jeans, and across the jacket that flaunted his strength. Theo grinned and shot her a knowing look. Shit. She turned away and scowled. He'd caught her.

She studied the panels of the ceiling, looking anywhere but at him, when he asked, "So are you going to tell me?"

"Tell you what?" Ramona asked.

"Whatever had you running to the library on a Friday."

Oh, that. He was still curious, was he?

"Maybe I like the company there." Ramona shrugged and checked the clock. Three minutes.

Theo snorted. "Sure, that's it."

Ramona bit her lip to stifle her laugh as she locked eyes with him, and her heartbeat quickened. Gosh, he really was handsome. What she wanted to ask was why he wanted to know her, his claim from the other night lingering in her mind, but that felt too bold. Instead, she asked, "I recall a certain someone saying something suspiciously similar when I asked about The Foes."

"So you want to trade?"

"Maybe," Ramona murmured. "I'm not sure how much I care anymore."

Lie.

Theo's eyes bore into her, rising to her challenge. She couldn't look away as he shifted a step closer beside her, and her toes curled in those damned sneakers.

"Freedom of expression," Theo whispered. "It's what we stand for. The Free Speech Movement. Protesting the war. Olly thought of the name. He's cleverer than people give him credit for, and it stuck."

Ramona smiled. It made sense.

"Your turn." Theo shifted closer to her until his shoulder was mere inches from hers.

"I'll think about it," she teased.

He scowled.

Shaking his head, she thought she heard him mumble something that sounded an awful lot like "what are you doing to me" under his breath. She didn't dare ask. Doing so would risk losing the feeling of lightness expanding through her … a feeling so fragile and new.

Instead, she squeezed her eyes shut and gripped the leaflets against her chest.

"Nervous?" Theo asked.

"A little."

"Don't be. You know what to do."

She did. A half hour earlier, they'd been at the pool where Betsy had gone over the plan with enthusiasm that encouraged them all. Rather than handing out the leaflets one by one, or leaving stacks in common areas around campus, their method would garner more attention.

The group had split up, and each pair stood at the top of the staircase of the most crowded buildings on campus. Once the bell rang at noon, they would drop the leaflets down the center of the staircases, where the papers would cascade and drift into the arms of the students rushing from classes for lunch. As soon as they released the leaflets, they would blend into the crowds of students and meet back at the pool.

It wasn't exactly that they were doing anything against the rules. It was more that they wanted to fly under the radar. The school administration had a way of making life difficult for students who rebelled. Also, Betsy had promised that the anonymity would be more exciting. People want to know about the things they're excluded from.

It sounded simple enough, but Ramona worried she'd mess it up.

Ramona nodded at Theo. He brushed her shoulder ever so softly, and the gesture sent sparks bouncing through her like a pinball machine.

"Why didn't you speak up yesterday?" Theo asked.

"Maybe I didn't have anything to say."

"Could be." Theo shrugged. "But I don't buy that."

Then, to Ramona's stunned delight, he reached out as if to tuck a piece of hair behind her ear, but instead lightly traced his thumb across her cheek. The feel of his touch set her skin alight.

"I would've liked to hear what you were thinking," he encouraged.

She tried to suppress her smile.

"Next time," she said, "if you're lucky."

Emboldened by his touch, she wanted to know something in return.

"Why did you choose me to be your partner today?" Ramona asked.

Theo had volunteered before anyone paired off.

His serious expression turned playful. "For the charming company."

"Seriously?"

"Well, in that case," Theo answered with a wicked gleam in his eyes, "to check out your legs in that skirt."

Ramona huffed. "I'm being serious."

Theo lowered his head an inch closer to hers and stared straight into her eyes. "So am I."

Ramona opened her mouth, but no words came out. Instead, she felt heat spread across her cheeks at his admission.

"Ten, nine, eight …" Theo's eyes were on his watch as he counted down.

The shrill sound of the bell rang out. "Now."

Ramona raised her arms and held the leaflets out from her chest and over the opening of the staircase. As soon as she saw a head below, she let go and the leaflets rained down. Some separated, and the single sheets floated through the air, while others cascaded down around the students who filled the staircase.

She looked back at Theo, expecting to see his eyes on the leaflets, but they focused on her instead.

"Let's go!" She hurried toward the stairs.

Students spilled from classrooms, and Ramona and Theo joined the throng descending the stairs. The students looked around in confusion and grabbed at the flying pieces of paper. They rushed down the steps, floor after floor, until they reached the entrance, and Theo pushed the door open for them.

Just as they burst from the building, he held his hand out to her. Surprised, Ramona stared at his palm for a beat before taking it in hers. The steady weight of his warm palm felt like the most natural thing in the world. In a sea of raining leaflets and shocked students, Ramona and Theo laughed and ran. They wanted attention, and now they had it.

As they crossed the quad, leaflets were visible in dozens of hands. Ramona felt like she was on top of the world, and the only thing keeping her from floating into the sky was Theo's hand in hers. They dodged students reading leaflets as a strong gust of October wind nudged them on their way.

Once the old gymnasium building was in sight, Ramona saw Mable's blonde head from afar with Dimitri and Olly close behind. As they slipped inside, they checked over their shoulders. Ramona let go of Theo's hand and followed the others. When they were all gathered, they joked and vibrated around the empty pool in celebration.

"Betsy, that was fantastic. We should pass out all our leaflets like that. Good work, everyone!" Theo congratulated.

Ramona felt breathless as she turned to Mable.

"How did it go for you?"

"A teacher almost saw us, but Dimitri was really quick on his feet and hid the leaflets before she could see them."

Across the pool, Olly picked up Dimitri and swung him around the space until Dimitri, laughing, swatted him away. Then he turned for Cat, who dodged him, and Mable crossed her arms before looking away.

Breathlessly, Ramona asked the group, "So what's next?"

She wanted to keep going. Her limbs felt lighter, as though she had enough energy to pull a double shift. This feeling was power. Theo considered her.

"What do you think we should do?" Cat mocked. "If you're a part of the group now, you tell us what you think. There aren't instructions. We're making this up as we go."

Ramona looked across the circle at Mable, who nodded. She couldn't have asked for a better opening, although she could've done without Cat's judgmental gaze.

"I have an idea." She paused beneath their curiosity. "Mable and I wrote an anti-handbook. A *Women's Anti-Handbook*."

Before her, the group remained quiet, looking thoughtful. Ramona twisted her hair and waited.

"What's an anti-handbook?" Olly asked.

"It's a play on the official *Women's Handbook* that all female students receive. It basically brushes off all the ridiculous rules and advice, demanding equal rights for women."

Beside her, Mable nodded and Betsy looked impressed. Cat seemed a tad less hostile.

Of the four females and four males standing in the empty pool, the latter half didn't seem to understand the idea. No surprise there. The girls got it because they'd experienced the need for one. The boys didn't have a clue. Still, their curiosity was encouraging. Theo, Dimitri, Olly, and Don all appeared to be focusing intensely. Ramona would give them that. They wanted to understand.

A knot formed in Ramona's stomach. She wanted them to like her idea. Taking a deep breath from a chest that felt too small for her lungs, Ramona asked, "What do you think?"

"So this would be in protest of the curfew?" Theo asked.

"Yes," Ramona confirmed. "But not only that, the current handbook is a guide to life on campus—clubs and activities, academic programs, stuff like that. It also gives advice on how female students should act, sound, look, date, make friends. Basically, it's a rulebook for being the picture-perfect collegiate girl."

"And then there are the enforced rules." Cat stretched the words out.

"Exactly," Ramona agreed. "It also contains rules that cover females living on campus, like the curfew. My roommate, Patsy, the vice president of AWS, says it's a good thing, but—"

"Wait, wait," Betsy interrupted. "Patsy Connell is your roommate? She's awful!"

Beside Betsy, Cat's eyes narrowed.

"And Cat here went to high school with her," Betsy continued.

"Really? What was she like?"

"Different," Cat answered tightly.

When Cat didn't elaborate, Ramona turned back to Theo. "You see, AWS works with the school administration, with Dean Redley. Their *Women's Handbook* is another way for the school to control students."

Theo leaned against the pool wall, one leg crossed over the other, and tapped his fingers against his thigh as he considered.

"Help me understand how the *Women's Anti-Handbook* relates to the curfew in particular," Theo said.

Ramona looked at Mable for confirmation. When she nodded, Ramona knew they'd have to share their secret.

"Mable helps me sneak in after my waitressing shifts," Ramona said, hoping she could trust them. She'd have to. "And it works. At least, it has a dozen times. I can't be the only one who needs to sneak in after curfew, so we were thinking the *Women's Anti-Handbook* could give advice for sneaking into the dorms."

From only a few feet away, Ramona could see Theo's eyes glint with excitement, and everyone else looked toward Mable with admiration.

"That's righteous," Olly praised.

"Yeah, it is." Theo added, "That's exactly the type of thing we need to do. It's bold. It's risky. It's what students need."

Across the pool, Betsy clapped her hands together and yelped with glee. "I know … I know what we should do! It should be a secret, duh, but only selected students who we can trust will get a copy. It will make AWS crazy to know there's a *Women's Anti-Handbook* out there that they can't get their hands on. Oh, I'm so excited!"

"That's really important," Ramona added. "AWS and the school can't find the *Women's Anti-Handbook* and see the tricks for sneaking in. Otherwise, they'll tighten security, and then I won't be able to sneak in."

Betsy raised her finger in the air to mimic writing. "Noted!"

"Remind me why you can't get a new job," Don asked, and everyone turned to him.

His face reddened from the attention.

"Because I don't want a new job. Dusty's is in between home and school, so I can work there year-round, and I make good tips," Ramona said, her voice sharper than she'd intended. "Besides, that's not the point. I shouldn't have to get a new job."

"Hear! Hear!" Betsy lifted a fake glass in salute.

Don hunched forward and raised his hands in surrender. Theo pushed himself off the wall and paced back and forth.

"How long will it take you to write it?" Theo asked Ramona.

"It's finished," Ramona answered. "Mable edited it this morning."

Theo looked at her as if she were a map to buried treasure. "Even better. Cat, if Ramona is willing, will you take a look? Betsy, think about how we'll distribute ... who will get it and how we'll get it to them. Olly and Don, you'll get them printed once ready, and I'll do some scouting to make sure there won't be any problems with the student government." Theo paused and smiled. "What am I saying? You know the drill."

The group nodded in agreement and collected their things, their work effectively done. Ramona's stomach growled, and she hoped the cafeteria wasn't serving meatloaf again.

As they all walked toward the exit, Betsy called out to Ramona, "What do you think of this sweater? I just bought it."

Before she could answer, Theo appeared on her other side in the dark hallway leading away from the pool.

He whispered in her ear, "You did good today. Really good."

Ramona's skin prickled at his compliment. She tipped her head to face him. The edge of his mouth lifted, revealing gleaming teeth in the darkness, and Ramona couldn't help imagining the feel of them on her.

Then, just over Theo's shoulder, Ramona saw Dimitri watching them. Watching how close Theo's mouth had been to her ear and her resulting smile. Dimitri frowned. Theo followed Ramona's glance and stiffened as he looked between Ramona and Dimitri. Without hesitation, Theo shifted away from her and bounded forward to walk beside Don.

A sinking suspicion dawned within Ramona as she looked between the brothers. Did Dimitri have a problem with her getting to know Theo?

Ramona mouthed, “What’s wrong?” to Dimitri, and he mumbled back, “Nothing” before ducking his head and continuing to the exit. Staring at the back of his head, Ramona felt a potent mixture of frustration and worry swell within her.

Beside her, Betsy asked again, “So do you like it?”

The question about Betsy’s sweater snapped her out of the exchange.

“Yeah, it’s great,” Ramona answered as each step felt heavier than the last.

CHAPTER 9

Dark ink covered the pads of Ramona's fingers by the time she'd finished reading the local section of last weekend's *The Seattle Times* from her desk. The reading had been dull. The only article that struck her was a piece on the opening of a new department store downtown that boasted having everything anyone could want.

"Doubt that," Ramona mumbled.

She wiped off her fingers with a napkin and found a blank piece of paper.

Dear Editor,

While this Sunday's edition of the local section was fine (I would rate it 3 out of 5 stars), your article on the addition of Melvin's to the downtown corridor lacks depth. As your reporters regurgitate the promotion of the new department store's wares, there are troubling issues happening all across the city with no coverage in your paper. May I make a suggestion? Before you publish another glorified advertisement, investigate what's happening in this city.

Sincerely,

Petition girl

Ramona folded the letter and slipped it into one of the preaddressed envelopes she kept on hand. She licked the lip to seal it shut and hurried toward the mailbox closest to Gangly Hall, where Cat and Betsy expected her. Once Cat finished editing, Don and Olly would print the *Women's Anti-Handbook*. Her idea would be real. It both thrilled and terrified her.

With the letter safely sent, Ramona found Cat and Betsy sitting at a table a few minutes later. She wiped her palms against her sleeves before approaching them. Cat glared at the drafted *Women's Anti-Handbook* as though the words had stolen something from her, with an uncapped pen dangling from her mouth. Beside her, Betsy smiled at Ramona's arrival.

"Hey!" Betsy chirped.

Cat scowled. "Be quiet."

Betsy rolled her eyes conspiratorially as Ramona sat at the table with them. She took a large sip of apple cider, which she was really beginning to like, and waited.

"It takes time for her to work her magic," Betsy whispered. "No offense! Cat's just the best."

"It's fine." Ramona shrugged as Cat shook her head without removing her eyes from the pages.

Still whispering, Betsy said, "We can plan while Cat does her thing." She looked around the lobby once, then twice, before writing "The List" on a blank page.

In the four days since Ramona had shared the idea, Betsy had been eager to start the distribution plan, adamant that in order for the *Women's Anti-Handbook* to get the attention they needed to make change, to change the curfew, and to get equal rights for female students, it had to be notorious. "And exclusive," she'd emphasized. "That's critical! Nothing works better at getting attention than leaving someone out."

Now Betsy wrote out a long column of names before crossing out most of them.

"Dana P. obviously needs one. She's the coolest girl in Pine Hall and can keep a secret. I would know." Betsy raised an eyebrow. "Amelia C. should also get one. She owes me a favor and won't spill. Tina D. could actually really use one. She's dating a guy who lives way off campus and is always complaining about having to leave his parties early."

And on and on it went until they had a list of ten women, not including Cat, Betsy, Mable, and Ramona.

"These are our girls. They'll get the job done, just like women did in the war. We'll make sure everyone on campus hears about the *Women's Anti-Handbook*, but only ten will be lucky enough to receive a copy."

Ramona's stomach tightened in anxiety. The fear of getting caught overtook the excitement for a moment.

Betsy noticed her expression and patted her shoulder. "It's going to be fine. We do stuff like this all the time."

That's easy for her to say, Ramona thought. *She isn't the one risking everything.* But still, Ramona took a deep breath and nodded. It would be fine. This was too important to stop. It's not like what she was doing now didn't have risks.

Cat closed the notebook and looked up at Ramona. "What you're feeling now? Like you're about to jump off a cliff? That's the whole point."

Before Ramona could respond, Cat carried on. "I'm done. Take another look with fresh eyes, and we'll give it to the boys tomorrow."

Ramona agreed. Cat handed her the pages but didn't let go when Ramona reached for them.

"You're all right," Cat said, her voice softer than Ramona had ever heard it, before letting go.

Across from them, Betsy beamed.

Had Cat accepted her presence? Feeling dazed by the sudden shift, Ramona gathered her things and followed the girls outside into the cool, afternoon air. Soon the light would be lost for the day.

"What are you doing now?" Betsy asked Ramona as they walked away from Gangly Hall.

"Going to the library," Ramona said, pointing in the opposite direction.

"Not anymore!" Betsy wrapped her arm through Ramona's and pulled her toward Cat. "We have plans. Come on."

"What plans?" Ramona asked.

"It's time to make things official." Betsy winked.

Ramona gulped, intrigued and hesitant at the same time.

"Hold still," Cat said as she wrapped a piece of cloth over Ramona's eyes, blindfolding her.

"Seriously?" Ramona asked, but the girls only laughed before spinning her twice and hauling her forward.

Ramona's chest tightened, wondering whether Theo would be at their destination. She hadn't seen him since Monday, and the way he'd bolted from her side in the hallway still stung.

They led her across campus with the buzz of students as her only anchor. Then they went down some stairs, and a door opened. Stale air greeted them inside, and hands gripped her arms to pull her forward. Giggles erupted from the left. Betsy.

Ramona couldn't see a thing through the blindfold and stumbled along. Another door opened and shut before they stopped.

"Betsy, Cat," Ramona pleaded, "what's going on?"

"That's what I want to know."

Ramona whirled around at the sound of Mable's voice.

"These two brutes practically dragged me out of Psychology class for this," Mable continued.

Laughter erupted from the same direction as Mable's voice. Olly.

"Come on," Ramona urged. "Let us take these off."

"Oh all right." Betsy sighed and then said sardonically, "But it's not because you asked nicely."

The fabric slipped off her face, and Ramona squeezed her eyes against the sudden brightness. She blinked until her eyes adjusted. Then her breath caught. There, at the bottom of the empty pool, were balloons and a large, purple banner. In fact, it looked familiar, and it clicked into place as Ramona read, "Welcome to fall term '65."

"We borrowed it," Olly said, grinning.

A large cake sat on one of the chairs, and Ramona tried to understand the occasion.

"Is it someone's birthday?"

Olly laughed and bumped Don's shoulder.

"No, silly! This is your and Mable's initiation," Betsy explained.

"You're not going to try to haze us, are you?" Ramona asked, sensing Mable tighten beside her.

Cat seemed to consider the idea, but Betsy came to their rescue. "No! No. It's a welcome party more than anything."

"Well, it's about time," Mable said, relief clear in her voice. "We've done a lot for you lot."

Warmth filled Ramona at the gesture. They'd done this for them.

She scanned the group, and her eyes lingered on Theo, leaning against the wall, an invisible barrier seemingly between them.

"Mable's right," Theo continued, pushing off the wall without looking at Ramona. "You're part of our group now."

Betsy clapped her hands together and rose on her tiptoes with excitement. "I made the cake! Let me serve you each a slice so you can tell me how much you like it."

Soon the cake was cut and passed around. As Ramona sucked a chunk of remaining frosting from the fork, she realized the space looked different. It wasn't just the decorations. It took her a moment to understand why. They had cleaned up. There were no scattered gum wrappers, which Betsy chewed obsessively, or basketballs strewn across the floor where Olly left them. Even Theo's sketches on the sides of the pool walls were covered by the banner and balloons. Ramona stifled the smile that wanted to break out at their effort.

Once their paper plates were empty, and Betsy had asked each of them how they liked the cake, Olly spoke up.

"Now for the most important part—"

Cat cut in, "You're not going to get all sappy on us, are you?"

"That'll come later," Olly teased. "For now, Earl's lemonades!"

Don said, "Disgusting" at the same time Betsy said, "They're the best!"

"No one knows exactly what is in them, but there's definitely vodka and rum. I know a girl who convinced the bartender to tell her that much," Betsy continued.

"The final part of the initiation is to go to Earl's for a lemonade," Olly said.

Don groaned but went along grudgingly with Dimitri and Theo, who shrugged at the order. Everyone climbed out of the pool and shuffled toward the door, but Ramona hesitated.

"As good as a lemonade sounds, I really do need to go to the library. I'm so behind in school, and I still have to find a speech to watch in the next week."

"What kind of speech?" Betsy asked.

Ramona looked back at her, confused by her interest. "Any speech."

"Theo!" Betsy practically shouted. "Aren't you driving down to Portland to hear Angela Parker speak at the rally?"

"Yeah, so?"

"Well, take Ramona!"

Theo's face soured, as though he smelled bad milk, and across the circle, Dimitri's expression hardened. Either Betsy didn't notice or she didn't care.

"I don't know," Ramona began. As much as the idea thrilled her, his reaction didn't.

When Theo still hadn't replied, Betsy shoved him. "What's wrong with you?"

Theo glared at Betsy, and Ramona's stomach dropped. The shift from his warmth to this distant manner unsettled and infuriated her. Was this all because of Dimitri's reaction to them talking? When Ramona thought she would implode from the awkwardness, Theo turned toward her.

"I'm driving down tomorrow if you want to come."

Ramona's stomach dropped. She couldn't imagine a more hesitant invitation.

"I don't want to put you out," she said, giving him an opportunity to back out of what Betsy had pushed upon him.

"It's fine," he said. "I'll be back by curfew anyway."

"Okay, then sure."

Theo nodded once in acknowledgment before crossing the pool toward Don and Olly.

"It's just like my mama says," Betsy mused. "Boys are all fools. But now you can come to Earl's!"

By the time they got outside, the sky was dark, and Ramona shivered in her thin jacket as The Foes bumbled and bumped their way the few blocks to Earl's. The lemonades were even stronger than everyone had said, but hard as she tried to stay present, Ramona's head was already hundreds of miles away in Portland. Theo didn't talk to her once the entire night.

CHAPTER 10

Ramona perched on the windowsill, tracing her eyes with black liner in the early morning light. Not an easy task with her beloved mirror in one hand and eyeliner in the other. She examined her work and sighed. She looked like herself, but today was different. She wanted to look special. She wanted to feel like someone else.

She lifted the eyeliner to add a wing on her eyelid, moving ever so slowly to get the detail just right. But her hand shook so badly, the black kohl resembled a brick more than a wing.

"Shit."

Ramona wiped the brick away.

Then, remembering, she glanced across the room and sighed with relief to see that Patsy continued sleeping. She looked harmless like that. How would Patsy react when she learned of the *Women's Anti-Handbook*?

While celebrating at Earl's the night before, Ramona had managed to review Cat's edits before giving the pages to Don and Olly for printing. The final version was great—better than what she could've come up with alone—and Ramona felt grateful for the help. In a few days, there would be a real

Women's Anti-Handbook, and Ramona would work a double shift to be there to see Patsy's reaction when she heard of it.

Ramona donned her jacket. Theo would arrive any minute. She wasn't sure what she'd need for the trip to Portland, so she chose from the clutter scattered across her desk until her purse was filled with lip balm, gum, a few bills, and some loose change. That should cover her for the day.

Patsy's alarm clock blared, and Ramona jolted upright. Shit. She'd been hoping to get out before Patsy woke up. Patsy tipped up her eye mask and looked surprised to see Ramona standing there.

"Where are you going?"

"What are you doing awake so early?" Ramona asked instead.

"Me? You're the one who sleeps in every day," Patsy retorted, and Ramona worked to hold in a scowl. "I need to write my speech for the AWS elections."

Ramona moved toward the door when Patsy asked again.

"Portland."

"For what?"

"What do you care?" Ramona asked without reining in her anger. "You already think the worst of me."

Patsy's mouth dropped open, and Ramona left the room feeling satisfied.

When Ramona rounded the bend on the tree-lined path from Wolden, she saw Theo's gray Chevy idling in the parking lot just as he'd said. Her heart thudded at the sight of him, the same way he looked when picking up Dimitri at the end of a shift. But this time, she was the one getting in the car. So much had happened in these past few weeks, and yet, they felt like strangers again. Ramona sucked in a shaky breath and got into the car.

As she settled in the seat, Theo handed her a cup of coffee and nodded toward a paper bag on the floor.

"I hope you like scones."

Ramona nodded, appreciating his thoughtfulness. "Love 'em."

She took him in, his wet hair and freshly shaven face, as the scent of soap and his cologne filled the car. He returned her look for just a moment before shifting his eyes back to the steering wheel.

The silence stretched between them until Theo said, "We should get going."

By the time they drove onto Interstate 5, Ramona had drunk half her coffee. As Theo merged lanes and accelerated, she ignored the tension to focus on the expanse of downtown Seattle passing by. In the soft morning glow, the buildings glittered where they nestled beyond Lake Union.

"I've never been to Portland, you know," Ramona said. "I've never been outside of Washington."

"Is that so?" The shock in Theo's voice was audible. "Well, I guess it's good that you're coming today."

The statement hardly reassured her, and disappointment clawed at the coffee in her stomach.

A few minutes passed before Theo asked, "Are you excited? To see Portland, I mean."

"Sure."

"It's a nice place," Theo remarked. "Not like Los Angeles or San Diego, but nice."

"You've traveled a lot?"

"Yeah." Theo turned to her for a moment before gazing back at the highway. "My dad's in the navy, so we've lived in a lot of places."

Dimitri had never mentioned that.

“That must’ve been hard,” Ramona said.

Theo shrugged. “There are worse things. Nobody should stay in one place their whole life. Where’s the fun in that?” When his eyes met hers then, there was a glint of the playfulness she’d grown used to.

Ramona imagined herself boarding a plane, wearing one of those expensive dresses that filled catalogs. One day, she would.

“So your family is from Washington?” Theo asked.

She nodded. “I grew up in the same town as my mom and my grandparents. It’s about an hour north of Seattle. Even in the same house.”

Answering this question always made Ramona’s skin itch because of what came next. She gripped her hands together in her lap.

“Pacific Northwest, born and bred,” Theo commented. “What about your dad?”

“I don’t know.”

Theo shifted to look at her, and his concern was familiar. Ramona had been asked this question in one form or another more times than she could count, and she usually answered with her well-worn script. But something about Theo made her want to be honest … as though she knew he could handle the truth.

“He left before I was born. He’s not a part of my life.” *He doesn’t want to be.*

As long as she could remember, not a day had gone by without Ramona wondering why he had left her mother and why he’d never come back for her. When she was little, she would stay up at night, imagining elaborate scenarios. He was stationed abroad, leading an army. He was a traveling salesman. He was a scientist, researching across the world. Always far, far away. So it broke her heart as a kid to discover that not only did he know she existed, but that he lived in Seattle with a family.

Against her will, a tear formed at the corner of her eye, and Ramona wiped it away. She hated crying about him. He didn't deserve it.

"I'm sorry." Theo's voice, so tender that it made her throat ache, pulled her back.

With one hand white-knuckling the steering wheel, Theo reached the other across the console and gently held her hand. They didn't speak, and he brushed his thumb across her skin in comforting strokes for a long while. Until she found her way through the fog that descended every time she talked about her dad.

The Beatles played on the radio, and Ramona realized that at some point, the tension had dissipated between them. Between the vulnerability and hand-holding and maybe even the scones, their glittering connection was back. She relaxed as the Chevy sped fifteen miles above the speed limit down the highway.

***

Theo pulled off the highway two and a half hours later. The University of Portland nestled against the Columbia River just north of the city. After circling the lot and parking, Ramona and Theo joined the flow of people walking toward the center of campus. The deep echo of a bass thrummed through Ramona's chest as the music got louder, and she crossed her arms to contain the warmth from the car.

After rounding a bend in the path, a large stage came into view with a crowd pressed up on all sides toward the band that played. Students filled the walkways and sat on tree branches, and even looked out from windows of the quaint, brick buildings lining the quad. Anticipation twinkled through the air, and Ramona felt herself leaning into it, even as the whole scene threatened to overwhelm her. She wondered how many of them, like her, were at their first rally. Everyone seemed seasoned with the confident air of those who knew what was coming.

"A concert?" Ramona shouted to be heard over the music.

Theo leaned in, and his breath tickled her ear. "It's the pre-show. Sometimes rallies start with a band to get the audience energized before the speakers come on."

If crowd size was any indication, then Angela Parker must be popular.

"So what makes Angela Parker so special?" Ramona prodded.

"She's an activist for civil rights, women's rights, and the anti-war movement. People say she's an incredible speaker, and that you can't call yourself a real activist until you hear her."

"Good thing we're here then," Ramona teased. "I wouldn't want to be a fake."

Theo grinned. "C'mon. Let's find Mark."

He turned toward the densely packed crowd and hesitated. Ramona could see him calculating before he reached for her hand.

"So I don't lose you."

Ramona nodded and gripped his hand as Theo made a path through the people toward center stage. They twisted to fit between the jostling bodies. A waft of smoke passed over them, the smell rich and pungent and not at all like the tobacco that lingered around her grandfather day and night. She'd never smoked marijuana, but she recognized the scent, particularly from the cars of hungry customers who came to Dusty's stoned, late at night. Lectures in school had warned that the drug was dangerous, but Ramona couldn't help feeling curious. The scent of sweat lingered beneath the smoke, and she warmed as they moved deeper into the crowd.

Somehow, they found Theo's friend, who threw an arm around his shoulder.

"You made it!"

"It's Angela Parker," Theo said, like that made it obvious. "Mark, this is Ramona."

"It's a pleasure, Ramona. I'm this guy's oldest friend."

Mark had a wide smile and warm eyes, and Ramona wondered if he was always so happy or if this was a special occasion due to a certain speaker.

"Yeah, yeah." Theo chuckled, rolling his eyes.

"You can help me understand him then?" Ramona teased.

"Sure can! Just tell me what you want to know," Mark agreed as they shook hands in the tiny space allotted between them in the crowd.

Theo's eyebrows stitched together as he turned to her, but she ignored him and focused on the stage where the band played on. Despite not recognizing the music, she liked it. It was upbeat and funky in a way that made her hips and arms sway on their own. Song bled into song. Ramona lost track of time, and it was bliss to let go.

She didn't know how long she'd been dancing when something collided with the side of her neck. She yelped and turned to see a beefy guy wearing a sleeveless T-shirt pull his elbow back from where he'd banged against her. She didn't have a chance to react before Theo grabbed the front of the guy's shirt.

"Hey," Theo said. "Be careful."

"Whatever, man," the guy said with hazy eyes.

Theo's grip tightened. "I said, be careful. Don't knock into her again."

"All right, all right," the guy said with hands raised, stepping back. "It was an accident."

Theo watched him until he was a few feet away before turning back to her.

"Are you okay?" Theo asked, quieter now.

"I'm fine. It just surprised me is all."

Theo nodded. He studied her, and she saw something in his eyes shift. They softened. Slowly, he raised his hand to replace her own on the sore spot of her neck. A tingle spread across her skin at his warm touch.

"I couldn't stand you getting hurt."

Ramona's breath caught in her throat. *How is it possible to feel so safe with someone so new?*

"Do you know how much I think about you?" Theo whispered. He gently gripped the nape of her neck, threading his fingers through her hair. "Ever since I first saw you at Dusty's, lit up behind the window. And now, I see you everywhere."

Her stomach dipped deliciously as she imprinted his words in the part of her mind where she stored her most precious moments. She'd never let herself imagine that he felt as consumed by her as she felt by him. Like he was the center of the universe. And that was a problem because she couldn't focus on anyone else right now, on anything besides her mission. But that didn't mean she didn't want to kiss him.

Before she could respond, trying to form the words to describe the complexity of her feelings, the music faded away in the background. Silence echoed in its absence, and the crowd's anticipation swelled.

They both looked toward the stage, where a man stepped up, gripping a microphone.

"Welcome to the Students Against Violence Rally!"

The crowd erupted.

"I don't have to tell you that we have a fantastic lineup of speakers today, but I will anyway." The host chuckled at his own joke. "First, we'll have Professor Mark Avery, who will be followed by …" The host listed a string of names before getting to the person they all listened for. "Finally, we're honored to have Angela Parker."

The cheering increased at the mention of her name.

"Please help me in welcoming our first speaker to the stage," the host said, passing the microphone to a gray-bearded man in a brown suit.

One speech rolled into another and then another. With each passing minute, Ramona was more eager to see Angela Parker speak. And finally, it was time.

The microphone passed from hand to hand, and then Angela Parker stood center stage. The woman glowed, literally. The sun had lowered in the sky, and it seemed to shine directly on her. Ramona looked up toward her in awe. She had short, brown hair with chopped edges hanging at her ears, chunky, gold earrings, and was dressed in a T-shirt and wide-legged trousers.

"My name is Angela Parker, and there's something that each of you need to hear."

Standing elbow to elbow in the crowd, Ramona was surprised by the conviction in the woman's voice. Besides her female teachers, she couldn't remember a single time she'd seen a woman speaking in front of a crowd. And never a crowd like this.

"Times are changing. That won't come as a surprise to any of you," Angela said, raising her free arm as if to encompass the entire crowd, "but change is not happening quickly enough. The injustices faced by many across this country are too high to count, and we have to do something. Otherwise, these horrible conditions will continue. Our Black brothers and sisters are facing horrendous discrimination in every part of this country. Our sisters and mothers of all races across this country are limited to roles that men feel comfortable enough to give them … roles in the home and roles in the most limited careers. The few control the many, and it's far past the time to change that."

The crowd roared.

"I was in Alabama and was honored to see Dr. Martin Luther King Jr. speak. He spoke of peace and participation and hope, and I hope to share this feeling with you all and extend his message even further."

A hush fell over the students whose ears strained to listen closer.

"It's through education that understanding is bred. It's through understanding that empathy is bred. It's through empathy that change is made."

Murmurs of agreement rippled through the crowd, and beside her, Theo clapped. The crowd quieted down, mesmerized by Angela Parker, a woman who didn't look all that different from herself. Ramona couldn't imagine speaking this way, let alone having the opportunity to.

"You might be asking yourselves what you can do to help fight these injustices," Angela Parker called out. "I ask myself the same question. What I've learned is that we have to listen to others. We have to listen to their stories and experiences, from where people have come and where they hope to go." She moved from one side of the platform to the other, walking slowly back and forth as the audience tracked her. She owned the stage. "How can we learn without listening? It's not possible.

"Listening is the first step. The next step is to participate. Be an active member of this movement for better. Participation could be voting." Angela Parker paused, then looking serious, said, "And everyone should be voting. Whether it's voting, writing, marching, volunteering, educating, or speaking, there's room for all of us to be active. In fact, our world demands involvement from us. Civil and equal rights are the responsibility of us all, no matter your gender or race. No one can sit by. Justice demands your involvement. You cannot sit idly by, waiting for the change to happen. You have to grab it by the balls and take it."

The crowd erupted. Cheers. Claps. Whistles. Ramona rose on her tiptoes.

Theo leaned over. "Can you see?"

"Not really."

Suddenly, Theo's hands wrapped around her waist, and before she could comprehend, he had scooped her up and held her in the air. Breaking out of the line of heads, she now had a full view of the stage and crowd that had doubled, maybe even tripled, in size. Theo lowered her back down to the ground, and his grin made her glow from the inside out.

"Get a good look?"

She nodded. "This is incredible."

Ramona turned back toward the stage in awe and clapped her hands together loudly like a child would at the sight of presents. As soon as it ended, she wanted Angela Parker to start again. Theo lifted her to see Angela wave to the crowd. They were close enough to be visible from the stage, and when the activist looked in their direction, she nodded at Ramona. Ramona froze, her heart racing.

The band began playing again, and the crowd resumed dancing. Ramona buzzed as if she'd drunk a pot of the burnt coffee from Dusty's. *Is this what it feels like to be high? Angela Parker saw her.* If this woman, with nothing but a microphone and a makeshift, wooden platform, could advocate for equal rights, could Ramona do the same? She wanted to. She hadn't intended to be part of this movement, but she couldn't ignore the signs in front of her to do something for the rights of female students on campus. The *Women's Anti-Handbook* was only the beginning.

Ramona swayed with the music, somehow ending up in Theo's arms with her back pressed against his chest, and forgot that she was a student, and a waitress, and a daughter. Instead, she was just Ramona. Nothing and everything all at once.

***

It was only when the sun had set, glistening for a few final moments against the water of the river, that the students dispersed. It was dinnertime, after all. Even so, people crowded around the stage as another band played when Theo suggested they eat. Ramona wanted to stay but couldn't deny the dull pangs of hunger in her belly. Sighing, she agreed, and they said goodbye to Mark.

As soon as they reached the parking lot, though, Theo grabbed her hand and pulled her away from the car. "Come on."

He moved confidently in the darkness, and she hurried to keep up, her hair flowing behind her.

"Where are we going?" Ramona giggled.

"I want to show you something." Theo grinned, his eyes bright.

They ran for a few minutes along the street, just until her lungs started to burn, before he slowed. They reached a path leading into the woods. Still gripping her hand, Theo led her into the trees. He pushed aside a branch blocking their view, and Ramona sucked in her breath at the sight revealed. The river lay beyond with the moon glittering on the water's surface. They ducked under branches until they were at the river's edge. They'd passed into another world made up of just the two of them.

"How wonderful," Ramona beamed, crouching down to soak her fingers in the water. She did this every time she was near the water, always expecting it to be warmer. The coldness bit, and she pulled back her fingers. She glanced back to see Theo studying her.

He knelt beside her and reached for her hand. He wrapped her dripping fingers in the front of his T-shirt, warm from his skin, and dried them. Ramona stared, mesmerized by the glimpse of his stomach.

"You're beautiful," Theo whispered, inches away. "Do you know how beautiful you are?"

A spark spread down her spine, and goose bumps formed across her body like a thousand invisible threads plucking at her skin. She'd never wanted anyone so badly. She hadn't known this feeling existed.

His dark hair fell across his forehead as he tilted his head toward hers. Still holding her to him by her fingers wound within his T-shirt, he reached his other hand to the side of her neck. His deep-blue eyes, dark as the night, searched hers.

"Tell me what you want."

Ramona's heart thudded. She couldn't look away. She saw a glimmer of vulnerability in his eyes. Was he as nervous as she was? That thought made her brave.

She dragged her thumb across his bottom lip. "This."

Theo groaned. He opened his mouth to lightly lick her thumb. Jolts of desire shot through her.

Once he released her thumb, Ramona brought it to her mouth, rubbing it across her lips. Theo's eyes flashed. His lips curved up ever so slightly at the edges. It was shyer than the grins she'd grown accustomed to. It was desire.

She smiled back.

Beneath his T-shirt, Theo's chest rose and fell. She wanted more.

Ramona leaned in slowly and watched something shift in Theo's eyes just before she pressed her lips to his. The kiss lasted only for a moment before she leaned back to gauge his reaction. It felt like everything hung in the balance as they stared at one another.

"Fuck it," Theo growled, grabbing her head between his hands and pressing his mouth to hers. His mouth was hot, and he sucked on her bottom lip ever so slightly, just enough to part her lips. She grabbed the back of his jacket to pull him closer. They moved together, the feeling familiar and new all at once, and she pressed herself against him to close the distance between their bodies.

This. This is what she'd wanted.

"Hold on," Theo murmured, his voice rougher than before.

Still crouching, he reached for her thighs and lifted her from the ground. With her legs wrapped around his waist, Ramona could feel every part of him, and when he pressed her against the closest tree trunk, her eyes flickered shut. Her body had never been drawn to another's like she was to Theo's. She tightened her hold on him and kissed him harder, faster. More. She wanted more.

Surfacing for air, Ramona took a deep breath, and Theo moved his mouth to her neck, where he traced his tongue toward her ear. Stars erupted from her core. She ached for him.

He nuzzled her neck as though he wanted to be buried there.

"I love your hair," Theo murmured against her ear as his hands held the back of her head, fingers threaded through her curls.

Theo set her down and gently turned her around. She looked back at him and opened her mouth to ask what he was doing, when he said, "Trust me." She nodded.

Her hands gripped the tree as Theo ran his fingers down her neck, then down her shoulders and arms. He reached for her stomach and stilled. She breathed hard, nervous and eager all at once for what his hand implied.

"Can I?" Theo whispered. "Please let me touch you."

Ramona knew she should say no. She should stop things where they were, but she didn't want to. She might faint if he stopped. So she pressed herself against him and said, "Yes."

Another rumble came from somewhere deep in Theo's throat, and his hand explored from her stomach downward, finding its way beneath the waist of her jeans. His other hand held her chin, tilting her mouth toward his. His touch was everything, and when he reached the spot, she moved with him. She gripped the tree to hold herself upright as he touched her and kissed her, whispering words that set her skin alight.

At first, his touch teased, but as her desire built and the pressure felt like it would end her, his touch became demanding. Familiar threads of pleasure built within her, and surprise flooded her as she realized that Theo was getting her where she'd only brought herself before.

His lips pressed against her ear, causing tingles to shoot up her spine.

"Let go, Ramona." Theo quickened his grip. "Feel me."

Her stomach tightened sharply until suddenly she was plunging, this feeling devouring her whole. They moved together as she rode the wave that he'd given her. She'd been touched by boyfriends before, but never like this. The intensity left her breathless.

Ramona blinked as she turned around to the view of the river. She could make out the dull thrum of music they'd left behind in the distance. Theo kissed her forehead before adjusting himself. A hint of embarrassment hovered at the edges of her consciousness, but Theo's warm smile chased that fear away.

He leaned against the tree, looking more handsome than anyone had any right to be. She wanted to touch him … make him feel just as she had. Ramona wrapped her arms around his waist.

"I want," she whispered, suddenly nervous again. "I want to touch you back."

Theo's eyes searched hers. "You have no idea how many times I've imagined you saying something like that."

Ramona reached for the waistband of his pants, eager to feel his warmth, but the thought of pregnancy intruded just as her fingers grazed his stomach. She stiffened in his arms, trying to push the thought away. It was fine. You couldn't get pregnant from touching someone.

"What is it?" Theo asked.

She wanted this. She wanted him. But guilt filled her, despite her best attempts to hold it at bay. She pushed on, wanting to give him this, and continued reaching.

"Hey." Theo cupped her cheeks in his hands and leaned down to meet her, eye to eye. "There's no pressure to do anything. Hell, I'm just happy I got to touch you. I've been wanting to for a long time."

"I want to," Ramona said. "I just started thinking about getting pregnant, and I know that's ridiculous, but—"

"It's not," Theo assured her. "It's not ridiculous."

Ramona was hit with such a swell of appreciation that she hugged him to her and pressed her face against his chest.

"Come on." He wrapped an arm around her shoulders and led her back the way they'd come. "Let's get dinner."

As they left the riverside, the guilt subsided, and lightness filled Ramona again. They walked to a nearby restaurant with a view of the city, and she couldn't help thinking about what she would do once she got her hands on Theo. Because one day, soon, she wanted to.

In the restaurant, they sat across from each other in a booth. Thoughtfully placed candles lit the room. After they'd ordered, Theo's blue eyes centered on her, and his attention felt like home. Still, something tugged at her.

"Can I ask you something?" Ramona asked.

Theo nodded. "Anything."

"Why were you acting so"—she searched for the right word—"cold for the past week? You didn't want me to come to Portland, and then this?" She waved a hand between them, feeling her cheeks heat.

Theo bit his lip and looked at her just like her grandmother studied a chessboard… concentrating and calculating.

"You can tell me."

His shoulders drooped at that, and he sighed. "I was trying to stay away from you."

"Why would you do that?"

He rubbed his thumb across his chin.

"You have no idea how long I've wanted to know you," Theo explained. "And then once we'd met, I was done for." He smiled wryly, as if he'd won a game he hadn't intended to play.

"And then that idiot knocked into you, and I couldn't stop watching you watch the rally, and then you kissed me …" Theo gripped his hands together on the table, cracking his knuckles in the process. "And I figured that if you liked my brother, you wouldn't have done that."

There it was. She'd suspected as much, but hadn't wanted to assume.

Ramona reached for his hands. "You know, Dimitri is great, and I do like him, but only as a friend. It's always been just friendship between us. At least from my side."

Theo nodded, something between guilt and acceptance battling in his eyes.

"When I realized he liked you, I tried to stop. But this," he said, nodding at their intertwined hands, "I've never felt like this."

"I feel it too."

Ramona felt relieved to have confirmation of why he'd acted so strangely and accepted his reasoning. Soon their food arrived, and between bites of steaming pasta, Theo asked what Ramona thought of the rally and Angela Parker.

"She's an incredible speaker, like you said, and so powerful. I was really impressed."

"Me too," Theo agreed. "I had high expectations based on everything I'd heard, and she was even better than I could have imagined. I wonder whether she'd consider coming to Seattle."

Ramona could picture it … Angela Parker standing on another stage with another microphone in Gauld Square.

"Let's ask her," Ramona encouraged.

She wanted to be a part of this world. Go to rallies and demonstrations and sit-ins. Make leaflets and picket signs and a *Women's Anti-Handbook*. Something bigger than herself—something that mattered and would make the world a better place for all.

"You know what I've been thinking about since her speech? I want to be seen as a student, not just as a female student. We're all students, and we should be looked at the same way."

Theo's expression grew serious. "You're right. What happens next with the *Women's Anti-Handbook*?"

They spent the next hour talking in depth about the *Women's Anti-Handbook*, the content, and how to distribute it. Theo talked about his frustration with the school administration and how he wanted to plan a big demonstration—something that would be impossible to ignore. Angry with the limitations placed upon their free speech, he was determined to do something. And he wanted to do something more than an expected sit-in or rally.

"So then, what do you want to do?" Ramona asked.

"I have an idea, but I need more time with it." Theo chuckled when Ramona scowled. "You'll be the first to know, I promise. And make no mistake—it will be something they won't be able to forget."

The way he'd said it, so intensely, gave her chills. For the dozenth time, Ramona admired his passion for this work. And while she knew that what they did came with risks, she hoped his plans didn't go too far. There were limits to the risks she'd take. She just didn't know what those limits were yet.

They left in order to make it back before curfew and took turns choosing songs on the radio on the drive home. As Theo sang along to the radio, to her, she marveled at how much could change in less than twelve hours.

CHAPTER 11

As Ramona walked toward the old gymnasium building, she thought through her to-do list. She hadn't studied enough before her shift yesterday, and the new assignments passed out during classes today added to the anxiety that swelled within her. As soon as Don showed up with the printed *Women's Anti-Handbooks*, she'd go straight to the library.

"Petition girl!"

Olly bounded up the path behind her with wide, purposeful steps. She couldn't help smiling at his goofy grin, until she saw what he carried.

"What are you doing with all those eggs?"

A devilish glint flashed across his eyes at the three cartons of precariously stacked eggs.

"I've got a date with the faculty parking lot."

"Oh, Olly," Ramona said. "You can't be serious."

"Couldn't be more serious if I tried." Olly raised his eyebrows as he fell into step beside her.

Ramona sighed, but it certainly wasn't the worst thing he'd done, so what did it matter, really?

Mist fell from the sky, and Ramona tucked her chin to her neck. They were only a few minutes from the abandoned pool, but Ramona searched her bag for her scarf anyway. Before feeling the wool, her fingers brushed against the edge of the letter she had to mail. Ramona had been disappointed while reading the paper yesterday when she realized that Editor Gruffly hadn't heeded her advice, so she'd written to him again.

In 1958, Grant Gruffly had been promoted to editor of the local section of *The Seattle Times* and has held the position ever since. Every time she saw his name printed in the paper, she wondered about what had happened in his life to get him into such a position. Educated, with a well-paying and influential career. Not too shabby. A smart man, no doubt. For all Ramona knew, he hadn't read her letter at all because there wasn't a single article of substance in his section. Instead, the front page showcased an elderly woman who knitted blankets for soldiers. A touching article for sure, but not enough. And that wouldn't do.

Dear Editor,

Maisie Jay sounds like a sweet person ... and those blankets. What a talent! But you've once again neglected to focus on the issues at hand in our city. You're a learned man, but I'll give you a hand. Look at the college. You've made mistakes, I'm sure, but it's not too late to correct.

Sincerely,

Petition girl

Ramona wished she was cozied beneath one of those hand-knitted blankets now as she shivered from the rain.

Soon, Olly and Ramona arrived at the pool, Ramona having held the doors open for Olly as he balanced his eggs to join the others. Everyone gathered there except Don, and anticipation filled the space as they waited for the *Women's Anti-Handbooks*. It had been two days since the trip to Portland, and every drop of anxiety disappeared from Ramona's body as soon as she locked eyes with Theo.

He crossed the room to her, and when he cupped a warm palm to her cheek, she leaned into his touch.

"Hey," he said softly as he studied her face.

"Hey yourself." She took a step closer, softening into the crook between his chest and shoulder. She forgot about everyone until a chuckle sounded. Olly.

"Look at you two," he said. "A trip to Portland, and you're going together already."

A ripple of nerves ran through Ramona. She didn't think they would notice so quickly. She looked around the room, from Olly, to Cat, to Betsy, to Mable, whose expressions ranged from encouraging to indifferent. Ramona turned to Dimitri. He looked up from the textbook in his lap with wide eyes. Tension thickened the air, and Ramona wished for him to smile, to do anything that would melt the awkwardness, but instead, his face deflated as though he'd aged ten years in an instant. Ramona's heart fell. She didn't think she could bear it if Theo turned away from her once more to safeguard his brother's feelings.

Theo wrapped his arms around her shoulders, tucking her to his chest.

"What can I say? Portland's a romantic place," Theo answered Olly with a grin.

"Yeah, it's fine. Now, I want to know who's going to help me egg the cars."

"I'm in," Betsy volunteered before turning to Ramona. "I have a great arm."

"Thatta girl!" Olly scooped Betsy into the air and bounced her for a few steps before looking at Theo.

"Don't give me that look." Theo groaned. "I'm planning our next demonstration. We can't just do another protest. We need to make them pay attention. And not just the faculty. Students at this school have no idea what's going on. If they knew about the restrictions to their free speech, then they'd be pissed, I know it."

They hadn't made much progress in the Free Speech Movement since their rally had been shut down by the campus police. Despite reaching out multiple times, the administration still had neither budged nor responded to numerous letters and requests for appointments, and Ramona could sense the frustration simmering in Theo.

"So what's your idea, big guy?" Cat prodded.

"I'm still working on it." Theo scowled. "But while we're on the subject, how does everyone feel about breaking into the administration building?"

Cat scoffed. "That'll definitely make them pay attention."

Ramona stiffened at the suggestion, her stomach bottoming out. Rallies and sit-ins were one thing, but breaking into the school administration offices was illegal. They could get into real trouble. She gulped at the thought of being suspended and losing her scholarship. No, she wouldn't do it.

"Oh yeah?" Olly replied to Theo. "And what will we do once we're inside?"

"We'll take something," Betsy said as though it was the most obvious thing in the world. "Like one of Redley's beloved awards. You know, the ones he keeps behind his desk."

"Exactly." Theo grinned.

Ramona gawked at Theo. This conversation felt like a train picking up speed. Surely, there had to be another way. Breaking the law wouldn't make the administration any more amenable to their position on free speech and equal rights. If anything, it would likely make things worse and make them look like a bunch of criminals rather than student activists.

Ramona said as much, "I won't do it. We'll only give them cause to suspend us—or worse."

"True," Cat added as she stretched her arms above her head. "Best-case scenario, we don't get caught, and what good would it do?"

Theo rubbed his hands over his face. "I don't know."

The group was quiet for a minute until Olly suggested, "We could do another petition."

"That's not going to make a bit of difference. Think of Ramona's petition against the curfew."

Ramona stiffened. He wasn't wrong, but her failure still stung.

"How about we make more signs and protest outside the administration building?"

"We did that same thing last spring," Theo said, shooting down the idea.

The only noise was the sound of Cat's nails clicking together until she spoke. "Well, what are they doing at other schools? Like, have any of you heard about what they did down at Berkeley? A friend of mine told me all about the way they'd stopped a protester from getting arrested by surrounding the cop car until the police gave up."

Theo turned to Cat as though she were the rising sun at dawn.

"That's a great idea," Theo said, pacing the pool. "We're not the only ones fighting for free speech. Better together and all that, huh?"

Ramona studied Theo, wanting to know where his head was going, when the door flew open with a bang. They all looked up in alarm, but it was only the sturdy form of Don walking quickly toward them, looking smug with a package in his arms.

"Do you have them?" Betsy asked.

Don nodded, and Betsy grabbed at the package. "Well, let's see them!"

Don opened the package to reveal a stack of booklets. He handed the first one to Theo, who immediately passed it to Ramona. The *Women's Anti-Handbook*. As soon as it was in her hands, all other thoughts fell away. The words *WOMEN'S ANTI-HANDBOOK* popped in red font on the laminated, black cover. She flipped through the pages, skimming the words that she, Mable, and Cat had written. It felt surreal to see her own words printed. So official. The black typeset ink had transformed her writing into something worth paying attention to. The *Women's Anti-Handbook* was better than she'd imagined.

"You did it," Ramona said, looking toward Don with awe.

Don simply shrugged. "*We* did it." Ramona surveyed the group.

Cat rolled her eyes but smiled with the rest of them.

There were fifteen copies—ten for the female students selected with a spare left over. The group crowded around her, passing copies and flipping through the pages. Their animated chatter echoed in the cavernous space. Ramona felt buoyed to see them as excited as she felt.

"So what happens next?" Olly asked.

"Leave that to me," Betsy said, collecting the ten copies into a stack. "I'll get them to the chosen girls."

They looked around at each other, considering what the release of the *Women's Anti-Handbook*s meant. Once they were out there, they couldn't take them back. As excited as Ramona felt, the implications weighed heavy. The risk of sneaking in after curfew would be that much bigger with others attempting the same, but it was worth it. It had to be.

"Oy!"

Ramona jumped, as did the rest of them, at the loud, unexpected sound that broke through the moment. A middle-aged man stood above them at the edge of the pool.

"What do you think you're doing in here?"

The man held a set of silver keys and wore a workman's jacket and boots. His face tightened as he surveyed the space, revealing balls, juice boxes, and skid marks in the pool from many rubber-soled shoes.

When no one answered, he yelled again, "What are you doing in here?"

"Run!" Olly shouted, scrambling toward the shallow end of the pool.

A split-second later, they followed him, grabbing their bags and jackets and making for the shallow end too. As Ramona hoisted herself up over the edge of the pool, she felt hands pushing her up and looked back to see Theo's hands on her thighs. She didn't have time to react because the man scrambled toward them. As soon as she was out of the pool, Theo had her hand in his. They all sprinted toward the exit and down the hallway, arms pumping and hair swinging. They burst from the building, laughing, and scattered in all directions across campus without looking back.

CHAPTER 12

The bell rang just as Ramona opened the door to Malt Hall. She braced her bag against her body and ran down the hallway as the bell blared. She reached Classroom 105 and launched herself inside just as the bell stopped. Professor Scott and the entire class turned to stare at her as she, red-faced and breathing hard, held up her essay triumphantly. Ramona placed it in the wire bin on Professor Scott's desk before finding a seat.

The professor looked at Ramona for a moment longer than was comfortable before starting class.

"Good afternoon," Professor Scott said. "We're going to spend the first half of today's class discussing the speeches you chose. Please find a partner, and we'll check back in twenty minutes."

Chairs and table legs scraped against the floor as students rearranged the room. Ramona looked toward Molly, a kind girl whom she'd partnered with for the last few in-class assignments, who nodded. Ramona pulled her chair across the room, sitting close enough to hear each other over the chatter.

"So what speech did you choose?" Ramona asked.

Molly told her about one from JFK.

After a few minutes, though, Molly glanced around the room before lowering her voice. "Have you heard about the *Women's Anti-Handbook*?"

This would have shocked Ramona a few days earlier, but word of the *Women's Anti-Handbook* had spread like wildfire throughout campus over the last week since they'd distributed the ten copies. Still, she felt just as thrilled as the first time she'd heard someone mention her book. Ramona shook her head and motioned for Molly to continue.

Molly's eyes gleamed as though she'd found the last cookie in the jar. "My roommate's older sister's classmate swears she saw a copy last night."

"You're kidding," Ramona said, feeling like an actress. "What is it?"

Molly's voice dropped into a hushed tone. "Apparently, it's a rebuke to the *Women's Handbook* that we all got on the first day of term. It's really harsh on AWS, and I heard that the whole thing is done in deep-red ink to look like blood."

"You don't say!" Ramona answered, raising a hand to her mouth. She hadn't heard that version yet.

"It's quite bold, don't you think?"

"Definitely," Ramona agreed.

Eventually, they got back to talking about their speeches when Professor Scott came within earshot. But Ramona's mind kept returning to the *Women's Anti-Handbook* throughout the rest of the class. She hadn't expected Betsy's plan to work so well.

Soon, the bell rang, and just as Ramona was saying goodbye to Molly, Professor Scott called out to her.

"Ramona, may I have a moment?"

Ramona fidgeted until the classroom cleared.

"I couldn't help noticing that you seemed distracted in class today."

Ramona ducked her head in embarrassment. Always a stellar student, a professor's scorn made something inside Ramona wail. Sure, between work, school, and the *Women's Anti-Handbook*, things had slipped a bit recently. But it wasn't anything she couldn't handle.

"Yes, Professor. It's just that … well, there's a lot going on."

Professor Scott's eyes softened. "I understand. Attending any university, especially one this large, is difficult. And we understand that each student faces their own set of challenges. Still, it's important to prioritize wisely. Please know that you can come to me if you find yourself in need."

Ramona was surprised by the offer. She barely knew Professor Scott.

"Well, thank you, Professor. I appreciate that."

A look of concern and disapproval, swirled together like a soft-serve cone, remained on Professor Scott's face, but she nodded to signal that Ramona could go. Ramona adjusted her bag on her shoulder and went to look for Theo, all the while wondering how the professor could help her.

The temperature had grown colder during the hour she'd been in class. Ramona buttoned her jacket up to her neck when she arrived in the quad a few minutes later. She scanned the area for Theo. With all the students bundled up, it became more difficult to tell everyone apart. Then she spotted him, leaning against the side of one of the buildings, reading a newspaper.

Ramona crept up from the side, enjoying a moment to take him in before he saw her. Desire hit her so strongly that she couldn't help smiling. He concentrated on what he read, and the seriousness of his expression made her want to throw her arms around him. So she did.

"Boo!" Ramona whispered as she flung her arms around his waist. Despite their heavily padded jackets, she could feel his sturdiness as he twisted toward her.

"Didn't anyone ever tell you it's not polite to scare people?" Theo murmured into her hair.

"Yeah, well, I don't listen to them."

"Of course you don't," Theo said before gripping her and kissing her forehead. "I have a surprise to show you."

Theo led her toward the entryway of the building beside them. They walked up the front steps, and after Theo held the front door open for Ramona and two other students behind them, they continued walking down a quiet hallway. Ramona's curiosity grew with every step. Theo paused at a non-descript door and looked both ways before opening it to reveal a set of narrow, dusty stairs leading up.

"Some surprise," Ramona teased.

Theo's eyes crinkled and he nodded upward. "Go on."

Theo closed the door, sealing them inside the dim stairwell. Gripping the railing, they walked up the four flights, their breath shortening with each creaking step. Ramona frowned when she saw what waited for them at the top.

High ceilings soared above them with a wide wall of windows that cast light onto an attic filled with dusty, brown boxes and stacked furniture.

"What do you think?" Theo spread his arms wide and spun around in a circle.

"Of what, exactly? It looks like an attic."

"This, baby, is our new headquarters." Theo came to her with a glint in his eye. "At least, it can be … if you like it."

Ramona surveyed the space with their group in mind. Clearly, it was abandoned. The fact that it was four floors up made her calves burn, but that made it secluded enough.

"No one will find us here?"

"My friend said that it hasn't been used for years and is rarely checked, and he would know." Theo chuckled. "He's the one in charge of cleaning it."

Theo's knowledge of the ins and outs of the campus continued to amaze her. He knew which doors were unlocked and which rooms were filled with dust. Ramona wandered over to the windows and peered outside. The sprawling lawn of the quad lay below, with students moving here and there and everywhere.

"I think it's wonderful. And not a bad view," Ramona said, still looking outside.

Theo came up behind her and rested his hands around her stomach. "I'd argue it's got the perfect view," Theo whispered. "We can see them, but they can't see us. I tested the theory earlier."

She turned around to face him and stood on her tiptoes so that their eyes were closer together. "Does that mean we're alone?"

Theo nodded and ran a thumb up her neck, making her skin prickle with goose bumps. Privacy was almost impossible to come by on a campus filled with thousands of people. And ever since they'd returned from Portland two weeks ago, Ramona longed for Theo so much that it scared her. There was no risk in touching, though—no risk of an unwanted baby at least—so Ramona let herself go.

"Kiss me," she urged.

Theo bent to meet her request, and as soon as their lips met, she gripped the back of his shirt to pull him closer. They kissed slowly, exploring the shape and feel of each other. Desire swelled in her belly, and she could feel how much he wanted her in return. But just as she tightened her grip, he flipped her around so that she faced away from him. She gasped in surprise at the sight of all the people milling about in the quad below.

He reached for her hands and pressed her palms up high against the glass, whispering, "Leave them there."

Theo ran his fingers softly from her wrist down her arms, causing her to twitch as he traced the sensitive skin beneath her arms before moving down to the sides of her stomach. He kissed her neck, whispering sweet words under his breath that she could barely make out but absorbed like sunlight. She was eager for him, loving the slowness but also wanting more all at once. His hand stilled at her hips.

"Tell me what you want."

She knew what she wanted, but she couldn't possibly say it. Embarrassment overtook desire, even as she felt his breath on her ear.

"Ramona … tell me."

He rubbed the tip of his nose along her neck and squeezed her hips gently. Without realizing it, she'd started moving against him to get toward the release that she was craving. She barely recognized her body, but she was almost past caring. And he was patient, unrelenting. Finally, Ramona couldn't stand it anymore.

"Touch me," she whispered. "Please."

Theo made a satisfied noise and obliged. He slipped his hand inside her pants, and she melted against him. Her eyelids fluttered in response to his touch, and her head tilted back against his chest. It was the strangest sensation, being exposed by the window to those outside and yet feeling completely alone with Theo. They moved together, and she could feel her blood thrumming faster and faster until he captured her moans with his lips.

Ramona had never felt this good before, and her feelings for Theo swelled. She couldn't resist touching him any longer and turned to reach for his waist. She waited for his permission, and it came when he unbuttoned them for her. She'd thought about this moment a lot since Portland. She was ready.

At first, she was hesitant in her movements, unsure of herself, but she stroked him to his whispered requests. His reaction to her touch made her confident, and she continued until Theo's hands gripped the windowsill and his body bucked beneath her grip. Until he groaned and pulled off his undershirt with wicked speed to capture his desire. Until they collapsed to the ground in a heap of touches and smiles.

***

Twigs poked through a small hole in the ceiling. While the blood rang in Ramona's ears, she heard chirping too.

"Is that a nest?" Ramona asked from her own comfortable perch between Theo's shoulder and chest. They hadn't moved from the attic floor, each enjoying the peace and contentment of being together.

Theo, who may have fallen asleep, cracked one eye open and surveyed the ceiling. She pointed at the corner, and he squinted in the dim light.

"Mable's going to be thrilled to see those."

"Huh?"

"She loves birds." Ramona gestured toward the nest.

"She can name them," Theo said. "I have a good feeling about this place. The start of a new chapter for us, I think."

"For you and me?" Ramona asked.

Theo grinned.

"I was thinking of the group, but we seem to be off to a good start too." Theo cocked an eyebrow.

Pleasant heat filled Ramona's cheeks, and she forced herself to focus.

"I can't wait to see the reaction to the *Women's Anti-Handbook*," Ramona remarked. "So far, I feel like a spy every time I pretend to hear about it for the first time."

"And what a spy you are." Theo nuzzled her neck. "Has Patsy said anything yet?"

For the past week, Ramona had been waiting with dread and anticipation for Patsy to catch wind of her book. If Patsy heard of the *Women's Anti-Handbook*, she would surely report it to the administration, which would bring this whole thing to a new level. They needed that to happen, but a knot of worry still filled Ramona's chest at the thought.

"Not yet."

Theo tilted his head from side to side as though weighing out his thoughts on a scale. "She will soon," Theo said. "Everyone will."

"Are you going to tell me what you're planning yet?" Ramona teased. The more Theo kept his idea under wraps, the more she wanted to know.

More than a minute passed before he answered.

"What if we do something like they did at Berkeley?"

"Like what?"

"You know, how Cat said that the students forced the police to back off by surrounding their cars? What if we use the power of many to do something similar with the administration?"

"We would need a lot of people," Ramona remarked, trying to envision it.

"I'm not worried about that."

Theo gently shifted out from beneath her, moving to stand up. He paced around the room, his shoes clicking on the floor with each step.

"Do you think we need to do more?" Theo asked.

"What do you mean by more? More frequent?"

Theo shook his head. "More intense. Bigger."

"Maybe," Ramona answered. "But the bigger, the riskier."

"Nothing will change if we don't take risks."

He made it sound possible. The idea excited and terrified her all at once. But images of Angela Parker with a microphone reminded her that this was all possible. Students had power if they chose to use it.

Theo's cheeks flushed pink as he gestured with his arms.

"Students are stepping up all over the country, and I'll be damned if I'm not a part of it."

His tone shifted, hardening into fierce determination.

"We are a part of it," Ramona encouraged. "But I can't risk my scholarship."

Theo crouched before her, holding her face between his hands, and kissed her lightly.

"I know, baby. Don't worry. I won't let anything happen to you."

She knew that. But something else gnawed at her.

"Can I ask you something?"

Theo nodded.

"Why do you care so much?" When his eyes widened, she hurried on. "Don't get me wrong. I love how much you care, but I'm wondering where it comes from. What started all this for you?"

Theo stood up and went to the window. He bent at the waist, gripping the windowsill, facing away from her.

"Most of my father's friends served. Spend enough time with them, and you see what war does to people. It's brutal. A lot of kids from military families are expected to enlist, but my father always warned Dimitri and I away from it. I thought we were safe, until the rumors of a draft started."

Ever since the war in Vietnam began, rumors had run rampant and tormented males of a certain age.

"So last year, we'd started seriously protesting against the war. And it was fine, all very quiet, until this one time in the spring. We were protesting ROTC recruiting on campus in front of Zuccaro. It was pretty calm. There were maybe two dozen of us with signs, and we'd chanted, 'Gory, gory, what a helluva way to die,' and a crowd started. That's the best part, you know? The attention is better than getting high."

Theo turned to face Ramona from her spot on the ground. He'd never opened up to her like this before, and she soaked up his words like a sponge.

"A bit later, a pair of campus police officers had approached us. Olly got to them first and, being cheeky, said, 'What can we do for you, Officers? I'm afraid we don't have extra signs, so you'll have to make your own if you want to join.' They didn't like that." Theo laughed dryly.

"They'd told us that we needed to disperse, which caught me off guard. Usually, campus police officers observed to ensure nothing got out of hand and, if not, would leave everyone be. And that protest was the opposite of rowdy. So I told them so."

"'This is a peaceful demonstration,'" I'd said to them. "'There's nothing to disperse.'"

"Then they'd laughed to each other, like we were a joke. One got in my face and said that he'd given me an order and that we needed to stop. Don didn't like that, and I had to pull him back."

"I bet they would've been sorry to face Don," Ramona said.

"And believe me, I would've loved to have seen that officer get punched. I know firsthand how hard Don hits, but I didn't want him—or anyone—to get into trouble. So I'd tried one more time and asked what their cause was for shutting us down. They snickered before saying that we were 'endangering the peace.' I was so mad. So disappointed."

The veins in Theo's arms popped as he flexed his hands at the memory. Ramona got to her feet and stepped toward him.

"It felt like we were finally doing something—anything—to make an impact, and those officers could stop us like we were nothing. You asked why I care? Because I don't want Dimitri to go to Vietnam. Or Don. Or Olly. I don't want to go." Theo's voice cracked, and Ramona felt a corresponding twinge in her chest. "And I want to make those mother-fucking officers feel as small as they made us feel. The restriction of political protesting on campus was announced soon after that."

The picture she had of Theo focused like a film on screen at the drive-in after adjustments. She felt closer to him than ever before.

She wrapped her arms around his middle. It took him a moment to soften, but eventually, he melted against her. They held each other close.

"Thank you for trusting me," Ramona whispered. "We'll make those officers sorry."

Theo kissed the top of her head.

"Come on," he said. "Let's go. The dining hall opens soon."

He was right. As much as she wanted to stay there with him, she was hungry and had a lot of studying to do before she could call the day done. As they left the attic, Professor Scott's warning repeated in her head.

They walked across the quad, hand in hand, before branching off toward each of their homes. Something felt off as soon as Ramona reached Wolden. Nothing looked out of place, but tension filled the crowded lounge. Ramona found Mable across the room and moved toward her. Mable's eyes widened, and no sooner had she mouthed "Patsy" than Ramona heard her roommate's voice behind her.

"I need everyone's attention," Patsy snapped like a sergeant calling roll. All conversations in the room stopped. The only noise was the sound of the television.

Patsy's control was impressive. Ramona had to give her that.

Ramona whipped around, her heart speeding up, before freezing in the place near the doorway. Patsy's face flamed red, and her eyes went to Ramona, standing only a few feet away.

"It has been brought to my attention that there's a blasphemous *Women's Anti-Handbook* circulating around campus. This is an extremely serious matter, and I can confirm, without a doubt, that this act was not condoned by AWS. In fact, it's in violation of the official *Women's Handbook* and should be ignored at all costs."

Ramona felt removed from her body, as though looking down at the scene from above. Was this it? Was this the moment when they would get caught, and everything she'd worked to save would be taken from her?

"Has anyone seen this anti-handbook?" Patsy asked, her voice shrill.

The girls in the room shook their heads adamantly, and Patsy looked fractionally relieved.

"All copies of this *Women's Anti-Handbook* will be destroyed, and the creator will be brought before the council and administration for punishment. We will not stand for rule-breaking and any resulting chaos. I'll see to it myself, I can assure all of you."

Relief filled Ramona. If Patsy knew it had been them, they would have already been called to appear before the council. But that relief was short-lived. Patsy's eyes blazed with determination.

Speech complete, Patsy smoothed out her jacket before storming out of the common room, followed by two other members of the AWS council, like a mother and her ducklings. Everyone began talking at once about the scene. If there'd been any doubt about word not spreading fast enough about the *Women's Anti-Handbook*, it was gone now.

CHAPTER 13

Hairspray hung thick in the air like fog. The dorm room, already quite small, felt even more cramped as the five girls got ready for a night out. Ramona, Mable, along with Mable's roommate and her friends crowded around the limited mirror space and sat on any available surface. Music blared from the radio, and Mable swayed from side to side as she generously sprayed the curlers that she'd wound into her flat hair.

"The ends have to be curled," Mable declared. "Otherwise, the whole costume will be wrong."

One of the biggest parties of the term, a Halloween party, began in a few hours. As had become their routine, Ramona got ready in Mable's room. Patsy had been a nightmare to live with since she'd learned of the *Women's Anti-Handbook* last week and spent every waking moment in the room squawking about how awful it was or scribbling in her notebook.

Now, Ramona watched as Mable concentrated on her reflection. Mable had chosen to go as Dorothy from *The Wizard of Oz* and planned the costume down to the last detail, even sewing the blue-checkered dress herself. The dress, white blouse, blue hair ribbons and, of course, the glittering, red shoes waited in the closet. If only her hair would stay curled.

Letting out a puff of breath, Mable said, "You're so lucky to have hair like that."

"Don't be silly. You've seen it in the morning. The frizz?" Ramona's eyes narrowed.

Mable scoffed, and Ramona surveyed her own hair. She'd parted it down the middle because that looked the best with the black witch hat she had. She wore a long-sleeved, black, V-neck dress that narrowed at the waist and fell to her calves.

Across the room, Anne, Mable's roommate, asked Ramona, "What lipstick will you wear?"

Ramona shrugged. "None."

"That won't do," Anne said firmly, rifling through a basket in her closet. She emerged a few moments later with a glossy tube in hand. She uncapped it to reveal a deep shade somewhere between red and purple.

Ramona frowned. She rarely wore lipstick, let alone one so dark.

Anne held it to Ramona as though it was a paint swatch and she the wall.

"This is perfect. You have to try it."

After some cajoling, Ramona relented and painted her lips. She smiled at herself in the mirror. The dark shade made her teeth appear whiter than usual, and she had to admit that it suited her ivory skin and dark hair.

Mable clapped her hands together in delight, and Anne's satisfied smirk confirmed she knew she was right. As the rest of the girls finished getting ready, Ramona couldn't help glancing in the mirror again and again, each time surprised by the dark shade and how much she liked it.

"I wonder whether Olly will be there," Mable thought out loud as she made final adjustments to her costume.

"Do you *want* Olly to be there?" Ramona asked.

"No," Mable answered. "I wouldn't mind, though."

"Sure you wouldn't," Ramona teased. While double-dating with Mable and Olly would be fun, Olly seemed to like Cat.

But Ramona didn't have long to worry because soon, the girls were ready to go. They each signed out in the entryway before merging with other groups of girls heading out for Halloween parties. Their destination was a large, off-campus house infamous for throwing the best parties. Ramona had never been, but it was no surprise that Theo and the rest of the group were friends with the hosts. Within a few minutes, they heard music from down the block.

Anne led the way inside, but soon, Ramona and Mable lost the others and searched for their friends. People crowded the space, their bulky costumes making the problem worse. It was impossible to get through without brushing against everyone they passed. Finally, they found Theo, Dimitri, Olly, Don, Cat, and Betsy standing in the back room. Mable looked in Olly's direction and smiled.

"Spooky." Theo lifted his pirate's eyepatch to get a better look at her. "Are you trying to scare me again?"

"Is it working?"

"Without question." He wrapped his arms around Ramona and rubbed his scruffy beard, which he'd grown since they'd returned from Portland, against her cheek.

"Want a drink?" Theo asked. Both Ramona and Mable nodded.

Theo filled two cups with the purple liquid from the huge punch bowl, and the girls accepted them.

"What is this?" Ramona asked.

Olly laughed and raised his own cup to tap Mable's. "Call it witches' brew. It's strong enough."

Ramona sipped and immediately had to blink back tears. "Holy shit."

It was some combination of grape juice, soda pop, and liquor. Very possibly multiple types of liquor. Ramona drank again, and luckily, the second sip didn't bite as much as the first.

The group laughed and re-formed a circle. When Ramona caught Dimitri's eye, he looked away quickly.

"I need some air," he mumbled before hurrying toward the back door.

Ramona scowled. Enough was enough.

"I'll be right back." She followed Dimitri outside.

It wasn't as crowded in the yard, so Ramona easily caught up with him.

"Dimitri! Wait up."

To her relief, he stopped midstep. She figured he might flee, considering the way he'd been acting lately.

"Dimitri." Ramona paused, realizing how harsh her voice sounded and worked to soften it. "This has to stop. Are you going to leave every time I walk in the room?"

He considered the question before giving her a wry smile. "Not at work, I won't."

"It's not funny."

He took a deep breath before asking, "You know I care about you, don't you?"

Ramona nodded. "Of course I do."

"Please don't take this the wrong way"—he drew a deep breath—"but you should be careful around Theo."

Dimitri's expression looked apologetic, but determined. The warning surprised her.

"What are you talking about?"

Immediately, her imagination ran toward horrible scenarios. Had Theo done something wrong? Was he seeing other girls? She was certain he wouldn't do that to her.

"I'm not sure how to explain it, but when Theo gets his mind set on something, he doesn't let up. He can be intense. Really intense. And he doesn't always care about how he does it."

Ramona's eyes narrowed. She'd seen how hard Theo pushed for what he believed in, but she couldn't believe that Dimitri would describe it as a bad thing.

"He's your brother … how can you talk about him like this?"

Dimitri shrugged. "*Because* he's my brother. I know you think you know him, but I know what he—"

Ramona cut him off, raising a hand for him to stop. "Don't do that. I know you're not thrilled about Theo and I. Don't deny it," Ramona added when Dimitri opened his mouth to respond. "But I never thought that you'd go behind his back and speak badly of him to me."

She resented his claim. Of course she knew Theo. She'd spent hours and hours with him. He knew her mind and her body. He knew her heart.

Dimitri looked as though she'd hit him, but neither could respond before their friends spilled from the house. Theo headed in their direction with two full cups, and the others followed. In the back of the group, Olly tugged on Mable's braid in delight.

"You look just like her!" Olly said.

Mable blushed in response, and Ramona noticed the way the pair leaned toward each other.

Ramona did her best to forget the encounter with Dimitri, and soon, one cup of witches' brew turned into two, and then three as the night passed in happy chaos. Eventually, they found themselves in front of the crackling bonfire, sitting in a row of mismatched chairs. Ramona settled on Theo's lap and sunk into the warmth of his chest.

"Hey, who has the joint?" Olly called out.

Don pulled one from his pocket.

They passed it back and forth a few times before Theo reached out his hand and accepted it. He sucked on it like a sanctuary, and smoke billowed from his mouth.

"Do you want any?" Theo asked, and Ramona's stomach dipped. She did, but she also didn't.

"I don't know how," she admitted.

"I've got you. Let's try something."

Theo took another drag and held his breath for a beat before gently gripping the back of her neck and pressing his mouth to hers. Then he blew smoke into her open mouth and throat. It burned just a bit, but it also set her skin on fire, and she gripped Theo's forearm.

Ramona couldn't hold back a cough and looked toward a grinning Mable, whose hair was still curled perfectly at the ends. Theo patted her back, and a cup of witches' brew appeared before her.

When her coughing stopped, they all sat for a moment in relaxed contentment.

"Everyone, meet in the quad tomorrow morning. I have a surprise." Theo's eyes glinted in the firelight. "It's time for our next move."

"Are you fucking serious with the mysteries?" Olly moaned. "Tell us what we're doing, man."

"All right, all right. Remember the protest at Berkeley? We're going to do our own version here."

"No idea what you mean, but I'm in," Don mumbled between sips of witches' brew.

Ramona wasn't going to let Theo leave it at that, but then a group of giggling girls pulled her attention away. There were a handful of freshman girls whom Ramona recognized from Wolden standing across the bonfire, each gesturing wildly. Ramona squinted. What were they holding?

Books. They each held a small book. Identical books with red covers. Then one of the girls raised her arm and threw her book into the fire. Ramona gasped. Then another girl threw her book, followed by the third girl. Soon, they'd gotten the attention of the crowd, who watched in shock as if they were trespassing on a strange ritual. When the last girl with a book stepped forward, Ramona recognized it. A jolt of fear and delight shot through her.

The last girl threw her book into the fire and shouted above the crackling pops of the fire and hushed whispers, "Fuck Associated Women Students!"

Hoots and hollers and applause resounded. This group of freshman girls had just burned their copies of the *Women's Handbook* for anyone to see.

CHAPTER 14

A pebble rubbed Ramona's heel from the bottom of her left sneaker. She shifted her foot from side to side, attempting to move it, because she couldn't exactly take her shoe off in her current position. She stood shoulder to shoulder in a chain of hundreds of students surrounding the administration building. Finally, the pebble shifted, and the pressure on Ramona's foot released. She sighed in relief.

The morning after the Halloween party, the eight of them had met in the attic for their first meeting in their new headquarters. The feeling of abandonment disappeared as the friends filled the dusty space. Ramona had blushed at the memory of her hands pressed up against the windows overlooking the quad, until the task at hand forced her to focus. In the end, they'd planned this demonstration and rallied all these students in three days to recreate their own version of the protest Cat had mentioned. Hopefully, this attempt would finally convince the school administration to remove the restriction on political free speech.

And now, here they were, a human barricade surrounding the administration building. The sky darkened by the minute, and soon it would be 5 p.m., the time when school faculty usually left. But not tonight. Not unless they could break through the chain of students locked arm in arm. The wind whipped against them, but their packed bodies provided cover. Behind them, curious students gathered, and their closeness only reinforced the chain.

In the ten minutes since they'd formed their chain, no one had emerged from the building. Every passing minute ratcheted up the tension as linked arms squeezed tighter. Ramona stood between two baseball players who were, unsurprisingly, friends of Theo's. Supposedly, one of them had hosted the Halloween party.

Recruiting enough students in such a short time had been difficult, but they'd done it, mostly thanks to Theo's ability to bring people together. Eight students could get into trouble, but two hundred were much harder to pin down. And technically, they weren't breaking any rules. That's how Ramona justified being there. She wouldn't break the law, but she could participate in her right to free speech.

The guy on her right tapped his foot. A bead of sweat formed at his temple.

Leaning an inch closer, Ramona whispered, "What's your name?"

The baseball player stiffened. "Paul."

"Nice to meet you, Paul. I'm Ramona. I like to meet my partners-in-demonstration."

She could feel his gaze on her face, but before he responded, the front door of the administration building opened. Everyone froze. A group of school officials walked out, wearing coats and carrying briefcases and purses. Ramona felt a jolt of excitement. They'd waited all day for this moment, but that excitement quickly soured when Dean Redley appeared in the back of the pack.

The man at the front of the group wore wire-framed glasses, and his thick, white hair blew in the breeze. Ramona didn't recognize him, but he clearly led the rest.

"All right, you all. You've had your fun and kept us inside a few minutes after closing time, but it's time to let up now." The man's voice was gentle, as though the demonstration was a prank he was in on.

The students tightened their arms around one another.

The man sighed, ducking his head for just a moment. "I'm impressed by this show of unity, but you've been out here for almost half an hour, and I'm sure you've got better things to do with your time."

Ramona glanced at Theo, who stood about thirty people away, wearing an expression that darkened by the minute. He tipped his head in the direction of someone across the circle. The signal to start.

"We'll leave as soon as you give us what we want," called out one of the students in the chain.

"What is it, might I ask, that you want?" the man asked, his impatience showing now.

A different student spoke, "Lift the ban on political activism and free speech on campus."

The man scowled and switched his brown, leather briefcase from one hand to the other. He wore matching gloves.

"Now, you know I can't do that." He almost sounded sorry.

"You mean you won't," snarled a third student. "You're the president of the university!"

Ramona looked at the man with new interest. Of course she knew of President Howard, but she'd never seen him before. She gulped.

Calm down, she told herself, *you're not breaking any rules.*

"This is not how these things are done. I understand that you're frustrated with the limitations. I can see that now. Schedule an appointment with my secretary, and I'm sure we can come to a mutually beneficial agreement."

"Do you think we're stupid? We already tried that and were basically told to fuck off. So we're trying it our way now."

The remarks ping-ponged around the chain, different students speaking up so that the faculty had to turn from side to side to keep up. The tightness in Ramona's chest grew.

President Howard turned around to confer with his colleagues in hushed tones. After a few minutes, they sat on the front steps of the building, signaling that they'd decided. They would wait them out. Ramona chuckled. They'd soon see how stubborn students could be.

Thirty minutes became forty-five, and then an hour. When it was well past six p.m., Ramona wondered how long they'd stay. When you're standing in silence, without moves by either side, there's a lot of time to think. Ramona wished President Howard would engage with them. A real conversation where they were taken seriously as equals.

But instead, the president watched the students calmly. When his eyes came upon her, Ramona had the crawling feeling of being cataloged. And somehow, that made her proud and uncomfortable with this realization that he'd associate her face with this political demonstration. Dean Redley sat beside President Howard, looking like he'd just eaten something spicy.

Ramona realized her jaw ached from clenching her teeth so firmly. She caught Theo's eye and raised her eyebrows as he shook his head firmly. They would not let up.

The sun set, and the lights hanging on the administration building and walkways turned on. Finally, a woman with short, coiffed hair stepped forward. She wrung her hands together and appeared to be on the verge of crying.

"Please let us through. I need to pick up my children. They'll be scared."

The students glanced between the woman and each other. The school officials hadn't budged, so why should they let up? Ramona surveyed the woman's exhausted face and wondered why the children's father couldn't pick them up. She wondered whether they had a father at all. Despite their determination, it was feeling less and less likely that they would reach an outcome tonight. But wasn't it good that they were making the school officials uncomfortable?

"Shoulda thought of that before you revoked our first amendment right, shouldn't you?" Olly said with a smug smile.

"Hey, now," Dean Redley said, moving to stand in front of the woman. "No need to get nasty. Sandra here didn't do a thing to you all."

The dean walked right up to Olly. "I've had enough of this. We're going home."

He reached for Olly's arm and attempted to pry it from the student beside him. Olly jerked away and shouted, "Don't touch me!"

Students surged forward to reinforce the chain, and still, Dean Redley struggled with Olly attempting to break through.

President Howard jumped to his feet toward Dean Redley and Olly. Across the circle, Ramona saw Theo looking furious but unable to break his own position. Many students were shouting now in frustration, urging the president to call off the dean.

"Make him stop!"

"We just want to talk. Can't you see that?"

"Why won't you listen to us?"

President Howard's stern expression deepened. Just as he reached the pair, the whooshing sound of water broke through the clamor. Everyone turned, students and faculty alike, to see campus security guards standing at the edge of the chain, holding a huge hose. They aimed at the students.

The students held steady for a moment, but as the spray pummeled them, they eventually dropped their arms and the chain fell apart.

The hose turned toward the section of students where Ramona stood. And before she could prepare herself, frigid water struck her, hard, on the side of her body. She immediately tightened her arms around the baseball players and tried to stay in place. The security officer walked closer, and the pressure of the water increased until Ramona's hold on the baseball players loosened and she fell to the ground. Water hit her face, and all she could do was close her eyes to brace against it. *Is this really happening?* The wetness spreading across her skin felt like failure.

In the background, Ramona heard students shrieking with shock, frustration, and the bitter cold of water in the chilly night air. Suddenly, hands grabbed Ramona by the shoulder and hoisted her up to her feet and out of the spray. Blinking, Theo's blurred image appeared.

"Are you okay?" he yelled over the chaos.

Ramona coughed, her throat burning, but nodded. Theo's brows furrowed, and he looked furious. He turned around, and Ramona could see that he intended to confront the security guards. She grabbed his arm.

"No! It's not worth it!"

Hitting an officer was definitely illegal.

It was clear he wanted to go after them, but he stayed by her side. Students scattered in all directions. The campus security continued to spray anyone who remained too close to the administration building. President Howard, Dean Redley, and the rest of the faculty stared out at them. Ramona was pleased to see that both the dean and the president were soaked through and hoped the forceful water had stung their skin just as it had hers.

"Come home with me?" Theo asked.

Ramona nodded, taking Theo's hand, and they sprinted, refusing to look back to see whether they were being chased. The fear pushed them to move faster despite heavy, soaked clothes.

Soon, they reached the house and ran up the stairs to Theo's room. Ramona hesitated just inside the door, not wanting to track in water. Theo had no such worry as he stomped through the room, peeling off his jacket and shirt and throwing them on a heap of clothes in the corner.

"The fucking hose," Theo growled. "I should've seen that coming."

Water dripped from Theo's hair onto his chest, which rose and fell quickly. Ramona's lips parted as she tracked the droplets from his shoulders down his torso. Then he turned and crossed the room to pull her to him.

"I almost lost it when they sprayed you. Those bastards."

"I'm glad you didn't," Ramona answered, her voice muffled against his chest. "You don't need to get into trouble over me."

He cupped her head in his hands and teased, "But you're the best reason to fight."

"I'm fine," Ramona said. "But I appreciate you looking out for me."

"You better," Theo teased, gripping her sides now in a ticklish hold.

Jolts of delightfully uncomfortable electricity shot through her as she wiggled in his grip. "At least we got their attention, even if they haven't repealed the restriction yet. That was important."

"True. And did you see the look on Dean Redley's face when the water hit him? Fucking magnificent."

Theo picked her up and swung her into the room, and while Ramona felt like she might melt against his body, she shivered.

"Jesus, you must be freezing." He grabbed a towel from the pile in his closet. "Come here."

He wrapped the fluffy towel around her shoulders. Ramona sighed. Her hair was just as wet as Theo's, and her soaked sweater clung to her body.

"Theo," she whispered after a moment. "My sweater's soaked. I'll never get dry like this."

He stilled.

"I should take it off." And when his eyes widened, she added, "To get dry."

"Oh, sure," Theo said, eyes on her throat.

Ramona handed the towel back to Theo and slowly peeled the sweater over her head. She stood before him in her bra and soaked jeans. She could have reached for the towel again. She could get dry with her bra still on. But she didn't want that. She wanted Theo to see her. So while holding his gaze, Ramona took off her bra and dropped it. Theo sucked in a breath as his eyes went to her chest.

"Ramona," he said slowly. Reverently.

"Can I have the towel now?"

Theo gulped before wrapping the towel back around her shoulders, covering her from view. Instead of letting her go, Theo rubbed his hands across her shoulders and arms, drying her. When he finished, he dried her back. He was thorough, and when he was done, he released her. Being with Theo felt like dipping into a warm bath after waiting naked in a cold bathroom.

With her back to him, Ramona asked, "What about my front?"

A beat passed.

"Good point."

He rounded on her and slowly dabbed the towel against her collarbones. Theo rubbed her arms and then her stomach. Until only one area remained.

"Missed a spot," Ramona whispered.

Theo smiled and raised his hands to her breasts, rubbing them softly with only the towel between their skin. Ramona swayed toward him. She gasped when he pinched both nipples. Ramona's back arched, pushing her body farther toward him, and when she met his eyes, they gleamed delightfully.

"Like that?" Theo asked under his breath, his hair falling over his forehead as he kissed her.

She was about to nod when she remembered to speak. "Yes."

She shrugged off the towel and raised it toward his chest. "My turn."

Ramona dried him off just as methodically as he had done for her. Once they were both drier, they faced each other, neither making a move to part.

"What now?" Theo asked.

She wanted him. His mouth and his hands and his body. She wanted more with him than she'd ever had before. Logically, she knew the risks sex posed. Of course, she of all people did. But for the first time, she could sense her priorities shifting. Instead, she wanted to come together with him. Her first time.

A flitter of nerves danced across her skin as Ramona answered, "I want to be with you."

Her words set him loose. Theo dropped the towel and lunged, scooping her in his arms and carrying her to the bed. They landed in a jumble of blankets, pillows, limbs … two bodies fighting to close the distance. Ramona grabbed the back of his neck and kissed him as though he could be taken from her. His hands roamed her body as if sculpting a statue, and she shivered beneath his touch.

When she couldn't stand it any longer, she fumbled with the button of her jeans before pulling them off. Theo followed her lead and removed his own until nothing separated them. Their bodies collided, and as soon as her hips moved seemingly on their own toward the friction she knew she'd find at his waist, she froze.

"Condom!" Ramona blurted.

A flash of dread slashed through her. She'd forgotten for a moment. Thoughts of pregnancy flitted through her mind, and she squeezed her eyes shut, pushing them away. She wanted this, and she'd have it. Safely.

"Are you sure?" he whispered, brushing a curl behind her ear. "I only want this if you do too."

"I do," she breathed. "I just need a minute."

They lay face to face, eyes locked. And boy, did she love looking at him. He represented everything she loved and feared all at once. And for the second time that night, she couldn't wait any longer. She pulled his mouth to her, kissing him hard.

"Now," Ramona urged.

Theo nodded and opened a small package. When he reached for himself, though, Ramona paused him.

"Can I do it?"

Theo's eyes were heavy upon her. He handed the rubber to her and slowly, terrifyingly, she sheathed him, feeling thrilled as his hips bucked under her touch.

"Am I doing it right?" She had to make sure it was on. She had to.

Theo stilled. "Is this your first time?"

Her cheeks warmed, somehow feeling embarrassed for something that wasn't embarrassing.

She nodded.

"And you're sure?"

"You already asked me that," Ramona whispered against his throat.

"I think it's important that I make sure."

Love swelled within her. "Yes."

He held her face within his hands. "Thank you for trusting me."

Then his hands trailed down her neck and shoulders until he gripped her waist. They were kissing again, until all Ramona could think of was him. His touch. The smell of his skin.

"Theo," she said, holding him tight.

"I know, baby." Theo grinned wickedly. "I'm going to make it so good for you."

Theo laid her on her back and nudged her legs open, his hips cradled between her thighs. He hovered above her, and Ramona gripped his biceps tightly. He waited and looked at her expectantly.

"You know what to do," Theo said, his eyes not leaving hers.

He'd make her say it, huh? So she did.

"I want all of you. I want everything with you."

And on her next breath, they came together. Slowly, excruciatingly, beautifully slowly, they moved together until they were joined. And for a time, Ramona forgot about everything but Theo and the sensation that she chased within his arms, a hot shower long forgotten.

CHAPTER 15

Hours later, after Ramona and Theo ate a dinner of room temperature pizza, Ramona took the front stairs of Wolden, two at a time. She'd been quiet as Theo walked her home, her feelings threatening to take over. It felt like her chest had been filled with cotton candy, with shame and fear hovering at the edges, melting it down to nothing. They'd been careful, but the risk was still there. She'd resisted letting go of Theo's hand until she couldn't delay going inside any longer. Now the roots of Ramona's hair were damp as she crossed the threshold.

She headed toward the stairs when a large poster on the bulletin board caught her attention. As she got closer, she read the bold lettering:

THE WOMEN'S ANTI-HANDBOOK IS BANNED. ANYONE WITH A COPY, OR WHO HAS SEEN A COPY, MUST REPORT IT TO AWS BY NOVEMBER 8. ANYONE FOUND WITH A COPY OR IN ASSOCIATION WITH THE WOMEN'S ANTI-HANDBOOK AFTER THIS TIME WILL APPEAR

BEFORE THE AWS COUNCIL UNDER THREAT OF SUSPENSION.

Her throat dried. Shit. Ramona grabbed the banister to steady herself. Patsy wasn't playing around. She would kill Ramona if she found out that she'd authored the *Women's Anti-Handbook.*

"You're blocking the way."

A girl stood behind her, shaking her head.

"Sorry," Ramona mumbled before bolting upstairs.

She hurried down the hall, grabbed a towel from her room, and headed to the showers. She turned the water on to the hottest setting and, after stripping off her damp clothes, stepped in. Her teeth chattered as her body temperature normalized. Then she startled when she saw the large pink mark on her side from the hose. It resembled the mark she'd had after belly-flopping into the lake the summer before.

After washing her hair, Ramona paused on the spot beneath her ear. The spot where Theo had kissed her so tenderly, she thought she'd stop breathing. She should feel different, shouldn't she? She'd always thought that she'd feel like a new person when she had sex for the first time, but instead, she felt more herself than ever. Ramona brushed her hands across her body.

After a while, and despite the joy, exhaustion plucked at her, so Ramona finished and dried off. A wave of homesickness swept through her when she caught a whiff of the shampoo that she and her mother each used. She hadn't been home since school started almost two months ago and wondered what her mother would think of the demonstration.

With the terry cloth towel wrapped around her middle, Ramona went to her room, intent on going straight to bed.

Patsy scribbled in a notebook at her desk. She wore a light-green cardigan buttoned up to her throat with a matching headband, one of many in her pastel-colored collection. Normally smooth and well managed, Patsy's hair looked as if she'd ridden in a convertible with the top down. She was so focused on writing that Ramona slipped inside and dressed unnoticed. Her warm pajamas felt like heaven.

The wood frame creaked as Ramona tucked into bed. Patsy looked up.

"Oh! I didn't hear you come in."

She scanned Ramona, taking in the damp clothes piled on the floor.

"Why are your clothes wet?" Her eyes narrowed. "You weren't at that horrid demonstration, were you?"

Ramona felt surprised that word had spread so quickly but lied as she settled under the covers. "The shower leaked and soaked my clothes."

Ramona pulled the blanket to her chin and asked, "Were you there?"

Patsy scowled before snapping, "Of course not. Melanie told me how awful it was."

"What do you mean?"

Patsy shifted toward Ramona and leaned forward. "Students surrounded the administration building to block people from going home. Apparently, they all just stood there until one of the students got into a fight with Dean Redley. Can you believe that?"

Ramona shook her head, fascinated by the retelling. "And then," Patsy continued, "they sprayed the students down with a fire hose and they ran away."

Using her best acting, Ramona gasped. Good thing Melanie hadn't recognized her in the group of students.

Taking in Ramona's faux-shocked expression, Patsy looked pleased. "I know how you're feeling. I felt the same way when I heard. These people are going to cause chaos one of these days."

And here was yet another example of her viewpoint differing wildly from Patsy's.

"Do you know what they wanted?" Ramona asked.

Patsy tilted her head before answering, "Melanie didn't say. What does it matter?"

Interesting. Their demonstrations wouldn't be effective if students didn't understand their purpose. She'd have to talk with Theo about that tomorrow.

Ramona noticed Patsy staring at her.

"Sorry, what?"

"I said," Patsy emphasized, "did you see the poster we put up on the bulletin board?"

Ramona dulled at the reminder of another issue to deal with. Forcing her voice to remain neutral, Ramona asked, "The one about the *Women's Anti-Handbook*?"

"Yes," Patsy said. "After what happened on Halloween, I had to do something."

So Patsy knew about the burned *Women's Handbooks*. Ramona had wondered whether she'd find out.

"Were you there? Did you see who did it?" Patsy asked like a detective on the case.

Ramona shook her head and repeated Patsy's question. "Does it matter?"

"What kind of stupid question is that? Of course it does. Obviously, this is a huge problem." Pasty shifted, turning her back to Ramona. "And Dean Redley doesn't understand the seriousness of this delinquency."

Ramona took a deep breath, her patience thinning by the minute. "What's he done?"

"Nothing!" she burst out like a balloon meeting a needle. "Not a single thing. We need to find out who did this and punish them."

"I told him that we could get a list of all the female students living on campus who'd received the handbook at the beginning of term and require them to report in with their copy. Anyone who couldn't would be convicted as one of the girls who'd burned their handbook."

Horror filled Ramona the longer Patsy spoke. AWS didn't possibly have that power, did they? It was absurd. And what exactly did she mean by 'convicting' students?

Then Patsy sighed. "According to Dean Redley, burning the *Women's Handbook* isn't actually breaking any rules. It's despicable, he had assured me, but as long as the rules outlined in the handbook are still followed—and we apparently don't have any evidence that they aren't—there's nothing to punish."

If leading the Associated Women Students' council was Patsy's purpose, then authoring the *Women's Handbook* was her child. There hadn't been a day since Ramona met Patsy when she hadn't talked about the handbook or AWS or both. She took this personally.

"Between that wretched *Women's Anti-Handbook* and girls burning their *Women's Handbook*s in a bonfire, we have to do something. And now this demonstration at the administration building. What's wrong with everyone?" Patsy huffed out a breath.

"Something definitely is wrong with people," Ramona answered.

"I'm launching a special commission of the best AWS members to take down the *Women's Anti-Handbook*." Patsy's blue eyes brightened. "We're going to put a stop to these antics."

A pit of dread hardened in Ramona's stomach. Increased attention increased the risk. It also meant that their efforts were having an impact.

"That's great," Ramona choked out.

"Now, I've got an idea! Why don't you join us tomorrow? A few members of the commission are putting up more posters in female dormitories across campus, and we could use the help."

Ramona couldn't think of anything she'd rather do less, but Patsy smiled expectantly. Before she could think of an excuse, she had an idea. Working with Patsy would give Ramona direct access to know what she was planning. She'd be like a spy.

So when Patsy said, "I'm sure this is something you'd be happy to do as a member of AWS."

"Count me in," Ramona offered.

"Great choice!"

Patsy explained when and where the girls would meet the next day. Ramona nestled farther beneath her covers, but one thing gnawed at her.

"Why is this so important to you?" Ramona asked.

"We have these rules for a reason. Besides, elections for AWS council are later this month, and I will not lose because of this insubordination."

Patsy adjusted her headband, smoothing it over her hair. Her voice softened as she said, "I've wanted this position for a long time."

So Patsy had a personal stake in this too. Dread wavered at the edges of Ramona's mind, anticipating conflict. They couldn't each get what they wanted. One would lose. Soon, sleep overtook Ramona after a day that had felt so much longer.

CHAPTER 16

Leaves in every shade from yellow to brown covered the lawn. Someone had attempted raking them into piles, but the wind had its own plan. Ramona considered stashing the stack of posters prohibiting the *Women's Anti-Handbook* she held in one of the piles, but she didn't have a chance with the rapid pace that Patsy kept them moving.

As agreed, Ramona had met Patsy and a few other girls in the Wolden lounge that morning to put up posters. After covering the lounge, bathrooms, and hallways of Wolden, they now marched among the fall foliage to another dormitory. This whole exercise was turning into a big advertisement for the *Women's Anti-Handbook*, and Ramona couldn't help smiling to herself. She couldn't have planned it better if she tried. Of course, the risk of getting caught lingered, but they'd been careful to hide their identities.

Surprisingly, the other girls were more down to earth than Ramona had expected. They wore similar headbands to Patsy, and two had fraternity pins on their sweaters. They didn't seem to have the same passion as Patsy about upholding the mission of AWS. Instead, it seemed they were there out of loyalty.

Ramona recognized about half of them. As big as the school was—over thirty thousand students—moments like this made it feel small.

When they reached the next dormitory, Patsy led them inside.

"Becky and Jane, you're on the top floor. Hannah, you've got the bathrooms, and Ramona, cover the lounge."

Ramona clenched her teeth, not liking taking orders, especially not from Patsy, but she took her stack of posters and tape to the lounge. Girls studied at the tables and lounged on the couches, watching television. It looked just like the Wolden lounge with a different set of faces.

A bulletin board hung on the wall, and Ramona quickly put up a poster on the side. Not feeling like adding any more, Ramona walked toward the exit.

"Seriously?"

Ramona froze just as she was about to walk through the doorway. Two girls stood before the poster.

"Great, now there's another thing they can write us up for. Whoever made that thing should cut it out," one girl said to the other.

"I know, right? What are they playing at? It's not like anything is going to change, and it's only going to make things harder for us as AWS cracks down."

Ramona's chest tightened, and her heart thudded uncomfortably fast. She'd never meant to make things worse … to make things harder for those who already had it hard. She fled before hearing anything else.

The rest of the girls were gathered in the lobby, waiting.

"Have you chosen a dress yet?" Jane asked.

"No." Becky groaned and rubbed a hand across her cheek. "I can't decide between two."

"Wear the better one," Jane suggested.

"Duh," Becky said. "The problem is that I can't decide which one is better for a dance."

Ramona's interest piqued.

"What dance?"

Each girl looked like an owl with a pair of wide eyes.

"The homecoming dance! It's the biggest of the term. And I have less than three weeks to decide," Jane muttered.

She hadn't heard about it yet. Ramona wondered whether Theo and the rest planned to go. Unlikely.

Soon, Hannah arrived. Before Patsy could march them to the next dormitory, Hannah spoke up.

"What if it's just a rumor?"

Patsy looked taken aback. If the *Women's Anti-Handbook* was just a rumor, then Patsy would look like a fool for reacting so strongly. She'd made posters, for God's sake.

"It's not," Patsy said.

"Patsy, don't get huffy with me. I'm just saying, it could be a rumor. No one we know has actually seen a copy. You know how some people like to pull pranks."

Patsy's cheeks reddened to an alarming state. "It's not a rumor, I just know it."

The girl shrugged as though it was Patsy's burden to bear and simply asked, "Where are we going next?"

Over the next hour, Patsy led them from building to building until they'd covered every female dormitory. She specified that the posters be hung in high-traffic areas and only inside the buildings. Ramona suspected this was because she didn't want the posters to be seen by the wider student body.

After covering the final female dormitory, they reconvened outside next to another pile of leaves. The crisp air welcomed them and felt wonderfully cool after spending so much time bustling about in heated buildings.

"Good work," Patsy said, collecting the extra posters in a neat stack. "We're done for today, and I'll let you know what's next."

"That's my girl."

The group turned to see Archer walking toward them. He looked like he was due at the country club, wearing khakis and a button-down shirt covered with an open cardigan.

Patsy squealed quietly and leapt toward Archer, kissing one of his rosy cheeks.

"You're so organized," Archer said, pointing at the stacked posters and clipboard Patsy carried. He rubbed her shoulder. "Definitely wife material," he teased.

The girls swooned at that, but Ramona felt revulsion bubble in her throat. As Patsy and Archer kissed again, Ramona took that as a sign for dismissal and hurried away from them all. She headed straight toward the attic. Fifteen minutes later, she found Theo, Mable, Cat, and Don hanging out, just as she'd hoped.

"Ramona," Mable called out from her perch on one of the windowsills.

Theo sat backward in a chair beside Don and smiled up at her.

"Hey, baby," he mouthed, and if she wasn't so intent on telling them about the commission, she might have gone to sit on his lap, regardless of the others. She felt her cheeks pinken, thinking of the night before, but forced herself to focus.

"You're never going to believe what I just did," Ramona started as she pulled out the folded-up poster she'd hidden away. "Patsy invited me to put up *Women's Anti-Handbook* posters in all the female dormitories with her new AWS commission."

"What the hell?" Cat said first, sitting up from where she lay on the floor against her book bag.

They swarmed to the poster to read it.

"You're going to have to start from the beginning," Mable said.

Ramona told them everything that had happened from the moment she'd returned to their room last night to putting up the final posters that afternoon.

Raising a hand in the air to accompany the question, Theo asked, "So you're telling me that you, the creator of the *Women's Anti-Handbook*, put up posters banning it?"

Ramona nodded.

Delight took over the shock and Theo beamed. "That's brilliant."

"He's not wrong," Cat said, her expression resembling admiration, and Ramona's pride swelled.

"It's pretty cool," Don added before turning back to the game of solitaire he'd laid out for himself.

Over the next half hour, Theo, Cat, and Mable asked her countless questions about the commission and posters and what each member of AWS had said exactly. Feeling exhausted and having had enough of the retelling, Ramona finally put an end to it.

"That's it! That's the whole story." She laughed. "I can't remember whether Patsy said she was 'mad' or 'angry,' and what's the difference anyway?"

Cat whistled. "Good ol' Patsy, falling right into place."

"What do you mean?" Mable looked confused.

"We couldn't have planned this better if we tried. Patsy's little commission is going to make the *Women's Anti-Handbook* even cooler."

"Exactly," Theo agreed. "This is going to spread awareness, and get more people to want to be involved, and the more involvement, the more power we have."

Then the attic door opened, and they all froze. A second later, Olly's long, lanky form appeared, and they breathed a collective sigh of relief. They were still on edge after getting caught in the pool, ready to jump up and run at a moment's notice. But the attic's single entrance and exit didn't give them many options for escape.

Olly dropped his bag to the floor without a care and made a beeline toward Cat. "What are we talking about?"

"Ramona's psychological warfare on AWS," Cat answered.

Ramona immediately objected, "I don't know about that—"

"I've got to hear this," Olly said, and when everyone started talking at once, he hushed them. "Only Ramona, eh? I want to hear what happened."

Ramona gave him the abbreviated version and enjoyed the reactions of her audience.

"Damn." Olly whistled when she'd finished. "Good on you."

Olly crouched down on the floor right beside Cat's head. Her red hair was spread out around her head, and he gently picked up a strand.

"Should we go to Earl's to celebrate?"

Ramona shook her head, as did Mable and Theo. They all still had classes.

"Not a chance," Cat said, stretching her arms above her head. "I've got better things to do than drink with you all afternoon."

"Come on, *Elizabeth*, don't leave me hanging," Olly teased.

Ramona looked around. "Who's Elizabeth?"

Olly lay down on the floor beside Cat, his body parallel to hers and only inches away. "This lady right here."

"Your name isn't Catherine?" Ramona asked.

"No. Why would you think that?"

"Well, because you go by Cat," Ramona remarked.

"Olly thought I looked like a Cat laying in the sun in the quad one day during freshman year. What can I say? The name stuck."

It made sense now that she'd said it. Cat was exactly what Ramona imagined a feline in human form would be like. Elizabeth though? She'd never have guessed. Ramona felt a little thrown off by the reminder that she'd only been a part of this group for a few weeks, and in a lot of ways, she didn't know them very well. She bristled at the thought.

"My grandparents are English," Cat said by way of explanation. She sighed and sat up. Pulling her book bag over her shoulder, Cat turned to Olly. "All right, you big lug, one drink."

Olly jumped up in a flash and did a little celebratory shimmy as he followed her toward the door.

"Hold on," Theo called. "I got an interesting invitation today."

Everyone turned to him, and Theo continued, "Apparently, President Howard would like to meet to 'find middle ground' with us."

"No!" Mable blurted, holding her hand up to her mouth.

"So it worked then," Don considered, looking pleased. Don's older brother, a lieutenant in the Marines, was currently stationed in Vietnam with the intention of advising the South Vietnamese. As such, Don cared a lot about their ability to speak openly about the war … even if he said little himself.

"It seems so," Theo agreed. "But let's see what he has to say before we celebrate too much."

"Aye aye, Captain," Olly called. "Anything else?"

When Theo shook his head, Olly winked at Ramona and followed Cat out the door.

"I'd have a beer," Don said, leaving as well.

Still by the window, Mable looked crestfallen. Ramona wanted to go to her but couldn't say anything with Theo still there. So instead, she tried to give Mable a reassuring smile. But Mable looked away and stood up quickly to gather her things.

"I'm going to go too. Bye."

Mable hurried from the room with her head ducked so that her hair covered most of her face from view.

Theo and Ramona watched her go until he asked, "Is she okay?"

Ramona shrugged. She honestly didn't know.

Theo came to her and wrapped his arms around her waist to pull her close. He smelled like peppermint gum and deodorant.

"Well, let me know if I can do anything," he said before rubbing his nose along the side of her neck. "Interesting position we have here, all alone."

"Very interesting." Ramona shivered beneath his touch.

Thoughts of Patsy's commission faded as they kissed. Ramona leaned into him, and he cradled her head as though she was precious. With him, she felt like it. After seconds or minutes, who could say really, Ramona smiled against his mouth.

"How are you?" Theo surveyed her face. Checking on her. And again, her feelings swelled.

"Good," she confirmed. "Better than that, actually, but it's hard to describe. How are you?"

Before answering, he swooped her up in his arms and carried her to the window, pressing her back against it.

"Baby." He smiled against her lips. "I've never been better."

Ramona squeezed her legs around him, and they kissed until she'd lost track of time. Later, when her lips felt raw, she released him.

"As much as I love this, I have work to do," Ramona whispered, unwinding her legs from him and dropping to the floor.

Theo's eyes burned like embers for a moment before lightening. "Well, all right. I guess I can go to class. If you insist," he teased.

"I do."

He rubbed his thumb across her lower lip before letting her go. "See you later."

Once the door clicked behind Theo, Ramona took a deep breath and held the air in her lungs for a beat longer than comfortable. If she was going to do this, she'd need her wits. She pulled a chair toward the window where the light was best and curled up into it with her feet propped up on the ledge. Now that they had the attention of the students, AWS, and probably the faculty, she had to take advantage of the momentum. Releasing the *Women's Anti-Handbook* was just the start. She wanted to make life better, fairer, for female students.

Over the past couple weeks, she'd started thinking about how to make the college a more equitable place for them all, regardless of gender. Ramona couldn't contain those thoughts any longer. She spent the next half hour writing dozens of ideas, crossing most of them out before landing on the following list:

1. *Remove the curfew.*
2. *Equal representation of male and female students on the student body council.*
3. *Remove the dress code.*
4. *Lift restrictions on dorm room conduct (i.e. rooms could be as messy as a person pleased).*
5. *More women on the faculty.*

Ramona sat back, pleased with the agenda, and realized that her jaw ached from clenching her teeth. The list was more than reasonable, which made it even more ridiculous. She felt frustrated that she even had to make a list. Theo, Don, Olly, and Dimitri would never have to make a list like this. They were all White male students. And it wasn't fair. Suddenly, her skin itched with anger, but she tamped it down. No one was shamed more than an angry woman.

She shoved her notebook into her bag, planning to show the list to the group as soon as they came together again. There was so much to do for women's rights and student free speech, they would have to tackle it piece by piece. Professor Scott had said as much in a lecture earlier that week. To make an impact, language had to be simple and specific.

"It's okay to talk about big-picture ideas," Professor Scott had said. "But you need to tie that thinking back to specific talking points so that the audience can connect the idea to their own lives. You'll also want to speak simply, as though talking to children. This is the best way to ensure your audience understands."

That's what they needed to do. Ramona walked quickly across the attic, and even though every muscle in her body wanted to slam the door shut behind her, she closed it softly with a click.

The bell rang as soon as she reached the bottom of the stairs and entered the main hallway of the building. The classroom doors sprung open like the button on a pair of pants after a large Thanksgiving meal. The holiday was only a couple weeks away, and thoughts of turkey dinner weren't far off. Students swarmed the hallway, and Ramona navigated through them and back to Wolden, where she gently placed her agenda in the top drawer of her desk.

CHAPTER 17

Four sweaters were nestled neatly in a row in the closet. Ramona glared at them and blew out a breath. She'd already spent too much time choosing an outfit and stood in a black bra and fitted trousers. None of her options seemed warm enough. Fine. She'd do her hair and makeup first and choose a sweater afterward.

Ramona sat in her favorite spot beside the window, which undoubtedly had the best light in the room as well as the perfect view for watching people pass below. Despite the cold, Ramona warmed at the feel of the sun on her neck as she surveyed herself in the mirror. First eyeliner and then mascara, coating on so many layers she lost count, and finally, a dab of blush on each cheek. Her mother had always prescribed to the pinched-cheek method, but Ramona thought she looked like a corpse without blush at this time of year. Her dark hair made her pale skin look dramatic in contrast. And now the best part—lipstick. Mable's roommate, Anne, had given her the deep-mauve lipstick that she'd worn on Halloween, and Ramona painted it on now with pleasure.

Something shifted outside, catching Ramona's eye. A squirrel stared at her from its perch on the branch beside the window.

"Well, hello there, little one."

The squirrel squeaked. Then it went on with its business and climbed up the tree.

"And good morning to you too." Ramona laughed.

Then her gaze shifted beyond the empty branch toward a guy walking with a backpack slung over his shoulder. Just as she looked at him, he looked at her. And then he did a double take. Their eyes locked and Ramona froze. A jolt of adrenaline spread through her as she realized she wore only a bra. And he could see her. But instead of moving out of view, she raised an eyebrow at him, her heart thudding in her ears all the while.

Slowly, Ramona turned back to the mirror and sprayed her curls with Aqua Net hairspray. She could feel his gaze on her one-woman show. She liked it … the intimacy of him watching as though he was in the room. Power flowed through her as she had rendered a man frozen. Once her hair flowed around her shoulders as she preferred it, she turned back to the mystery guy. He still stood there dumbstruck.

That is, until a short woman appeared. Mrs. Garth hurried toward him with arms swinging at her sides. Mrs. Garth tapped his shoulder and he jumped, shifting his gaze from Ramona to the housemother. Ramona backed away giggling from the window, but not before she saw Mrs. Garth yelling and then glancing up toward her window. For the umpteenth time, Ramona wondered why adults needed a chaperone.

No longer caring, Ramona grabbed the closest sweater and dressed. She found Mable in the foyer a few minutes later to walk to class. Still flustered from the strange encounter, Ramona pulled Mable outside and in the opposite direction of

Mrs. Garth. She recounted the window incident and how exhilarating it had been before Mrs. Garth had appeared like a dragon guarding her castle.

Mable's eyes widened. "You've certainly had a more exciting morning than me."

Before Ramona could respond, they passed a circle of girls, and pieces of conversation caught their attention.

"Haven't you heard?" one of the girls asked before pulling a tube of lipstick from her bag. "There was a bonfire, and some girls burned books!"

"It wasn't a book, you idiot. Not really. It was the *Women's Handbook*," another said sharply.

"That's not all! I heard they burned their bras too," said a third under her breath.

"And AWS is putting together a special commission to find out who did it! It's going to be a witch hunt."

Ramona rolled her eyes at the exchange, and Mable stifled a laugh.

"Sounds like they saw the posters," Mable said.

"I'd be shocked if they hadn't." Ramona scowled. "Patsy made us put up a ton of them."

Soon, the pair split for their classes, and the next few hours passed quickly as Ramona focused on the lectures. She couldn't stand to fall any further behind. But focusing became harder when Betsy caught her between Public Speaking and Math to tell her to meet them in the attic as soon as she could. Theo had met with President Howard.

When classes finally released, and after eating a rushed late lunch, Ramona went to the attic. Her thick-soled boots thudded in the stairwell until she burst through the door to see the group assembled.

"All right, finally," Olly said as soon as Ramona appeared, nodding toward Theo. "She's here. Go on now."

Ramona sat beside Mable, and anticipation filled the attic as all eyes turned to Theo.

"He started by saying how impressed he was with our coordination," Theo began, pushing his hair off his forehead. "You know, trying to butter me up."

"Then he talked about the seriousness of the demonstration, saying that it could have been dangerous. To which I pointed out that the only physical harm done was by the hose his guards brought out. He didn't like that point much." Theo grinned.

"He apologized for not meeting to hear our concerns earlier and said that he wants to meet in the middle."

"How's he going to do that?" Don asked skeptically.

"That's the disappointing part," Theo said. "He offered to let us have one of the big lecture halls for a teach-in."

"As though we can't plan a teach-in ourselves," Betsy chimed in. "I can plan one in my sleep."

"What's a teach-in?" Mable asked.

"Let's see," Betsy said. "It's practically an unofficial, ungraded lecture. It started in Michigan, and now they're happening all over the country for the war."

Mable nodded beside her as Ramona considered. That sounded interesting. She'd like to attend a teach-in.

"President Howard could make things difficult for us," Theo continued, "and we don't want them pulling out the hose every time we plan something, so I agreed."

"Seriously? We're working with the man now?" Olly groaned and Theo gritted his teeth.

"Sure, it's not ideal, but it's better than nothing, huh?"

A thought occurred to Ramona and she spoke up. "It's a way to bring students into the cause who've been on the fence because they think our demonstrations are too radical. A teach-in, especially one supported by the school, is more accessible."

Admiration radiated from Theo, and Ramona felt herself light up like a candle.

"Good point," Betsy said. "So we'll plan a teach-in."

They discussed for the next half hour, talking through topics, timing, and hosts until Betsy assured that she had it handled. "You'll get your assignments soon enough," she said. "Don't you worry your pretty little selves."

Seeing everyone shifting to go, Ramona seized her opportunity.

"If we're done talking about the teach-in, I have something I want to share." Ramona wrung her hands together. "I've been working on an agenda for women's rights on campus and have come up with a list of five demands."

"Oh!" Betsy squealed and clapped her hands. "Let's hear!"

Ramona smiled appreciatively and recited the memorized list:

1. *Remove the curfew.*
2. *Equal representation of male and female students on the student body council.*
3. *Remove the dress code.*
4. *Lift restrictions on dorm room conduct (i.e. rooms could be as messy as a person pleased).*
5. *More women on the faculty.*

As soon as the last word rolled off Ramona's tongue, Betsy started clapping.

"It's fantastic!" Betsy cheered. Behind her, Cat nodded.

The praise warmed Ramona. She turned to Theo, hoping that he would agree with Betsy and Cat.

"It's really good," he said. "It will be hard though. And we can only get so much done at a time, so we'll need to prioritize the issues we're fighting for."

Ramona's chest crumpled slightly, just as Betsy swatted Theo's arm. "Don't be such a downer. We can do it all!"

Theo rolled his eyes at Betsy, and Ramona watched as though from the other side of a long tunnel. For a split second, Theo looked like a stranger rather than the person she felt closest to, and she scanned his face for a sign of familiarity. She didn't like to admit how offended she felt by his lack of enthusiasm.

Then Betsy's squeal pulled her back through the tunnel and into the moment. Betsy turned to Cat and raised her eyebrows. "Are you thinking what I'm thinking?"

When Cat nodded, Betsy turned back toward Ramona. "We need to get the word out about this agenda. We're throwing a party. This weekend!"

Ramona blanched. A party? She didn't see the connection, and besides, wasn't a party a surefire way to blow their cover? Ramona said as much, but Betsy hushed her to explain.

"It's going to be a secret party. Only girls who have a *Women's Anti-Handbook*. It's about time we brought them all together. Stronger together, right? Besides," Betsy said, seeing Ramona's unsure expression, "don't you want to know what they think?"

Fair point. It would be hugely valuable to understand what other girls thought of the agenda, the *Women's Anti-Handbook*, and women's rights on campus. Hearing from others had been the best part of doing the petition.

"You're right. That would be good."

"Even more importantly, we all need to let off some steam," Cat said with a head tilt, looking pointedly at Ramona. "Especially you. Let's get drunk."

Everyone left soon after, but not before Betsy made Ramona and Mable promise to be at their house at 8 p.m. on Friday. That gave Ramona four days to switch shifts at work. Betsy gave her a list of items to bring, including plastic cups and juice. They'd only given out ten handbooks, so the party should be small, which meant little risk of getting caught. Ramona tried to focus on the idea of having some fun instead.

Once they were alone in the attic, Theo chuckled at Ramona's expression. "Betsy moves quickly, huh?"

"She sure does."

Theo's grin transformed him back into the person she knew. "Well done with the agenda."

"It didn't sound like you thought so earlier." Ramona ducked her head.

"I think it's a great idea," Theo said as he stepped closer to her. "We'll just need to strategize how to act on it."

Fine. Ramona could accept that. His ability to see the big picture was something that attracted her to him.

She reached for him, and they pressed their bodies together. His shoulders were firm and wide beneath her hands, and she held on tightly as he picked her up and spun her around the large space until finally she begged, laughing, for him to stop.

"All right, all right." Theo set her on the ground but held on to steady her as she regained her balance.

Ramona stretched up on her toes to bite softly at his neck. Theo tightened his hands on her.

"I have to go," Theo groaned in her ear. "If I miss class again, Professor Dixon is going to fail me. Otherwise, I'd press you against the window again."

Ramona's spine tingled at the thought, but she let him go after a few shallow breaths. They left the attic together before parting ways in the middle of campus—Theo to attend class like a good student and Ramona to work on an English paper.

CHAPTER 18

A stack of *Ladies' Home Journal* magazines sat neatly on the shelf. Ramona twirled a curl around her finger as she lounged on her bed in the empty room. She rarely read magazines, but she was curious what she'd find in the pages that Patsy so dutifully read. And investigating sounded better than starting the new English paper that Professor Grant had assigned as soon as they'd turned in the last one. Ramona had spent hours over the past two days, researching and writing, and her brain refused to do more so soon.

She jumped up from the bed, pulled a magazine off the top of the pile, and returned to her perch. A beautiful woman on the cover stared back from close range with perfectly manicured nails. Ramona skimmed through the table of contents before flipping through the first few pages. Magazines were quite assertive, each sentence delivered with utmost certainty. Then Ramona's finger swiped right past a page, the material too smooth. She licked her finger just as the door flew open.

Patsy filled the doorway, her hair frizzed, and she gripped her headband in her hand.

"I've been looking for you everywhere," Patsy said as though she'd been stood up.

"What—"

Ramona froze. Her stomach curdled. She recognized the notebook Patsy carried.

"What do you have to say about this?" Patsy tossed the notebook into Ramona's lap.

Ramona caught her own notebook. And she knew she hadn't misplaced it.

"You went through my things?" Ramona asked incredulously.

"Yeah, and it's a good thing I did." Patsy's cheeks flamed with fury. "What do you think you're doing writing a thing like that? Are you trying to start a revolution or something?"

Ramona's hands clenched around the notebook so hard, the thick, cardboard cover bent. Anger filled her like steam in a shower. The violation. Patsy finding her notebook with the agenda only a few days after she'd tucked it away in her desk—a place that should've offered privacy—couldn't be a coincidence, and the realization pummeled Ramona. Patsy must've been snooping into her things on a regular basis.

"Why did I write it?" Ramona asked, fury rising in her own face now. "I want to make things better on campus for us. And somehow, the vice president of Associated Women Students doesn't want the same thing."

"Those things on your list will never happen. Not while we're here to see them."

Patsy slung her purse onto the designated hook in her closet.

"Why can't you be happy with what we have? Our generation already has so much more than our mothers did," Patsy said.

Ramona's mouth dropped open. Was she kidding?

"It's not enough." Ramona brought her hands together. "I won't settle, and you shouldn't either."

Patsy looked at Ramona with cold eyes. "You have no idea how hard I've worked to make AWS what it is today. You're just a freshman without a clue."

The air left Ramona's chest in a rush, and tears pricked at the corners of her eyes. *Don't cry. Don't cry. You better not fucking cry.* She wouldn't give Patsy the satisfaction. She raised her chin like she imagined the models did in photos where their necks looked a mile long.

"Until all students on campus have equal opportunities, it's not enough. You may have given up, but you can bet I'm not stopping."

Gripping the notebook as though she planned to hit Patsy with it—she deserved as much—Ramona stood up and got into Patsy's face, sticking her finger against her nose.

"If you think you're getting away with rummaging through my things, you're going to be wildly disappointed. You've definitely broken one of your precious rules here."

Patsy smiled, and from this close, her teeth held a yellow tinge at the edges that filled Ramona with satisfaction.

"You have no proof," Patsy said.

Ramona pressed her forefinger against Patsy's nose before stepping back and snapping her teeth together. It was true. And no one with decision-making power would believe Ramona's word over Patsy's.

"You're going to be sorry."

Patsy left, and Ramona paced the room like a caged animal. Her shoulders ached, as though too big for her body, and she rolled them to release the tension. Then a garment bag in Patsy's closet caught her eye … a particularly important garment bag that contained a dress that Patsy had been fawning over for days. Ramona smiled.

After what Ramona had in mind, Patsy would be very sorry indeed.

Ramona sat down at her desk, rested her head on her arms, and breathed deeply until the anger dulled. She wouldn't give Patsy a chance to talk to her like that ever again. Ramona thought of the party on Friday. Cat had been right. She needed a night of fun.

CHAPTER 19

"You're asking for the night off?" Randy asked across the telephone line.

Ramona gulped, imagining his beet-red face, knowing it would be funny if his anger wasn't directed at her.

"I'll find someone to cover," Ramona promised.

"After you've been late to multiple shifts over the last few weeks," Randy mused.

This party better be worth it.

Ramona shifted forward on her toes and suppressed her annoyance at his tone. "Randy, I get it. I haven't been the ideal employee lately, but I'm doing my best. I'm hoping for the night off to attend a special lecture."

A small lie. No way would she tell him about the party. She was a student, and a special lecture was feasible. It had sounded impressive even to her own ears.

Randy groaned across the line. He didn't hide his feelings toward college and higher education. Ramona wondered whether it had been an option for him.

"Fine."

"Really?"

"Yes. But you better find someone to cover."

"Yes, of course," Ramona said earnestly. "I will."

"I'll come right out and say it, though, Ramona. You're walking close to the edge here. I can find another waitress like that." The sound of him snapping his fingers deflated her lungs.

They clicked off, and after Ramona called another waitress to switch shifts, she left the phone booth. They had to leave for the party soon, so Ramona hurried toward the stairs to change out of the clothes she'd worn to class.

As she rounded the banister, the bulletin board caught her attention. Her stomach sank like a stone in water. Every notice had been removed from the board and replaced with a single sheet of paper in the center. Ramona read quickly, clenching her fists.

Wolden residents needed to close their window curtains from dusk until dawn each day to maintain privacy and decorum.

What. A. Fucking. Joke.

There wasn't a chance that this was unrelated to the incident earlier that week. Ramona shook her head, anger growing in her belly and her throat until she felt like she might breathe fire. You could sure as shit bet that girls weren't peeping in the boys' rooms. And yet, the girls were the ones with a new rule.

She hurried upstairs and flung herself inside her room. She shoved a pillow against her face and yelled as loudly as she could, only muffled noise escaping. How much more was she expected to take before she suffocated? Before they all did.

It took Ramona a bit to pull herself out of her funk. The idea of being with Mable and Betsy, and hell, even Cat, was the only thing keeping her from staying in bed. Ramona and Mable arrived at the party to an enthusiastic Betsy and music greeting them at the door.

Betsy and Cat lived in a small cottage house a couple blocks from campus with Cat's cousin, a chemistry major who spent most of her time in the lab. The house was in the same direction as Theo, Olly, and Don's house. Ramona couldn't help envying them all for that freedom. She couldn't wait to live off campus.

A large bowl rested on the kitchen counter with a liquid that looked suspiciously similar to the witches' brew on Halloween. Girls took turns dipping the ladle in and out.

"I'll get us drinks," Ramona said to Mable, following Betsy into the kitchen.

"Why isn't the ice in the bowl?" Ramona asked as Betsy took the ladle from a girl to first fill her cup before handing it to Ramona.

"It would water down the drink," Betsy said before taking a big gulp, leaving a purple tint above her upper lip that she wiped off with the back of her hand.

Ramona followed suit. The drink was intense, sharply sweet with the underlying bite of alcohol. She coughed and forced herself to swallow.

"What's in this?"

"It's good, right? There's cranberry juice, grape juice, apple juice, soda pop, and vodka. Mostly vodka."

"Yeah, I got that." Ramona laughed and took another sip, wincing less this time.

Girls crowded around the bowl, and Ramona turned her body sideways to make space. It seemed as though more girls arrived every few minutes.

"This is more than ten people," Ramona said loud enough to be heard above the music.

Betsy was looking at something in the backyard and only turned when Ramona tapped her shoulder.

"It might be," Betsy answered coyly.

Ramona scowled, not in the mood for Betsy's games. "It definitely is."

"Well, what's wrong with that?"

"Aren't you worried that someone will report us for the *Women's Anti-Handbook*?" Ramona's stomach had been in knots on and off all day thinking as much, and the window rule hadn't helped. She'd imagined getting dragged in front of the disciplinary committee and losing her scholarship—or worse, her admission—more times in the last few days than she could count.

"No one is going to say a thing. It's a secret circle we've got here. Every girl who's received a handbook was told to bring one friend. They have a stake in this just like us, so they don't want to get caught either. Besides, they are a part of the cause. We can't do this alone."

Ramona took a step back in surprise. Betsy was right. Still, Ramona felt annoyed that she hadn't talked to her first before doubling the *Women's Anti-Handbook* circle. She was losing control. Ramona pushed the feeling away and said, "Whatever. I guess this is fine."

"Of course it is." Betsy smiled and tapped their cups together. Then she gave Ramona a once-over and narrowed in on her face.

"Come with me." Betsy grabbed Ramona's arm, and she grudgingly allowed herself to be pulled into the bathroom.

Betsy opened the medicine cabinet and, after removing a pencil, nodded toward the closed toilet. "Sit down."

"If you insist," Ramona said, sitting on the lid.

"I do." Betsy then directed her to close her eyes. Her fingers felt cold as they pulled Ramona's eyelids to the sides. She traced her eyes with the liner before telling Ramona to open and then repeated the process on the bottom.

Betsy surveyed her work with satisfaction.

"There." Betsy capped the liner and went to put it away. "Just like in the magazines."

As Betsy rifled through the products on the counter, Ramona looked at herself in the mirror. The dark liner complemented her hair, and somehow, the thickness made her eyes appear bigger, rounder. Ramona smiled.

"Thank you."

Betsy waved her hand. "Don't mention it. Now let me take my pill, and we can go back to the party." She took a sip of water from the faucet, popped the pill, and swallowed. "Thank goodness for Margaret."

"Margaret who?" Ramona asked as she stared in awe at the packet.

"Margaret Sanger, of course! Without her, I'd be a heck of a lot more worried."

Ever since Ramona and Theo had had sex, and every time she'd felt a surge of longing for him, she thought about birth control. Two methods of protection would surely be better than one. She made a mental note to visit the doctor to ask for a prescription for the pill.

Betsy took her hand once more and pulled Ramona back toward the punch bowl before exiting into the backyard. Ramona didn't recognize a single person in the room. She filled a second plastic cup and wound her way through the girls toward Mable in the living room. It had all the makings of a classic college party. Packed full with loud music and strong drinks, excitement filled the air. But it also felt different … undoubtedly because there were no boys. Maybe she was imagining it, but they seemed less inhibited. Freer.

Mable stood next to the unlit fireplace with a couple girls. When she saw Ramona, she reached for the second cup and sipped. Her face crumpled as if she'd bit into a lemon wedge.

"Whew, that's strong."

"Betsy's a killer bartender," one of the girls joked. "I always get a gnarly hangover after going to her parties. But they're also the most fun."

The girls had big hair, and even though the front door opened and shut every few minutes, the living room reeked of hairspray.

"I'm Ramona, by the way."

"You're Ramona? I've been wanting to meet you!"

"I'm sorry to disappoint." Ramona smiled.

"No really! You wrote the *Women's Anti-Handbook*, didn't you?"

It felt like a hand tightened around her heart. Ramona could feel every pulse. The book was such a big part of her life, and she was so proud of it, but she'd never actually spoken about it to anyone beyond their group. Certainly not to a stranger. And now she wasn't sure whether she felt thrilled or scared. The anonymity protected her.

"Yes! She did," Mable beamed with pride.

"I love it! I've read it cover to cover at least three times already. I'm Gail."

"Wow. Thank you, but Mable wrote it too. It's nice to meet you."

"We, Sandy and I, have used the curfew trick a few times already. It works like a charm!" Gail gushed and pointed at her friend. They exchanged looks and laughed. Their lips, like all the rest in the room, were tinged purple.

Gail's short, bobbed hair bounced as she told the story of how she and Sandy had been taking turns staying out late and using the back door of their dorm to sneak in.

"Granted, our housemother is a bit of a dud. She'd sleep through anything, and I don't think she cares all that much. But still, it works!"

"Did you hear that?" Mable bumped Ramona on the arm and smiled. It was one thing to write the *Women's Anti-Handbook* and another to use its guidance to sneak in yourself, but it was something else entirely to hear about how others were benefitting. The smile on Gail's face made the risk seem worth it.

"I'm really glad." Ramona smiled. "What year are you?"

"We're juniors," Gail answered. "We live in Fredlund Hall on the east side of campus."

"Can I ask you something?"

"Shoot."

"Were things different when you were freshmen? I keep wondering what things were like a couple years ago."

Gail and Sandy exchanged another look, and Sandy spoke this time. "We met in Wolden Hall freshman year, and the rules were pretty strict then too. But we noticed the new freedom—far more than we had in high school—more than the rules."

"Tell them about the skirt, though," Gail prompted before taking another drink.

"Oh, yeah! I had this skirt, right? I bought it new for the school year. It was plaid in shades of red and brown, and it went perfectly with my favorite pair of Mary Janes. It was a little shorter than my other skirts, but not *that* much shorter. I usually pulled it down a bit before leaving the dorm, but one morning, I forgot, and I guess it had ridden up as I walked. I got a demerit for breaking the female dress code and had to go to detention for a week. Not to mention that I wasn't allowed to wear the skirt anymore. I still have it, though. I love that skirt," Sandy said dreamily as if she was talking about a long-lost friend.

All the girls standing in their circle wore the same frown. Finally, Mable said, "That stinks."

Sandy nodded, and Gail raised her glass. "A toast to all the skirts of past and future that won't see the light of day. They'll live forever shunned in our closets."

They tapped their plastic cups together.

"You think that's bad?" a raspy voice asked. They all turned around. The girl sat back on the couch, her knees bent and feet resting on the edge of the coffee table. "Boy, do I have a story for you."

"Go ahead," Gail said.

The girl leaned back and paused before beginning. The anticipation in the air increased, and more girls around the room turned to look. She rubbed her lips together and began.

"I'm taking Advanced Statistics this quarter, and we have weekly quizzes. I guess the class didn't do well on the first couple, so the professor started offering an optional study session that he'd lead the night before each quiz. Obviously, I went. I'm going to learn as much as I can."

Then the girl added with a half-smile, "Besides, I like stats. So I went to the first two sessions, and it was fine. I was the only girl who showed up. There were probably twenty guys, but I didn't care. I took notes and aced the quizzes."

The room quieted, as every girl stopped talking to listen.

"Well, I showed up to the third office hours' session, and before the professor started, he asked to see me in the hall. Once we were alone, he advised me that my attendance was causing a distraction. So I asked him what he was talking about because

I'd been sitting there, quiet as a mouse. He explained that the boys were having a hard time focusing on the equations with my presence. Apparently, I was distracting them by simply being there. Then he had the audacity to say that isn't the type of attention that I should want, and it would be better if I stopped coming to the office hours. He stood in front of the closed door, practically blocking my way back into the classroom."

Frowns deepened around the living room.

"I didn't see any other option because I was not in the mood to cause a scene. I took my things and turned to go. As I was leaving, he said that I was doing well enough in the class as it was and didn't need the extra help anyway. As though my learning had a limit and I'd reached it."

The girl took a sip, indicating that her story was done, and the room erupted.

"How dare he?"

"Bastard."

"What's his name? I'll show him what a distraction looks like … right before I elbow him in the throat."

Girls talked over one another as a new tray of drinks appeared, and cups were passed around the room until most everyone held two each. Ramona's anger blazed at the stories, which validated her own experience. None of them were alone in this. And that made her feel powerful.

Ramona put her drink down and pulled herself up on a chair, steadying herself with a hand on the ceiling. They'd given her an idea, and before she knew it, she called for their attention.

"Hey!" she shouted until the room quieted enough that she could hear herself think. Maybe it was the alcohol, but she didn't feel nervous as all eyes hung on her.

"I think we can all agree that"—Ramona pointed in the direction of the raspy-voiced girl—"that is fucked up." A few whoops let out and encouraged her.

"We all have stories like this. We've all been treated unfairly as female students at this school. The men do whatever they want. I mean, for God's sake, she couldn't study because boys were distracted? That sounds like *their* problem to me! I don't think we should have to worry about it."

"We're not the problem!" Gail shouted. "The men are."

"So what's wrong with this picture?" Ramona reached for a copy of the *Women's Anti-Handbook* from her pocket.

The girls looked at each other, curiosity blooming.

"Maybe there shouldn't be a *Women's Handbook* or a *Women's Anti-Handbook*, but instead one for the men!"

The room cheered. She wondered if Angela Parker had started in a room like this.

"We have an opportunity here. If you look at each of our stories together, there are common themes. Inequality for women, for one. Together, we can pool our power and make a difference on campus. We deserve to be treated fairly. And if we need to make them uncomfortable to do it, then let's make them uncomfortable. It's not our job to make men comfortable! Especially when they sure aren't worrying about our comfort."

Across the room, Cat leaned against the doorway with narrowed eyes. But beneath that skepticism, Ramona could sense approval, and it encouraged her to go on.

"The *Women's Anti-Handbook* is just the start! Now that AWS has put together a commission to take us down, we need to do more. We've outlined an agenda for women's rights on campus. Do you want to hear it?"

The girls cheered encouragingly, and Ramona took the opportunity to outline the five components of her agenda. Their agenda.

As soon as she'd finished, the girls erupted in whoops of agreement.

"Yes!"

"That's right!"

"Let's do it!"

Ramona beamed and took a moment to soak in the energy here. "We'll need all of your help in making it real."

Gail and Mable helped Ramona off the chair, and soon, the room was louder than before. The next few hours passed in a blur as the girls swapped stories, and more drinks were distributed. Time lost meaning, as it always seemed to do during a good party. Soon, stories turned into singing, and the girls danced through the living room and kitchen to "You Don't Own Me." Their feet tapped the floor, their arms swung through the air, and their hands clapped to the beat, banging walls in excitement.

It was only when someone noticed it was 11:30 p.m. that they came back to themselves. The curfew. After thanking Betsy and Cat for hosting, the girls filed outside, leaving in groups toward their houses and dorms.

The plastic tub had been emptied hours ago, so Ramona grabbed a half-full cup of the purple drink from the coffee table before hurrying after Mable. But she slowed when she noticed Cat watching her by the door.

"A *Men's Handbook*," Cat said. "Now that's an interesting take."

Ramona beamed drunkenly. That was the best compliment she'd ever gotten from Cat.

"Want to help write it?" Ramona asked.

Cat nodded and patted Ramona's shoulder before steering her outside. "Let's talk about it tomorrow. Go sleep it off."

Ramona hesitated, and the next words bubbled up from her throat without warning.

"Patsy found the agenda."

"She what?" Cat asked slowly. "How?"

"She found it by snooping through my desk while I was gone."

Ramona had spent the last forty-eight hours feeling like she would punch Patsy in the face if it didn't mean suspension. And her heart cracked at Patsy's claim.

"She said it would never work," Ramona squeaked out as a tear formed at the edge of her eye.

Cat ground her teeth before responding.

"That nasty thief." Then her voice softened, "Now, you listen to me. Patsy was trying to intimidate you. Don't let her, all right?"

Ramona nodded. And when Cat wiped the tear from her cheek, Ramona had to suppress a sob at the show of unexpected kindness. Cat would hate the display of emotion, and that made Ramona laugh. Crying to laughing. She really was drunk.

Cat looked at Ramona as though she might be losing it, but smiled.

"Go catch up with Mable before she trips down the stairs."

Ramona hugged Cat and squeezed tightly before stumbling toward Mable and wrapping an arm around her waist as the pair descended the stairs.

At the bottom, Mable twirled and held her skirt out with both hands. "That was soooo fun."

Dancing chased any lingering sadness away as Ramona and Mable spun on the sidewalk. Finally, when one of the two claimed to be sick, they faced the direction of campus. But before they took more than a few steps, Ramona turned around.

"Where are you going?" Mable asked.

"Let's go see the guys," Ramona said with a devious smile.

Mable raised her eyebrows. "What about the curfew?"

"We'll be quick. It only takes a few minutes, and we can run."

Mable skipped over to Ramona and intertwined their arms. "Let's go."

They ran down the rest of the block before tiring and slowing to a walk, giggling all the way. When they reached Theo's house, Ramona bent over at the waist to flip her hair back. Her curls cascaded around her head, and Mable clapped like a gleeful child. Ramona took a gulp. She was thirsty.

"Theo!" Ramona shouted. "Get out here right this minute."

Mable's giggles turned to cackles of delight. "Yeah! And bring Olly too!"

She felt warm after skipping and walking and drinking, so Ramona pulled her sweater over her head. The fresh air felt wonderful against her chest. She wore a tight, V-neck tank top that she knew accentuated her chest.

"Theooooo," she sang to the old house that had been abused from years of college residents who threw too many parties and did too little cleaning.

A window on the second floor opened, and Olly's face appeared. He rubbed his eyes and Ramona waved, just as Theo came to the front door, and thoughts of anyone else disappeared. Theo was shirtless, and his toned chest was wide and muscular. He looked delicious, and his olive skin shone under the porchlight. His jeans hung low on his hips and Ramona gulped. She stood frozen in place until she met his eyes, and his half smile pulled her toward him. She ran across the walkway, and he met her at the bottom of the steps. She jumped into his arms and wrapped her legs around his waist. Still holding the cup, the purple liquid sloshed down Theo's shoulder.

"Oh no!" Ramona lowered her face to lick it off of him without a second thought. His skin was warm beneath her tongue, and she took her time cleaning him off. In fact, she lingered a bit.

Theo trembled beneath her. He was ticklish, and said, "Ramona, baby, it's fine. It's fine."

Then he saw the color and laughed. "You were with Betsy, huh? How drunk are you?"

She pressed her forehead against his so that their eyes were only an inch apart and squeezed him so that his waist was pressed more tightly against hers.

"Very."

Theo held her up with one arm and gripped the back of her head with the other, holding her face against his as she kissed him with every ounce of energy she had left. He tasted like mint and beer and a touch of smoke, and she briefly wondered what he had been doing, but she was here now, and she wanted him so badly. She'd forgotten where they were and who they were with until Theo smiled beneath her lips and pulled away.

"Let's get you some water."

He carried her through the house to the kitchen and poured her a tall glass of water from the tap. He set her down, and as soon as her feet touched the floor, she dropped her plastic cup in the sink and reached with both hands for the water. She guzzled it as though she'd spent the day in a desert. When the glass was empty, she beamed at him.

"I love water," she said dreamily.

"I'll bet." His eyes crinkled the way that she loved when he smiled. "Now as happy as I am to see you, it's 11:52 p.m. And I'm pretty sure you don't want to miss curfew."

At the word curfew, Ramona stiffened. Shit! Where was Mable? Ramona stretched up to kiss Theo once more before bolting from the kitchen. She found Mable on the porch, sitting next to Olly on the front steps with their legs pressed side to side. She'd ask her about that tomorrow. As long as she didn't forget. For now, they had to go.

Ramona raced down the steps and shouted, "Come on! Curfew!"

Mable startled. She turned back to Olly, opened her mouth, hesitated, and simply closed it without another word to him. She raced after Ramona, and soon the two of them sprinted down the street in the direction of campus. They didn't notice that the two boys followed to see them home safely.

CHAPTER 20

In every dormitory, the entryway is visible from the front room. And that's exactly where Mrs. Garth sat as Ramona and Mable stumbled in the door at 12:02 a.m. Mrs. Garth glared at them as if they'd interrupted a particularly steamy romance scene in one of her erotic novels, which, by the look of the book cover in her hand, they may just have. She peered over her glasses to look from Ramona and Mable to the clock on the wall.

"Ladies." Mrs. Garth sighed as though this was the very last place she wanted to be. "It's past curfew."

Ramona's stomach cramped as fear flooded her body, all while focusing on staying upright. Beside her, Mable flung her hands out in dismay.

"It's only two minutes past midnight!" Mable sounded five years younger than she was.

Mrs. Garth set aside the book and reached for the ledger on the side table. "That's correct, Miss Mooney. It's two minutes past curfew."

After flipping through the pages, Mrs. Garth made a note in the ledger. The purple alcohol swirling in Ramona's stomach soured as the world spun. They'd just received a citation.

"This isn't a rounding situation. We don't round down to the closest hour. You ladies are late to curfew and will each receive a citation. Be glad that you aren't later. Breaking curfew by more than fifteen minutes results in two citations."

"Well, we wouldn't want that," Ramona mumbled.

"I didn't catch that," Mrs. Garth said.

"Nothing, Mrs. Garth," Ramona answered louder.

"This is a very serious matter. This is a prestigious institution, and we take our rules of conduct very seriously. Miss Bronson, you've already received one free pass. You won't get another."

Ramona looked at her shoes. She'd hoped the housemother had forgotten that in the flurry of new faces that first week. The instinct to fight back, to somehow talk them out of this situation, flared. But Ramona suppressed it. The walls were spinning something fierce now.

"Yes, Mrs. Garth. We'll go to bed now."

Ramona grabbed Mable's hand, and they unsteadily maneuvered the stairs. They separated to go to their own rooms. All Ramona could think of now was her bed. She braced her hands against the wall beside her room door.

"Please be asleep, please be asleep, please be asleep."

The only light in the room came from the edges of the windows where the curtains couldn't contain the moonlight. Patsy slept with her eye mask and ear plugs as usual, and Ramona sighed with relief. She hurried to her bed, pulling off her black boots along the way, when she noticed the glass of water on her desk and lunged for it. Droplets spilled down her chin as she drank deep. The spinning quickened, and Ramona dove into bed without a care that her clothes, jeans, and jacket were still on. Closing her eyes, she hoped for the steadiness of sleep.

It took less than five seconds for a wave of nausea to roll through her, and she bolted upright with eyes wide open. She focused on her closet door, urging the handles to remain still.

"What's wrong with you?"

Shit.

Patsy lay on her side, facing Ramona. One ear plug was out, and her eye mask rested on her forehead. Surprisingly, she looked more amused than judgmental.

"Oh my God! You're drunk, aren't you?"

Ramona groaned. It wasn't a crime to drink, but she knew Patsy would look down on her for it. She dodged the second question and answered the first. "I'm fine."

"Sure you are." Patsy reached for her wristwatch. She took it off every night, along with the gold bracelet that Archer had given her for their anniversary, and set them in a ceramic dish next to her bed. When she saw the time, her eyes bulged. "You missed curfew?"

This time, Ramona didn't answer. Instead, she turned away from Patsy to face the wall. She could feel Patsy's eyes on her for far longer than was comfortable until she heard the rustling of bedding, and then, only quiet. And in that quiet, Ramona lay with the knowledge that she'd been caught breaking curfew, not even for a shift, and had been written up. Not to mention that Mrs. Garth would pay extra attention to Ramona and Mable as she no doubt did for all the women who broke curfew. If she got five citations, she'd be brought before the AWS disciplinary committee. And if that happened, she could lose her scholarship. She imagined standing before them, a waitress who wanted more than anything to be a student. Gritting her teeth,

Ramona squeezed her eyes shut tight to ward off the tears that burned for release.

***

The headache from Betsy's cocktail had taken two days to wear off. And 'cocktail' put it generously. Ramona finally felt like herself again. She'd muscled her way through the shift she'd swapped, and the only good part about it was that Randy had been too busy to give her a hard time. Now she sat on the windowsill of the attic beside Mable as Betsy crossed yet another idea off the chalkboard.

"No, definitely not," Betsy snapped. "We're not making the environmental impact in Vietnam the theme of the teach-in."

Across the attic, Dimitri opened his mouth, but Betsy cut him off. "I don't care that it's an important issue. It's too abstract for the likes of the students here. I mean, I know this is a good university, but people can be so dumb."

Dimitri sighed and waved his hand. His expression was so defeated, Ramona couldn't help giggling, drawing his eyes to hers. They held each other's gaze for a beat, and when Dimitri gave an exaggerated roll of his eyes at Betsy's theatrics, Ramona laughed again. It felt nice. Almost like it used to be between them.

"I can't believe we're doing another fucking teach-in," Don complained, pulling Ramona's attention back to the moment. He pushed the sleeves of his sweater up to his elbows. "People are burning their draft cards, and we're sitting down to talk with a bunch of professors."

"It's not anyone's first choice," Theo said, "but it's better than nothing, and we're in this for the long haul. This is one step in that direction, so help or shut up."

Don clenched his fists and remained quiet, his cheeks pinkening by the second.

"We're overthinking this," Cat drawled from her spot, sitting against the wall. "All we need to do is talk about the war and the draft, and the conversation will flow from there. Then we wrap it up by explaining how the current restrictions mean we aren't allowed to protest openly about any of it. We want them to support removing the rule, after all."

Betsy smirked at Cat. "It's that simple? Well, gee, I guess you figured it out, Cat. Why do I even bother to plan this then?"

The pressure for a successful event had everyone on edge. And it didn't help that it was Monday or that the wind whipped viciously outside. They were each in a mood.

"Well, we need to finish planning the content so we can talk about Ramona's idea," Cat said.

"What idea?" Betsy asked.

Cat glanced Ramona's way. What was she talking about?

"We're going to create a *Men's Handbook*, and I think we should give out copies at the end of the teach-in."

Silence stretched as the blood pounded through Ramona's ears. She'd completely forgotten about the idea in the haze of alcohol, and Theo, and getting a citation. Ramona tucked her hair behind her ear and wondered what else she may have forgotten. She should stop drinking.

"What the bloody hell is a *Men's Handbook*?" Olly asked. He stood in the corner, spinning a basketball on his middle finger.

"Just as it sounds. There's a *Women's Handbook*, courtesy of our friends on AWS, and it's about time that we create a *Men's Handbook*. It's only fair ... a bit of satire, if you will."

Cat explained how the idea had formed at the party on Friday. That men were the source of so many problems women faced. Often, women minded their own business, and men made their own problems. So the *Men's Handbook* would tell them exactly how they could behave to avoid such hardship. The guys' faces clouded as they processed what she explained, clearly battling with feelings of defensiveness and support. Ramona wouldn't have expected anything else. Accountability didn't come easily.

Theo shifted toward Ramona and asked, "You think this will help?"

She nodded, appreciating how he checked with her.

"I can't say it makes me feel great about my gender, but all right, then we'll do it. I don't want it to take away from the message of the teach-in, though—to repeal the restriction on political free speech on campus. Are we agreed?"

Every head nodded.

Anticipation filled Ramona as a picture of the *Men's Handbook* formed in her mind. She couldn't wait to see the reaction.

Soon after, they packed up. All Ramona could think of was lying down for a quick nap before a long study session. Midterms were upon them, and she'd fail if she didn't focus. The stairs groaned as the group left the attic in a slightly better mood.

When Ramona arrived at Wolden a few minutes later, she could hardly step inside for all the women who gathered in the entryway.

What was going on?

Ramona craned her neck, searching for the cause. The women gathered around the bulletin board at the foot of the stairs—the bulletin board she'd grown to detest. No good news ever appeared there. Ramona edged closer until her breath caught as if she'd been punched. Smack dab in the center, beside an advertisement for the homecoming dance, was a large poster:

NEW! THREE CURFEW CITATIONS WILL RESULT IN AN AWS COUNCIL REVIEW.

Ramona's heart squeezed. *What the fuck?* It felt as though she couldn't catch a break. They'd reduced the number of citations from five to three. The typical outcome of a council review was community service or detention, but Ramona had heard rumors of serious cases impacting student scholarships. After all her hard work, any progress she thought they'd made evaporated.

And she had no doubt who'd done this. Patsy stood on the staircase, smiling down at them all, her position of power evident.

The women's voices echoed throughout the entryway as they reacted to the tighter restriction, but Ramona only registered an angry buzz. What to do next?

Then her eye caught on the pink homecoming advertisement, and realization struck her like lightning. AWS exerted control to keep everything in order, and the picture forming in Ramona's mind was anything but. She'd show them what chaos looked like. AWS had power on campus because they were recognized as leaders of female students. They didn't actually have any power on their own—that all came from the school administration. So AWS needed to lose that power. Maybe their image wasn't quite as picture-perfect as they would lead everyone to believe. And nothing ruins a reputation faster than public humiliation.

Patsy had been planning the homecoming dance for weeks, so Ramona would find a way to ruin it. She looked back at the stairs and was startled to see Patsy smirking at her with her chin raised. Clenching her hands into fists, Ramona narrowed her eyes. She'd make sure that Patsy wouldn't know a moment of peace as long as she continued to keep women down on campus.

CHAPTER 21

People and decorations filled the gymnasium. Glittering star cutouts covered every surface, and deep-blue streamers extended from the center of the ceiling out toward the walls, making the space feel like a makeshift circus tent. It almost disguised the basketball hoops. AWS had chosen the theme "Love at Midnight," which Ramona found to be extremely ironic.

She'd laughed dryly upon seeing the theme written in looping letters when Theo presented the tickets. After she'd explained her idea, Theo had immediately agreed before disappearing for a few hours. When he reappeared, he'd held a bouquet of red and orange dahlias, adopted his most serious voice, held his hand to his heart, and asked her if she'd do him the honor of accompanying him to the homecoming dance. She'd thrown her arms around his neck, kissing him between each answered "yes."

Now Theo led her through the entrance, where a coat check attendant offered to take her purse, and she politely declined. They moved through the throes of students to find their friends. Girls wore large dresses that took up more space than they were used to, throwing everyone off kilter. That and the booze. Ramona tugged at the bodice of her own dress and took as deep a breath as she could. It felt surreal to wear *the* dress. Her mother's.

Her mother's closet was one of Ramona's favorite places. Growing up, she'd rifle through the skirts and shoes and sweaters until her mother appeared to make sure she didn't have sticky fingers. Ramona still remembered when she'd found this dress. It hung in a garment bag in the back. Only nine years old, Ramona had unzipped the bag and stared in awe. It glittered gold—the shade Ramona now thought of as champagne—with a corset bodice and sweetheart neckline that cinched at the waist. From there, a cascade of ruffles, layer upon layer, flowed to the bottom. She'd never loved a dress more.

She hadn't planned to bring it to college, but her mother had insisted, saying, "You never know when you'll need a wow dress. Take it."

When Ramona slipped it on earlier that evening and twirled in front of the mirror, she smiled as the ruffles flew. She'd worn her hair tucked to one side with dozens of pins, and with her burgundy lipstick on, met Theo at the entryway of Wolden. His expression, mouth parted and eyes shining, made her feel as though she was the only person in the room. And now, standing among hundreds of others dressed just as fancifully, she still felt just as special as his hand tightened on hers. Her heart raced as she scanned him from head to toe. He wore his suit well.

Theo made a path for her through the crowd, just as he'd done at the rally in Portland. She gripped his warm, callused palm until they reached a pocket of space. Theo stiffened, and Ramona could see why once she peeked past his shoulder. Dean Redley stood alone by the wall a few yards away. She hadn't seen him since their chain demonstration a few weeks ago. He wore a brown suit that hung too far past his waist and a mustard-yellow shirt underneath.

The dean's hands perched on his hips with elbows bent outward as he surveyed the students. Then his eyes narrowed. Ramona wasn't sure if the dean recognized her, but he certainly recognized Theo. They stood, frozen, as though in a staring contest, and Ramona's skin crawled. She tugged at Theo's hand and pointed toward their friends. Nothing good would come of extending this silent exchange.

Theo followed her through a cloud of musky cologne before reaching Cat, Betsy, Olly, Don, Dimitri, and Mable. They stood in a loose circle, each holding a cup of punch.

Theo grabbed Don's drink and took a big gulp before smiling, shaking off the run-in with the dean. "Well, you all dress up nice," Theo said before turning to Mable, in particular, and said kindly, "That's a nice dress, Mable."

Mable wore a high-collared dress with cap sleeves the shade of a clementine. It cinched at the waist, accentuating her petite frame. Mable had insisted on meeting them here so that Theo could pick Ramona up "like couples do!"

"Why, thank you," Mable said with a small dip of her chin.

Theo stretched his neck looking around for anyone whom they didn't want to overhear. Once satisfied that they were relatively alone within the loud, crowded space, he whispered, "Does everyone know what to do?"

"You bet," Cat said with false brightness. Her blue, silk dress hugged her body, and she looked bored.

"What's with the attitude?" Theo asked.

"No attitude," Cat quipped. "It's only that you've gone over the plan a dozen times now. We're ready. Besides, Ramona has the biggest part."

It was true. The group had met multiple times throughout the week to plan. The dance was in full swing now with hundreds, maybe even a thousand, students pulsing throughout the gymnasium. It reminded Ramona of her prom, except now she stood next to a guy she really liked and was much more nervous. As excited as she was to take a stance against AWS, a lot could go wrong. If caught, Patsy would make it her personal mission to crucify Ramona, which could mean losing her scholarship.

Ramona gulped. She wouldn't get caught.

"What time did we say?" Olly asked after taking a swig of punch and wiping his mouth with the sleeve of his jacket.

Theo gave Cat a knowing look. Ramona answered.

"Ten o'clock. Late enough for most people to get here, and early enough that people won't be leaving for the after parties yet. It's"—Ramona tilted Theo's wrist to see his watch—"8:56 now."

Olly finished his drink and threw the cup behind him. "Plenty of time for dancing then." He reached for Mable's hand and pulled her to the dance floor. She yelped and giggled all the way there.

"Well, if they're dancing, we're dancing!" Betsy tugged Don along.

Then Cat dragged Dimitri, mumbling something under her breath about not being the only one left out, until Ramona and Theo stood alone. As much as she had thought about the dance, she hadn't thought of dancing. She didn't think they'd have the time or that she'd have the stomach for it. But when Theo extended his hand, she didn't want to do anything else. He led her to the dance floor where he swirled, twirled, and dipped her until her skin flushed. She really did love dancing.

"My Girl" by The Temptations shifted to "Ring of Fire" by Johnny Cash to "Do You Love Me" by The Contours, and on and on. Ramona was doing the twist when she glimpsed Theo's watch and froze. It was 9:48. They were behind schedule.

Ramona gripped Theo's shoulders and yelled into his ear, "It's time!"

Then she tapped each of her friends to get their attention before hurrying into position.

Now, sweat overpowered the mingled scents of perfume and cologne. If the space had been crowded before, it was packed now as bodies moved in full swing. Dancing forms took up more space than still ones. Ramona nodded with satisfaction. The more people the better.

Ramona pushed between bodies until she reached the draped silk curtains that separated the dance floor and the bleachers. She slipped through an opening and emerged on the other side. Her heart pounded as she searched the space. Once she confirmed she was alone, she sighed a breath of relief. She couldn't be seen and didn't have much time. According to Betsy's friend's sister, who'd volunteered for the dance planning committee, the drop would happen at ten o'clock on the dot. Ramona held up her skirt to move quicker and searched for the giant papier-mâché moon. Her purse, heavier than usual, bounced against her side.

Where was it? It had to almost be time.

She looked behind a stack of chairs before spotting a glimpse of white. She went straight for it and found a giant crescent moon the size of her body. It was hooked to a large cord and hidden beneath a swath of fabric. Ramona pulled off the sheet and opened her purse. She uncapped the jar of red paint before pulling the brush hidden between her breasts. She dipped it and went to work on the papier-mâché moon.

After a few moments, she leaned back to survey her work and smiled. Perfect. Without time for the paint to dry, she threw the sheet back over the moon and hurried away, her heels clicking. She heard rustling as she hid the paint and brush beneath a stack of chairs before returning to the dance.

Her friends were right where she'd left them, and she slipped back into Theo's arms for another dance. His arms wrapped around her, and she nodded in answer to his unspoken question. He laughed and pulled her closer to sway to the music.

Soon, a tapping from the speaker drew everyone's attention to the stage. Patsy gripped a microphone and leaned back against Archer. He wore a matching tie to her pink dress.

"Welcome to the homecoming dance of '65!"

The crowd gave a halfhearted cheer.

Patsy pouted and tried again. "Let's hear it for this homecoming dance, put on by our wonderful AWS planning committee!"

The crowd was louder now, excited to be riled up.

"As you all know, the theme of this year's dance is 'Love at Midnight,'" Patsy said into the microphone before smiling at Archer.

Cat mumbled, "Barf," making Ramona choke on her spit.

Ramona had to hand it to Patsy. It took bravery to speak in front of a thousand of your peers. She still got nervous speaking in front of the students in Professor Scott's class.

"Well, we have a surprise for you all. Hit it!" Patsy yelled, and the students waited in hushed anticipation.

At first, nothing happened. Then the sheet-covered shape rose from behind the curtain toward the center of the dance floor. Once in position hanging above all the students, someone pulled the rope attached to the sheet to reveal a bright-white, papier-mâché moon. A split second later, Patsy screamed, and her expectant face turned to one of horror. Written on the side of the papier-mâché moon, painted in red, were the words "REMOVE THE CURFEW!"

Half the students whooped and clapped, delighted by the prank. The other half looked too stunned to respond. Ramona and their group joined the first group and cheered, but not loud enough to draw particular attention to themselves.

Patsy stood, frozen. After a painful moment of awkward silence, Archer took the microphone and said with forced brightness, "Some prank, huh? Turn the music back up! Let's get to dancing again!"

The volume became so loud, the new song drowned out the murmuring. Soon enough, the students danced again, and Ramona with them. And as she danced, she listened to what the students said about the cool stunt and the outdated curfew. Still on stage, Patsy's shock hardened to fury. And Ramona had no doubt that somewhere in this gymnasium, Dean Redley's expression matched.

CHAPTER 22

The path sparkled with ice as Ramona hurried toward Lane Hall. Taking care not to slip, she stepped lightly and tucked her hands within the arms of her jacket to keep warm. To distract herself from the bone-chilling cold, Ramona recalled the homecoming dance a couple days earlier. Patsy's horrified expression, along with the gasps from the crowd, still put a smile on her face. She hoped today's teach-in—her first—would be as successful.

A few minutes later, hot air encompassed Ramona as soon as she stepped inside the building. Students buzzed about the lobby, surely a good sign. Ramona rose on her tiptoes to look for her friends but couldn't see farther than a few people. She sighed before spotting a bench against the far wall occupied with students wedged side by side.

Ramona reached the bench and said, "Pardon me," before leaning over a guy and pulling herself up to stand on the armrest.

"What are you doing?" the guy asked as though she'd stood on him.

She waved him off and scanned the crowd until Cat's red hair caught her attention. Ramona jumped down and smiled at the guy, who looked even more confused, before pushing through the packed bodies. Cat stood with Mable and Dimitri.

"Did I miss anything?" Ramona asked.

"Nope," Mable answered. "You're just in time. I cannot wait for this, our first teach-in. How exciting!"

Cat cocked an eyebrow, and Dimitri nudged her before Mable could notice.

Ramona nodded and lowered her voice, "Where are they?"

"Don, Olly, and Betsy have them in boxes in the back. They're going to leave them out for students to grab once the teach-in is over."

Cat had worked around the clock over the weekend writing the *Men's Handbook*. She'd grown attached to the idea. Ramona had never seen her care so much about something without a trace of her usual pessimism. The *Men's Handbook* mirrored the *Women's Handbook* and complemented the *Women's Anti-Handbook* by outlining the ways men should alter their behavior to, in short, leave women alone. Anticipation thrummed through Ramona. She couldn't wait to see the response.

The wide, wooden doors to the hall creaked open, and heads turned. The crowd filed inside to choose a seat among the hundreds available. Ramona, Mable, Cat, and Olly walked among the rest and found their seats in the front row, informally reserved by jackets and bags.

Theo stood alone on the stage surveying the growing audience as he swung the microphone from side to side. Beside him, a row of chairs awaited the faculty panel that they'd hustled to recruit. While planning for the homecoming dance, they'd also planned the teach-in for the earliest possible date. They didn't want to risk President Howard going back on his word. While there had been a handful of teach-ins last spring, as other universities across the country did the same, they hoped that this would be the largest to date on their campus.

Ramona craned her neck. The hall was filling quickly, and Theo would start any minute now.

"Here we go," Dimitri said. "Let's hope it works."

"Did Archer show up?" Mable asked.

Theo had been trying to get Archer to join in countless demonstrations over the quarter. As president of the student body council, Archer's presence would provide a large show of support, but he'd been hesitant about being directly involved no matter how many times Theo had asked or that they'd grown up together. It probably didn't help that Patsy was adamantly against demonstrations that threatened the status quo she tried so hard to maintain.

Dimitri shook his head. "We'll see."

Five professors from a range of departments walked onstage and took their seats. Professor Scott sat beside four male professors, and Ramona's respect for her increased. Each of them looked particularly scholarly, wearing a range of glasses, tweed jackets, and shades of brown and beige.

When almost every seat in the audience was occupied, Theo turned the microphone on. Ramona's heart squeezed at the sight of him standing beneath the spotlight, capturing the attention of hundreds. He tapped the microphone twice. The room quieted in anticipation.

"Welcome! This may not be the first teach-in on campus, but I have a feeling it's going to be one of our best. As always, a big thank you to our friends over at University of Michigan for kicking off the teach-in movement last March and for sharing that good thinking with us."

Theo, never one to stand still, moved the microphone from one hand to the other as he spoke. His eyes gleamed, and Ramona could tell that he was pleased with the turnout.

"For those of you who are new, a teach-in is a casual lecture led by experts in the relevant field." Theo gestured to the group of faculty. "Experts who share a similar sentiment to our cause. This isn't a lecture like you're used to, though. This is a discussion-based sharing of ideas. Please, interrupt and jump in."

Ramona wasn't sure how so many people could have a discussion, but she was eager to see.

"In recent months, the administration has attempted to block our efforts to protest the war in Vietnam by banning political protesting on campus, resulting in a direct violation of our rights to free speech." Theo pushed his hair from where it had fallen across his forehead with one hand. "Today's teach-in is supported by President Howard himself, so I can assure each of you it will be a safe space to speak freely on the war and, more specifically, the US government's recent election to send more soldiers. Now, it's my pleasure to introduce our faculty speakers."

In addition to Professor Scott of the communications department, the rest of the professors taught political science, international studies, philosophy, and economics. Theo had been set on including faculty from a range of departments with diverse perspectives on the antiwar movement. Of course, they all leaned in favor. Otherwise, they wouldn't be here.

"With that, let's begin."

The audience let out a few whoops, and Theo's smile electrified. He walked toward the faculty and raised the microphone again. "First, we're going to hear from Professor Egan from the political science depart—"

All eyes turned toward the exit as the door burst open. Archer appeared.

"Well, isn't this good news. Our student body president will join the faculty members." Theo gestured toward the empty seat on stage, and Archer hurried up the stage stairs to his seat. "Archer, buddy, cutting it a little close, don't you think?"

Archer shrugged apologetically as his cheeks flushed.

"Over to you, Professor Egan," Theo said before handing him the microphone.

The professor sat forward in his seat with feet spread wide. Head of the political science department with over thirty years of experience, he was smart and direct. He explained the catalyst that launched the Vietnam War—the history between the US, Vietnam, France, and China, a complicated international relationship. He spoke of the decisions that were made to increase the US involvement and of the political decisions that were made in Washington, DC to make that happen.

"Now, the problem is that the decision-makers do not have military experience and do not fully understand the context, and gravity, of their decisions. As a result, we're in a huge mess that's cost thousands of American lives."

The students hung on Professor Egan's every word. Some even took notes in a hurried hand. It was one thing to talk about the war with friends, but it was something entirely different to hear an expert, an adult, confirm your suspicions that the war was not thoroughly thought through, that the decisions made could be mistakes. Insinuating the possibility of a mistake from the US government was a huge deal in itself and not done lightly.

The longer Professor Egan spoke, the more justified Ramona felt about their demonstrations. Just the day before,

The New York Times printed that a battle in the la Drang River Valley had resulted in hundreds of American deaths.

Once Professor Egan finished speaking, the echo of the microphone was the only noise in the hall. A teach-in was like a party—it took a bit of encouragement to get it into full swing. No one wanted to be the first one to speak up, so Theo nudged them along.

"Professor Egan," Theo projected across the hall. "What alternate approaches could the White House have taken?"

Professor Egan tipped his head to the side and scrunched his lips together in consideration, his lined face wrinkling even more.

"A few things. The US could have stayed involved in formal discussions between France and Vietnam to form a peace treaty. This would have been involvement without military action. Another option would have been to bring a limited number of troops to Vietnam as a gesture of the threat that could come, without actual violence inflicted. Without warfare. There are always options and choices, even if not a one is good."

The students considered this, and Professor Egan let his words settle. Then a hand shot up in the middle section of the lecture hall.

"You don't have to raise your hand," Theo called. "Speak up."

A boy in a red T-shirt and khakis stood in the audience. Ramona recognized him as one of the boys she'd linked arms with during the demonstration outside of the administration building a few weeks before. Familiar faces at events like this meant that they were building a community, and Ramona warmed at the thought. Strength in numbers.

"I listen to the radio every day, and every day, Johnson says that we're making progress over there, but I'm skeptical. What do you think?"

Ramona was glad that he asked because she wondered the same. You can only believe words without action for so long before they ring hollow. Soon, they might not mean anything at all. Professor Egan answered the question, agreeing with him that there had been a lot of talk of claimed results with little proof. He said that there was even evidence emerging to the contrary with talks of a draft and more military troops needed abroad. The idea of a draft struck fear in them all. The teach-in rolled onward as the conversation flowed like a river.

Hours had passed, and Ramona was riveted, feeling her perspective expand as more people spoke.

Despite facilitating, Theo's energy didn't waver. He was just as upbeat now as he'd been when he welcomed the students to the hall. These moments when he shone bright made her love him even more. He had such a gift, and Ramona had no doubt these students would follow wherever he led.

On stage, Archer shifted in his seat. He hadn't spoken yet, but nodded along. Ramona wasn't surprised by this from how Theo had described him, but it soon became clear that Theo wasn't going to accept this.

The discussion had turned to the White House's response to the student protests all over the country when one of the students had asked a question. One of the professors opened his mouth to answer when Theo cut in. "Actually, Professor Thompson, I'm hoping that Archer can answer."

Archer's eyes bulged, and he turned sharply to Theo. They held eye contact until Archer cleared his throat.

"Yeah, all right. I think the massive swell of student protests has surprised the government, and they aren't sure what to do. I mean, it's not like they were listening to us before all this."

Theo circled the chairs on stage.

"Sure, sure. What do you think of their lack of response, though? Or let's get more specific here. What do you think of the school administration's response to our very own protests? Do you think it was right that they'd banned political protesting?"

The air in the lecture hall tightened, and Archer shifted in his seat, but Theo waited for an answer. He wasn't going to let up until Archer spoke out like Theo wanted him to. Ramona's hands tightened into fists. President Howard wouldn't like this line of questioning.

Archer closed his eyes and took a deep breath before resigning to his fate. "The school administration is restricting student free speech by banning students from political protesting."

Students shouted their agreement until the hall echoed loudly. On stage, Theo looked like a satisfied cat that had captured the mouse. As far as Ramona knew, this was the first time that Archer had openly sided with the students against the school administration. As student body president, his role was a balancing act between the students he represented, the students who had voted him in, and the school officials whom he worked with on a daily basis. Ramona wondered how long it would take for word to get to Patsy about Archer's statement.

Theo looked from Archer to the audience, and then his gaze shifted higher. Curious, Ramona turned around toward the back of the lecture hall. Dean Redley stood with arms crossed behind the last row of seats. Theo and the dean glared at each other, each refusing to break the stare, and Ramona wondered who had more power in that moment—the dean of the college or the student with influence.

A shiver ran down Ramona's spine. Theo always said that it was impossible to make change without pushing a few buttons, but she worried what would happen when he'd pushed too hard.

"Outside of this teach-in, the restriction on free speech is still in place on campus. You are not allowed to gather to voice your opinions on politics," Theo said to the audience. "We don't stand for this, so we're asking President Howard to repeal this restriction. That way, we can have more fine discussions like this one." Theo grinned.

"What do you all say to that?" Theo called out, only to be met with an onslaught of cheering.

Ramona clapped along with the rest, standing from her seat. Mable did the same, as did Cat and Dimitri. Then the rest of the students in their row stood, until the entire hall, filled with hundreds, stood in agreement. And that felt like power.

On stage, Theo laughed and nodded to the audience before narrowing in on Ramona and winking.

"That sounds like as good a note as any to end on. Let's hear it for our faculty guests," Theo said, opening his arms wide in reference to the five professors.

After more clapping, students gathered their things and moved toward the exits where boxes of *Men's Handbook*s waited. During the distraction of the closing, Olly, Don, and Betsy had opened them before disappearing. There were dozens and dozens of *Men's Handbook*s ... not enough for every single male in the room but enough to make the point.

Students paused near the boxes, curiosity not allowing them to pass by without peeking. They pulled out and passed around copies, staring at them like they were written in another language. Ramona smiled.

Too loud to hear anything in particular, Ramona filed out along with the rest until they gathered outside. Theo caught up to them, slinging an arm around Ramona's waist.

"Well done," Olly applauded, bumping Theo on the shoulder.

Theo smiled before turning to Betsy. "This one really deserves the credit. Thank you for planning it with me."

Betsy took an exaggerated bow.

Then Ramona caught a thread of another conversation.

"What the hell is this?" a gruff voice asked.

When Ramona looked, she saw the guy held a *Men's Handbook.*

His friend said, "This is offensive, right?"

"Yeah, it's offensive. Who the hell made this, and what are they after?"

Beyond this pair, all the students still gathered around the exit of Lane Hall appeared to be discussing the *Men's Handbook* with varying degrees of disbelief. Dozens and dozens of students. And it pleased Ramona to see it. They felt angry? Join the club.

When Ramona turned back to her circle of friends, she saw them all taking in the conversations with interested eyes as well. All except Theo. His eyes looked conflicted.

He frowned. "None of them are talking about the free speech restrictions."

CHAPTER 23

In the twenty-four hours since the teach-in, Ramona hadn't been able to erase the image of Theo's expression from her mind. Disappointment and conflict warred across his features outside Lane Hall. And while she understood his reaction, she'd hoped he'd be excited like the rest of them. Sure, the *Men's Handbook* may have stolen the spotlight for a moment, but the teach-in was unquestioningly a success. She'd tried to convince him of that as he'd walked her home, but his mood remained somber despite her best attempts.

When they'd reached Wolden, Ramona pulled him to her by wrapping her arms around his neck.

"You were wonderful tonight," Ramona said, remembering the way he'd owned the stage.

But Theo ducked his head and his hair fell over his eyes, effectively retreating.

"It's like they all forgot as soon as they saw the *Men's Handbook*."

"They didn't." Ramona brushed her thumb along his neck. "Please don't be upset."

He looked at her, and she could've sworn that his sea-colored irises stormed in front of her.

"Good night," Theo said before kissing her forehead, and the gesture that had made her heart swell these past couple months lacked its usual warmth.

Confused by his abrupt departure, she watched him walk away as a pit formed in her throat. A tear sprung from the corner of her eye, and she swatted at it. How silly of her to feel disappointed that he wasn't happier about the reaction to the *Men's Handbook. Don't take it personally.*

The pit had migrated from her throat to her stomach, and she carried it now as she returned to Wolden after a day of classes. With no Dusty's shift tonight, Ramona needed to spend the time catching up on schoolwork.

Once inside, Ramona saw an open table in the back of the lounge and wound her way through the occupied furniture. The women of Wolden adopted favorite spots that they returned to again and again. Ramona passed by one of the brass magazine holders usually filled with old copies of *Time*, *Ladies' Home Journal*, *Ebony*, and *Seventeen*. New copies got snatched before making it to the magazine rack.

Ramona slowed to a stop.

None of the usual magazines rested in the holder. Instead, there were a dozen copies of an unfamiliar magazine. Ramona crouched and pulled one loose. The cover read, "*The College Girl*, Edition 1" with an illustration of a slim woman in a collared dress that cinched at the waist. The woman held a book and smiled sweet as a peach. Ramona narrowed her eyes as a growing feeling of dread filled her.

Hardly a magazine, barely ten pages, Ramona flipped it open and read, "*The College Girl* is a modern magazine for the ideal woman. She's smart. She's punctual. She's well mannered.

She's well groomed. She's well liked. She's what every woman in college should aspire to be. This monthly magazine will have advice on the latest fashions, the hottest majors, and the coolest activities."

Ramona scowled. Whatever this was, she didn't like it. It went in the opposite direction that they should be going. There was no "ideal" woman, and to make that claim was a disservice to women and men alike. The tone made her skin crawl. Then it made sense when she saw that, "brought to you by Associated Women Students" was written on the bottom of the page.

Dammit.

She flipped through the pages, scanning with wide eyes. Sure enough, there were articles and advice on everything from how to wear a headband without losing your hair volume to the most flattering way to hold a stack of books.

Ramona snorted and stuffed the magazine into her bag. She should have seen this coming. Of course Patsy and the rest of the AWS council wouldn't let the homecoming dance demonstration go unanswered. Ramona hadn't expected them to move so quickly, though. And admittedly, she hadn't expected them to do something so smart. It would be difficult to rid the campus of *The College Girl* if the persona caught on.

Ramona stormed out of the lounge in search of its creator.

She found Patsy in their room. Patsy looked up with her hand as a makeshift bookmark in the large volume before her on the desk.

"What on God's earth is wrong with you, bursting in here like that?"

"This!" Ramona barked, throwing the magazine on top of Patsy's book.

Patsy adjusted her pastel-green headband, the color of an Easter egg, and smiled.

"So you found one of our first copies. Good for you. I'd hold on to this," Patsy said, lifting the beaten-up magazine. "I have a feeling the collectors may be after these one day."

Ramona huffed out a big breath, trying to keep a shred of her patience. "Do you realize how dangerous this is?"

"Dangerous?" Patsy replied, her volume growing. "That's silly."

"It's not." Ramona shook her head. "This sets unrealistic standards for how women should be. Women shouldn't 'be' anything. Things like this are going to keep us in the Dark Ages of gender roles where women are only seen in their service to men and making a home."

Patsy pushed back her chair and stood to face Ramona.

"And what's so wrong with that? Women have been in charge of the home for ages."

"That shouldn't be expected of us. Nothing is wrong with running a home, as long as that's what the individual woman wants to do! Don't you see? It's about choice and equality and autonomy."

"Now see here—" Patsy started, but Ramona cut in.

"I know those are big words for someone who writes about hairstyling and makeup, but try to keep up."

Rage flashed through Patsy's features, and it stoked the fire within Ramona. She wanted Patsy to fight back. She wanted the opportunity to shout and throw her arms into the air—anything to get this frustration-fueled energy out.

"How dare you speak to me that way," Patsy snapped, taking a step closer.

"How dare you speak to *them* that way." Ramona pointed toward the magazine. "How dare you set that kind of standard for any woman."

Patsy appeared to choke on her tongue for a moment, to Ramona's great satisfaction, before snarling, "You bitch."

Ramona's heart thudded heavily, shooting adrenaline to all corners of her body. She nodded before grinning slowly at Patsy.

"If a bitch fights for women's rights, then a bitch I am."

CHAPTER 24

Ramona could scarcely see for all the hair in her face as she rushed from Wolden toward the attic. The wind wailed, just as Ramona wanted to, twirling her curls out from their perch behind her ears and across her face. She had to get away from there, away from Patsy. Ramona had only lingered long enough to see Patsy's face drop before fleeing with her pulse in her ears.

A few minutes later, Ramona burst into the attic out of breath from the four flights of stairs. Olly, Cat, Dimitri, and Betsy crouched before a large, crumpled lump on the floor.

Olly looked up first and brightened. "Oy look, it's Ramona!"

"What's"—Ramona breathed in and out hard—"that?"

They all looked at her then, and Ramona couldn't help noticing a flash of concern on Dimitri's face at her own state of disarray.

Betsy answered, "It turns out that our old girl Patsy is throwing a pageant, and when we saw this mighty sign, we decided to … well, how do I put this—"

"We stole it." Olly grinned.

They shifted back to the lump and spread the fabric until it lay flat. At least ten feet long and five feet wide, the sign took up a majority of the open space. It was like the signs that filled the campus with the school colors and mascot, except this one was white with pink ink, the color of cotton candy. Dimitri smoothed out the wrinkles of the fabric as the rest stood back to get a better look.

Ramona gasped and raised a hand to her mouth.

"What?" Dimitri asked.

In large, block letters, the sign advertised 'The Miss College Girl Pageant.' Ramona groaned. Of course. Of course it wasn't just a magazine.

Ramona quickly regaled them with her discovery of the magazine and confrontation with Patsy, feeling proud, if a touch shaken, for standing up to her.

"There are posters about 'Miss College Girl' all over the bathrooms," Cat added once Ramona had finished. "It's so gross."

"And we stole their sign, so maybe no one will sign up for the pageant and it will be a total bust," Betsy singsonged.

They cackled like a bunch of hyenas.

"How did you get this?" Ramona gestured to the sign.

They each traded off telling the tale. They'd been walking through Gauld Square between classes when they had noticed two men with a large ladder. Curious, they'd listened to the men discussing how to hang a sign … a large, white bundle waiting off to the side. One of the men had groaned, annoyed at the task at hand because of the rain. He'd mentioned something about a pageant, and then said that their boss would be on them if they didn't get it up today because they'd promised the women's council. That's when they'd hatched their plan.

Olly had approached the men and asked if they knew whether he could rent the ladder for a home improvement project he was considering.

"My roof is looking mighty worse for wear," Olly had said as though he were the homeowner and not a college renter.

Apparently, the men had stared at him like he was a bizarre figment of imagination before one of them launched into a long explanation about why he most certainly could not rent the school's ladder for a personal project.

"... Besides, you look like the type to slip off a ladder and never get up again," one of the men had said.

And while Olly entertained this insult, Betsy, Cat, and Dimitri snatched the bundle and ran.

"When they'd mentioned the women's council, we knew it had to be AWS, so we figured whatever it was, we should take it," Betsy explained now.

"A good laugh that was," Olly agreed, clearly pleased with his acting.

Ramona smiled, delighted by the prank. Anything to get in Patsy's way.

"Now what to do with it," Betsy mused.

Glancing at her watch, Ramona shifted toward the door. "I wish I could stay and help, but I'm meeting Theo at the fountain."

As Ramona moved to leave, Dimitri called out after her. "I'll walk with you. I have to go to the library."

Surprised by the offer, Ramona waited for him to walk down the stairs. Once they got outside and into the drizzle, she couldn't stand waiting any longer. She'd counted him opening and closing his mouth three times without saying a word. Ramona sighed.

"What is it?"

He swallowed before answering, "Are you sure everything is okay with you?"

"Of course it is," Ramona said in a rush.

Dimitri rubbed a hand through his hair, looking a lot like Theo. "Ever since you've taken up with the group, it's like The Foes, AWS, the *Women's Anti-Handbook*, and the curfew are all you care about. What about school and your classes? I know how important getting your degree is to you."

Hearing Dimitri parrot her words from their long hours together at Dusty's over the summer frustrated her. She didn't like feeling so splayed open. Dimitri had always understood her in a way that unsettled her. So she snapped.

"I'm still doing that. In case you don't remember, I need to remove the curfew so that I can keep my job and pay for school. We don't all have the freedom to do whatever we want."

Dimitri stopped walking and stared at her as though she'd hit him. "Whatever, Ramona."

"Dimitri—"

He walked past her. Ramona rubbed a hand across her face, knowing she hadn't been fair. Dimitri wasn't working at Dusty's for fun.

She followed him around the corner, intending to apologize, when a large group of students came into view. They crowded around the new fountain on campus. It was shaped as a huge circle with water spouting from the center. A wide, cement lip encased the fountain where students lounged like mermaids up on rocks out of water.

"What the—" Dimitri said before taking off at a run toward the shouting crowd.

"Dimitri!" Ramona chased after him.

Dimitri shoved shoulders aside to wedge his way through the bodies, and Ramona followed in his wake. When they arrived at the center, she gasped. Theo was interlocked with another guy. The crowd of students shouted as though they were at a boxing match. Theo's arms gripped the guy's waist, who took the opportunity to punch Theo's head. Theo released his grip and stepped back as his face turned red. Dimitri ripped at the people who separated him from his brother, getting closer and closer. Ahead, Theo righted himself and lunged at the guy. He got a good grip and punched the guy in the face one, two, three times, until blood poured from his opponent's nose.

"Theo!" Ramona screamed, unsure if she was yelling for him to stop hitting or stop getting hit.

Finally, they reached the pair just as the guy raised his hand to hit Theo again. Dimitri threw himself between them without hesitation, taking the hit in his chest. Theo didn't look surprised to see Dimitri. If anything, he appeared to have expected his brother all along. Theo's eyes were glazed over, and it scared Ramona.

She ran toward Theo and raised her arms to surround him. Theo's chest heaved, and he wiped the sweat from his forehead. He glared at the guy and made a move to jump back toward him when Ramona shouted again. Dimitri shoved the guy hard enough to push him away as blood covered the bottom half of his face.

The guy laughed like someone deranged and pointed at Theo's chest. "You hit pretty good for a dirty communist hippie."

Theo lunged, but Ramona and Dimitri held him back.

The guy kept laughing. "That's right, take the hippie away. You're lucky I don't have my buddies with me. Think about that next time you plan one of your teach-ins." He wiped his face with the sleeve of his shirt before turning away.

The crowd broke apart to let the guy through. He almost fell more than once, but kept on. Ramona turned back to Theo. She scanned his body quickly and saw a bruise swelling around his left eye, then lifted his shirt to see a red mark covering his stomach. Despite the physical markings, she was most concerned about the fiery glaze coating Theo's eyes.

"You all right?" Dimitri asked.

Theo nodded and wrapped an arm around Dimitri's shoulders, pulling him in close. "Nice timing, little brother."

Ramona took a deep breath in to settle her stomach. Her hands trembled until she gently placed them on Theo's chest. "Are you sure you're okay?"

Theo raised a hand to her cheek and held her gently before the corner of his mouth tipped up. "I'm fine, baby. We might need a rain check on that restaurant, though. Not sure they'll appreciate the looks of me right now."

His angry mask disappeared, and Theo—her Theo—returned. Dimitri stood behind, his face etched with concern.

"Let's go home," Dimitri said and scooped his shoulder beneath one of Theo's arms. At first, Theo swatted at the offer but eventually leaned into Dimitri's support. Ramona took Theo's other side, and they walked in the direction of the boys' house.

Theo moved slowly and hunched slightly at the waist as though protecting his middle. They'd gotten to the edge of campus and crossed into the residential neighborhood when Dimitri asked the question that Ramona had been reframing over and over in her head.

"What happened?"

Theo closed his eyes and chuckled as if it was a personal joke. "Oh, you know … wrong place, wrong time."

"C'mon."

Theo sighed. "He's one of those pieces of shit who believes anything the government says. You know the type, patriot to the end. He recognized me from the teach-in. I guess you could say he had a different opinion on the subject."

They'd expected that there would be both objectors and sympathizers in attendance at the teach-in, especially out of curiosity, but it startled Ramona that this would be the outcome. The teach-in had been peaceful and unifying. At least, that's how Ramona had seen it. Now, the memory distorted like mirrors of a funhouse.

"He came up to me and started rattling on about communist this and not-a-patriot that. Then I decked him to shut him up. I wasn't really in the mood for talking, you see?"

"Yeah, no figure. Your eye's getting worse."

It was true. The red swelling around Theo's eye was shifting into the color of an eggplant.

Soon, they made it to the house, and Dimitri helped Theo up the stairs. Ramona hurried forward to push the mound of clothes off Theo's bed so he had space to lie down. Theo objected, swatting at Dimitri, but then relented once his back hit the bed and he relaxed. It appeared as though the guy had gotten more hits in than Theo had let on.

"I'll go get a bag of ice." Dimitri walked out and left them alone.

Ramona rested against the bed and looked down at Theo.

"Come here," he said, and she leaned closer until her forehead was resting against his. "That's better."

"You really got into a mess, didn't you?" Ramona whispered.

Theo made a noncommittal groan in his throat, so Ramona added, "I was scared for you."

"I'm fine. This isn't my first fight, and it sure as shit won't be my last. I can hold my own."

Faces pressed together, Ramona kissed him softly and then whispered, "You better."

A cough sounded from the doorway, and Ramona shifted back. Dimitri looked pink-faced, holding a bag of ice. He shrugged apologetically and handed it to Theo to place on his face.

"Thanks, little brother." Theo turned to look up at Ramona with one eye. "Do you mind if I shut my eyes for a bit?"

Ramona squeezed his shoulder. "Get some rest."

Dimitri and Ramona left the room and closed the door softly behind them. Not that he'd need the quiet. Theo could sleep through a concert when tired enough. When they got to the main floor, Ramona hesitated.

"Thank you for being there … for him."

Dimitri shrugged. "He's my brother."

The house was quiet. Ramona crossed her arms, trying to figure out how to ask what she wanted to know.

"Theo said that …" Dimitri waited patiently. "How many fights have there been?" Ramona finished.

"I don't keep track." Dimitri leaned back against the wall across from her. "A lot."

Ramona's stomach dropped as she considered this. She didn't like that. Finally, she said, "I didn't expect to see him like that."

"Yeah, well, that's Theo for you. He runs hot, and he's not one to let an insult go unmet. This is just what he does."

The memory of their conversation a few weeks earlier flashed across her mind. The conversation when Dimitri had warned Ramona that she didn't really know Theo. She still remembered the uncertainty she'd felt at the accusation. In some ways, she seemed to know him better than anyone else, but then she'd see a different side of him and question the foundation of their relationship. Could he be hers if she didn't know all of him?

Dimitri's shirt clung to his body after the exertion of practically carrying Theo home, and he pulled it away from his stomach now.

"Don't get me wrong," he said. "Theo's a good guy … the best guy that you can have in your corner. But you want him in your corner and not on the other side."

Ramona's hands were twisted together to steady them. She distracted herself by reaching up to twist her hair into a bun at the nape of her neck.

"I get it."

"Do you?" Dimitri's eyes searched hers, and she had the distinct feeling that she was not living up to his expectation.

"Yes," she answered firmly. Then she softened her voice. "How are you doing? It feels like it's been a while since we really talked. We're always with the group, and at work, you're busy in the back."

Surprise widened Dimitri's eyes, but he recovered quickly. "Fine. Just fine." Then she could see him closing up like a turtle in its shell. "I should study." He gestured with a thumb toward his backpack. "I've got a quiz tomorrow."

Realization dawned on Ramona. She was supposed to be doing the same.

"Sure, I'll see you later then," Ramona said before waving goodbye halfheartedly and walking down the front steps away from the Rhodes brothers, feeling like she'd lost something.

CHAPTER 25

The scent of tobacco wafted toward Ramona from the guy sitting beside her in class. He leaned back in his chair with boot-clad feet kicked out into the aisle. Every time they sat by each other, her nostrils filled with the smoke that lingered on him. He pulled a lighter from his jacket pocket and twirled it between his fingers. Ramona tried to pay attention to Professor Scott's lecture but couldn't help noticing the lighter from the corner of her eye. And when he flipped it open and shut, the sharp click reminded her of Theo's admission earlier that day.

When the group gathered in the attic, Theo had shocked them with his idea for their next demonstration. In order to make the administration take them seriously, Theo wanted to do something serious.

"We need to hit them where it hurts," Theo had said. "And what are they focused on this year?"

Ramona would've laughed at everyone's quizzical expressions if she hadn't been so worried about where Theo was headed.

Betsy was the one to finally answer, "Ruining our lives?"

"The student union building," Theo had suggested. "They're pouring all this money into it as the jewel at the center of campus. I've been thinking about this for a while. We should burn it down."

Click. The lighter snapped shut.

Ramona had stared at Theo. What had he said? Because it couldn't have been what she thought she'd heard.

Click.

She hadn't misheard. Arson. That's what he'd suggested.

Click.

And in the hours since, Ramona's body warred with itself—her love for Theo against her own morals. She knew what he'd suggested was wrong, and yet a part of her wanted to support him. Wanted to see him succeed. It was infuriating. This, along with the fight yesterday, made her uncomfortable.

Click.

"Please put away the lighter, Mr. Dobbs. I'm afraid I can't hear you listening over the sound of you snapping that thing shut."

Professor Scott wore her standard, beige-colored pantsuit, almost as though she didn't want to draw any unnecessary attention to her attire.

Despite looking annoyed, he put it away without complaint, and eventually, Ramona was able to focus back on the lecture. Professor Scott wrapped up thirty minutes later.

"Last thing for today, I'm going to pass back your persuasive speech essays."

When Professor Scott placed the essay on Ramona's desk, the first thing she noticed was the bright-red 'D' that hung at the top with "See me after class" written beneath. Ramona's stomach roiled. She'd never received such a low grade before, and that it came from her favorite class stung. She sank low in her seat as the rest of the papers were passed out.

Ramona hung back when the bell rang to meet her fate. It didn't bode well, knowing this was the second time Professor Scott had asked to see her.

"Thank you for staying, Ramona."

Ramona nodded and walked through the rows of desks until she stood a few feet from her teacher.

"Now, you'll see the notes I've left throughout your essay with feedback for how you can improve your grade on future assignments. That said, you really need to commit yourself. This is a challenging course, and I won't accept anything less than your best."

Why did Professor Scott single her out? She resented the guidance.

"Professor, pardon me for asking." Ramona hesitated and hoped her voice conveyed politeness, but she couldn't hold back. "Why do you care about how I do? I don't see you doing this for the other students."

A long moment passed during which Professor Scott's brown eyes flitted between Ramona and the window as though considering an escape.

"It's probably time I tell you."

Ramona's chest tightened, utterly thrown off by the familiarity of her words.

"Eighteen years ago, your mother and I were friends. Best friends, actually. I wasn't there for her during that time, and now I'm trying to do everything I can to help you to make it up to her."

Ramona's eyes bugged. Professor Scott and her mother knew each other? Then her words sunk in. Eighteen years ago.

"Hold on." Ramona frowned. "You're saying that you weren't there for her when she was pregnant?"

The ticking of the clock on the wall seemed to slow. Professor Scott nodded.

"We'd lost touch, but your mother came to my office at the beginning of the school year and told me that you were a student. It was so good to see her. She'd asked me to keep an eye out for you, and I've tried my best to do that."

It made sense. Ramona hadn't suspected a thing. Shock filled her at her two worlds colliding—home and university. But she pushed past the shock to the feeling beneath it. Anger. Her mother had described her time being pregnant as the loneliest of her life.

"You abandoned my mother during the hardest time of her life? You abandoned her at the same time that my father left? People were awful to her. They're still judging her."

"I know." Professor Scott nodded. "And I'm very sorry."

Ramona stepped back. "How could you do that?"

"I was scared." And when Ramona opened her mouth, Professor Scott quickly added, "I was studying to be a teacher and terrified of not living up to the expectations of women of our time. I didn't want to draw any attention, and your mother's pregnancy was all that anyone could talk about for a long while. My parents were very strict."

Professor Scott's brow furrowed, and Ramona felt even more furious. How dare she feel worried, when her mother had been treated as a pariah for so long.

"You didn't want her reputation to stain yours."

"Ramona, please—"

"No!" Ramona shouted. Everything came to the surface. The curfew. The *Women's Anti-Handbook*. The Free Speech Movement. Patsy. Dean Redley. It was all too much, and this shock was the final straw that pulled at wounds she'd thought had long since healed. Professor Scott became a target for everything that had gone wrong.

"She still insists on going to church every Sunday, the same church where everyone looks down on her like she's less than them. She still goes. She needed a friend."

"Ramona." Professor Scott's eyes drooped as though she hadn't slept in days. "I'm so sorry. I want to make this right. I've been trying to help you. I promised your mom."

Ramona held up a hand. "I don't need anything from you."

The lights above seemed to brighten so that Ramona could hardly see straight, and the air became so stale, she felt as if she could suffocate. She needed to get out. Ramona turned on her heels and fled from the classroom, rage burning through her.

Framed photos filled the mantel at home. One photo displayed her mother just before she was about to give birth. Ramona looked at that photo often, wondering how it was possible for her mother to look so beautiful and determined and scared and lonely all at once. Her mother's eighteen-year-old eyes were etched into her memory. And now Ramona better understood why. She really liked Professor Scott—hell, she looked up to the woman—and that image was now ripped to shreds.

Ramona stormed down the hallway, and when she came to an open locker, she slammed it shut with all her strength and kept on walking.

CHAPTER 26

Ramona continued seething into the next day, unable to understand how someone could do something so awful. She imagined what she might do if Mable got pregnant. She didn't know how they'd manage it, but manage it together they would … even if the idea of a missed period sent a lurch through her stomach. Ramona looked at Mable now as they walked side by side from the dining hall and smiled as she pictured a mini-Mable. Yes, they'd manage if it ever came to that.

"What?" Mable asked, feeling Ramona's gaze.

"Oh nothing," Ramona remarked, holding two fingers together to gesture something small. "I'm just imagining what your kids will look like and how I'm going to be the best aunt they'll ever have."

"Gosh," Mable considered, "to think that may not be that far off."

Ramona covered her ears. "Don't say that."

Mable sighed fondly. "All right, all right, not that soon either."

It had rained throughout the night, so the pair took careful steps on the slick path. At least Ramona's boots had a rubber tread on them. Mable's Mary Janes were no match for the slipping hazard.

"Can I ask you something?" Ramona asked, figuring it was as good a time as any to ask the question that had lingered for weeks.

"Of course," Mable answered, slowing ever so slightly.

Ramona cleared her throat. "What's going on with Olly?"

"Um," Mable said quickly before silence descended and her cheeks pinkened.

Ahead, Gauld Square came into view, and Ramona sipped apple cider from the canister in hand.

Finally, Mable answered, her voice lowered a few decibels, "I really like him."

Ramona whirled around, this being the first time Mable had ever confirmed her suspicions, and held her free hand out for Mable's. They clasped hands, and Ramona raised them into the air.

"That's great!"

Mable's blush deepened, and the corners of her mouth crept toward a hesitant smile.

"I don't know what to do," Mable continued. "Cat and Olly clearly have a connection, but he said—"

The rest of Mable's words were drowned out by the noise coming from Gauld Square. They approached a large crowd. It was typical for the square to be packed, but everyone stood still facing the grand steps of the library, jeering at whatever had just been announced. Someone whom Ramona didn't recognize held a microphone.

"Please," the man urged. "Let me explain."

All around, the students yelled and groaned. Ramona and Mable moved deeper into the crowd, drawn toward the energy like moths to a flame. It felt muggy, the body heat radiating in the still-damp air from the morning rain.

The speakers boomed as his voice echoed across the square.

"This program will begin effective immediately. Any student who sees another student breaking any university rule should report the offense to the program officers for investigation. The reporting students will be rewarded, depending on the severity of the offense reported."

What program? Ramona tried to ignore the clamoring around her to listen. It's not like this man was handing out free ice cream. Nothing good ever came from announcements like this. Dread rose within her.

"Now, you might wonder what type of offenses to report, and that's a good question," the man continued.

No one seemed to have been wondering that. Rather, they all looked like they were wondering how to take the microphone from him.

"Report any broken rule. However, you should especially report serious offenses like destruction of property, harassment, physical altercations, breaking and entering, political protesting, and breaking curfew."

Mable's head whipped toward Ramona so quickly that she almost laughed. Until the proclamation punched her in the stomach. The administration would reward students for snitching on their peers. So no longer did they only have to worry about faculty, but they also had to worry among themselves, no doubt ruining trust among students. And there would be rewards at stake.

"It's a vigilante program." Mable exhaled sharply, her lips pressed together in anger.

She was right. The administration had created a fucking vigilante program.

Around them, anger spread from person to person. Their faces reddened as they yelled and shook their hands in the air. Ramona yelled along with them.

"No fucking way!" a guy yelled from behind, and Ramona felt spittle hit the back of her neck.

Ramona had been thinking the same thing.

CHAPTER 27

At a certain point, anxiety becomes physical. And for Ramona, anxiety manifested in the form of a stomach ache that plagued her in the days since she and Mable had stumbled upon the announcement of what they now called the "Rat Program." Throughout the weekend, and through her two usual shifts on Friday and Sunday, Ramona's stomach knotted so tightly that she'd wince and press her nails into her palm to distract herself. Thank goodness for aspirin.

Luckily, Mable hadn't had any difficulty sneaking Ramona in after curfew over the weekend, but Ramona could tell that she felt just as anxious about the increased vigilance. Asking her best friend to do something so risky filled Ramona with guilt. That, on top of the anxiety, created a combustible concoction within her. The potential for failure clung to her skin like smoke after a bonfire, and more than once, Ramona wondered whether it may be better to give up before getting caught.

The only respite, distraction, she found came in the form of an article. Ramona had been considering the idea of writing for *The Daily*, the student-run newspaper on campus, and the fury she felt about *The College Girl* sealed it.

Ramona had written in a frenzy until an article emerged. She'd edited what started out as three thousand rushed words down to five hundred and felt proud of it. Especially now as she listened to Olly read the published version aloud across the cafeteria table. His hands gripped this morning's copy of *The Daily*, holding the pages wide enough to cover his face.

"If I told you that there was a time at this school when a group of students had vastly different rules from the rest, what year would you think I was referring to?" Olly voiced the words she'd written.

"You may think sometime in the 1940s. Maybe 1950. What if I told you that this group of students—the group that's held to a different standard—paid the same tuition? Would that change your mind?

"Today, in the year 1965, half of the student body is held to vastly different rules than the other. When men turn eighteen and go to college, they are considered adults. Women are treated like children until they marry, even at eighteen years old on campus.

"From the moment women step on campus, they are told what to do, what to wear, where to be, what to say, how to talk, and so on. There's a curfew in place for female students living on campus, but the school administration wouldn't dream of enforcing the same rule for our male counterparts. The term, 'control the girls and you'll control the boys' is outdated and ineffective. Women deserve equal rights on campus, from what we choose to study to the time we close our curtains at night. It's about the choice. Every student, every adult on this campus, deserves the right to choose and the respect of independence."

Olly paused, eyeing Ramona over the paper. She nodded as he continued to the closing passage.

"With the emergence of *The College Girl*, the danger to women increases. It makes a statement that there's one type of woman that will be prized on campus. Making the assertion that one 'ideal' type of woman exists is fundamentally anti-woman and anti-women's rights. Women should not be made to conform to a mold that society has deemed appropriate and pleasant. Every woman is an individual, and we will be our own selves."

Olly whistled long and low before folding the newspaper and handing it back to Ramona. He stretched back in the chair and kicked his long legs out as though lounging in a recliner rather than one of the rigid, plastic chairs that filled the cafeteria.

"Now that's an article."

"Does that mean you like it?" Ramona asked.

"Words have never been my strong suit, so I don't think it matters what I think, but I like it all the same." Olly reached for the bottle of Coke and took a long, lazy gulp. "And I'm sure the faithful readers of *The Daily* will feel the same."

"That's the intent."

After Ramona had told Theo about her idea, he'd contacted the editor of *The Daily*, who had eagerly agreed to run it. As soon as she'd finished writing it yesterday afternoon, she had sent it for printing in today's edition. She smiled down at her words, at her name in black ink. As she considered her article, Ramona once again wondered why Editor Grant Gruffly didn't publish articles like this in his section of *The Seattle Times*. Maybe she would submit her article there too. That idea made her feel better than she had in days. That and seeing Patsy's reaction.

She hoped Patsy was just as surprised by the article as Ramona had been by *The College Girl* campaign. Patsy may have more experience and connections on campus, but Ramona knew she could best her, and satisfaction swelled, knowing that she'd matched Patsy's latest attempt.

If Ramona was being honest with herself, she knew that pushing Patsy had become a major motivator beyond her initial focus to get the curfew extended. And she'd certainly gotten under Patsy's skin. Without realizing it, this had expanded to become more than just pushing back the curfew. This was about women's rights. Extending the curfew no longer felt like enough. It should be removed altogether. Ramona thought of the agenda she'd written. The administration should've accepted her initial request. She wouldn't settle for anything less than equality. Ramona hardly recognized herself.

Olly stood up from the table, drawing her attention back to the moment. "I've got to meet Theo and Don. Good job on the article."

"Thanks, Olly." Ramona nodded.

As he strolled away, Ramona had the urge to call him back and ask him about Mable, but she knew it wasn't her business. Even more, Mable wouldn't want her to. She'd have to ask what she'd been about to say a few days earlier before they'd been distracted by the announcement of the vigilante program in Gauld Square.

Ramona got up to go to the library. Final exams were only two weeks away. She folded the newspaper and slipped it in her bag, set to show it to her mother in a few days when she went home for Thanksgiving.

CHAPTER 28

A shiver ran through Ramona as soon as she stepped outside carrying trays of burgers, fries, and milkshakes. Thank goodness for the tights she wore beneath her uniform skirt. Still, it annoyed her to no end that the waitresses weren't allowed to wear pants as the temperature dipped to the low 40s.

A car filled with beefy teenagers crowded the windows as soon as Ramona appeared to accept their order, relieving her tired arms. Her shift was halfway through, and it felt as though she was on her last ounce of energy. Every day, she felt more tired. She'd been studying late every night, and even when she got to bed, sleep evaded her. She stifled a yawn as she hustled between cars to take new orders.

After dropping them off at the kitchen, Ramona checked in on her tables inside, refilling water along the way. One of her regulars sat at his favorite seat at the bartop.

"Hiya, Frank," Ramona said to the older man as soon as she'd rounded the bar and leaned on the counter across from him. "How's that cheeseburger treating you?"

"Cheesy." Frank grinned at his joke, and if he wasn't such a sweet guy who tipped well, she wouldn't have played along.

"What's on the menu tonight?" Frank continued along the route of their well-worn conversation. He always asked about her own dinner as she served him his.

"Let's see." Ramona took her time, wiping up a ketchup stain on the counter as she considered. "Charlie's hot on chili fries these days, so I gather we're having chili."

Frank nodded. "Chili is good."

"That it is," Ramona said as she scrubbed firmly at a stubborn bit of sauce. "Now that you mention it, I think it's time for my break."

She'd guessed correctly and took her steaming bowl of chili to the back room. Finding the room empty, she sat and held her hands over the bowl while waiting for it to cool enough to eat. Her to-do list rolled through her mind like movie credits. Her English paper needed editing, math homework needed starting, and laundry needing folding awaited her.

Suddenly, her neck felt too weak to support her head. She sucked in a deep breath and closed her eyes. It felt so nice, she decided she could rest them for a few minutes. With her arms folded into a makeshift pillow, Ramona laid her head down.

One sheep.

Two sheep.

Three sheep.

In her mind, sheep shifted to clouds shifted to cotton candy shifted to sand. Then only darkness remained, and she slipped inside as she would the clean sheets on her bed.

"Get up," a voice barked.

Ramona's eyes snapped open. Randy towered over her.

"Sleeping on the job?"

Randy's lip curled back from his teeth. What was Randy doing in her bedroom? She reached for her blanket to cover herself when realization hit her—she'd fallen asleep at work. The bowl of chili sat at room temperature before her. Shit.

"This is the last warning," Randy said. "Anything else and you're out."

Her ever-present stomach ache cramped deep in her belly, and Ramona nodded. She didn't have the energy to object.

"Finish eating and get back out there."

Randy left.

Ramona sighed before shoveling chili into her mouth. Soon after, she dropped the empty bowl off in the kitchen sink and returned to the hungry customers. It felt as though she was watching from outside her body as she hurried from car to car with shaky hands. How could she have fallen asleep? Something must be wrong with her to have messed up so badly. Her control was slipping, and that terrified her.

The next hour passed in a blur as she went through the motions until the bell above the door jingled and broke her trance.

"Ramona?"

Betsy, Cat, and Theo stood at the entrance of Dusty's, looking like they'd just lost their lunch money to the school bully.

Ramona froze behind the counter. "What are you doing here?"

When none of them answered immediately, Ramona knew. Something was wrong.

Theo glanced from side to side. "Is there somewhere we can talk?"

Yes, as long as Randy didn't see them. Ramona gestured toward the door they'd just entered. Randy rarely went outside while on the job, especially when it was this cold.

Ramona led them around the corner toward employee parking, where they had a small amount of privacy.

"Go on," Ramona urged. "I don't have much time."

"I'll tell her," Betsy volunteered. She smoothed the pleats of her maroon skirt and adjusted the belt cinching her waist before continuing. "Someone made copies of pages from the *Women's Anti-Handbook* and put them all over campus."

Ramona sucked in a breath like a pet's squeaky chew toy.

"How could that have happened?"

"Every page got copied, and there are hundreds of them floating around, including the one with the tips for sneaking in after curfew."

The world tilted. Ramona buckled over at the waist and gripped her knees to steady herself. She stared at her white sneakers. Her method for sneaking in had been outed.

"What if they find out I wrote it?" Ramona asked.

Who knew what sort of power AWS had now. Surely, Patsy would go straight to Dean Redley asking for Ramona's suspension, if not something worse. If she lost her scholarship—or worse, was expelled—then she could forget about her degree and her future. As her fears taunted, it felt like the walls of her mind were caving in.

Then she felt a warm palm press against her back and gently rub from side to side.

"Breathe, Ramona," Theo's voice comforted. "They'll never know it was you, or any of us. I'll make sure of it."

Ramona didn't know how he could carry out that promise, but she believed him. Theo always found a way.

He held her until the fears retreated to their home at the edges of her mind. She swallowed tightly before facing each of their pained, apologetic expressions. Anger replaced fear now.

"How did it happen?"

"We don't know," Theo answered. She realized now that his hair was disheveled, as though he'd been pulling at the strands.

"I want to see the copies," Ramona murmured.

She wanted to see what had been done to her beloved *Women's Anti-Handbook*, which she'd put her heart and dreams into over these past couple months. Which they'd all put so much work into.

"We're collecting some back at school," Betsy said.

Ramona nodded. She'd figured as much.

She had to find out how this had happened. They'd distributed ten copies, not including their own. Had one of the women betrayed them on purpose? Or perhaps they'd grown careless and left their copy out for someone else to find. There was a whole range of scenarios, and she'd probably never learn the exact cause. Ramona slammed her palm against the wall of Dusty's in frustration and closed her eyes.

"There's nothing you can do right here or right now," Cat said matter-of-factly. "But we need to learn what Patsy and Dean Redley are going to do next."

Ramona twisted her hair off of her neck because suddenly, she was overheating. Burning up outside in the cold. Dean Redley would be furious when he read the *Women's Anti-Handbook* pages.

"My shift doesn't end for another half hour."

"It's fine," Theo assured. "We'll handle it and meet up tomorrow to figure out what's next."

Needing to be near him, needing the comfort he offered, Ramona wrapped an arm around Theo. She didn't know how she'd get through the rest of her shift without mixing up orders, but she didn't have a choice.

CHAPTER 29

For as long as Ramona could remember, each member of her family sat in the same spot at their dining room table. Of course, the seats weren't assigned and they'd never discussed it. And yet, even now, Ramona, her mother, and her grandparents each sat in their designated places. Rich gravy pooled around mounds of mashed potatoes, soft stuffing, and supple turkey on the four plates before them. In the crevices between, green beans, cranberry sauce, and rolls found space. Too bad Ramona couldn't enjoy it.

The administration had acted quicker than they'd feared. The morning after the copies were released, a new declaration had been made, stating that suspension was the punishment for breaking curfew. Even worse, electricians had already installed alarms on the dormitory exits, which would likely be active by the time the students returned from Thanksgiving break.

She felt like a caged animal. At least Ramona had this long weekend at home where she could continue her shifts undisturbed, but that would only last until her shift one week away. And so, the delicious food that her mother and grandmother had spent hours preparing tasted bland to Ramona.

Across the table, Ramona's mother chewed slowly and watched her. Unable to bear her mother's attention, for Ramona already felt as though she'd failed, she looked toward her grandfather instead.

"All right, Grandpa," Ramona posed. "Are these the best mashed potatoes yet?"

Every Thanksgiving, the four of them focused on the mashed potatoes as the centerpiece of the feast. They'd experimented with the recipe, one that had been passed down rather than written in a cookbook, and the ratio of ingredients. In fact, Ramona first learned her fractions from her grandmother in the kitchen.

"Now let's see," her grandpa answered before taking another bite, as though he hadn't already finished half his plate. He shifted his shoulders from side to side, considering.

"No doubt, they're the best yet."

While all four of them were in on it, her grandma still seemed delighted by the proclamation.

"Dear, do you really mean that?"

Ramona's grandparents faced each other, beaming. "That I do, darling."

Ramona scooped another bite from her own mound of mashed potatoes and agreed with their assessment. They continued eating, the comfortable conversation shifting from the weather, to her mother's job, to the church potluck, and on and on. At some point over the next hour, Ramona's world narrowed to this room and she relaxed, her body loosening after many tense days.

Frank Sinatra crooned from the record player as they finished eating sometime later and shifted to cleaning. Ramona gathered and carried their plates in a neat stack to the kitchen.

"You two relax." Her mother gestured toward the couch. "Ramona and I will clean up."

She carried the wine glasses and remaining plates into the kitchen as Ramona filled the sink with warm, soapy water.

Rolling up her sleeves, Ramona set to work at the sink as dishes and cutlery filled the counter, thanks to her mother. They set a comfortable rhythm as Ramona washed and her mother dried. And as her hands scrubbed, her mind wandered back to campus.

She must have tensed up because soon, her mother asked, "What's wrong, sweetie?"

Ramona bit the inside of her lip, thinking of all that had gone wrong. Her failure to remove the curfew. The exposure of the *Women's Anti-Handbook*. Her slipping grades and the increasing pressure from Randy. The free speech restriction on campus. That other thing that she refused to consider at all. But instead of these, something else surfaced.

"You know Professor Scott?"

Her mother nodded as though she'd expected the question.

"She was my best friend in high school. We'd lost touch, but I stopped by to see her when I dropped you off at school."

"Lost touch?" Ramona scoffed. "She abandoned you when you were pregnant. That's not a friend."

Her mother opened her mouth and then closed it twice before answering, "That's true, and that was very difficult for me. I was furious with her for a long time. All these years later, though, I understand why she'd acted that way, and I can forgive her for it."

Soap bubbles dripped down Ramona's arm, chasing her sleeve.

"How?"

How could something like that be forgiven?

"It took a lot of time and space, but one day, I'd honestly forgotten about it. And then once I had thought of it again, it didn't hurt so badly. And I was fine. I'd made it through, and it made me stronger. Now I'm not saying that Deborah and I are going to be best friends again, but it's not worth my energy to keep holding on to the anger."

Her mother tossed the dish towel across her shoulder and leaned against the counter.

"In fact, that's how I forgave your father."

Ramona stiffened, feeling as though ice filled her veins, and dropped the dish she held into the sink water. She didn't want to talk about that. Every time her father, or rather his absence, had crossed her mind, she pushed it away as if it would infect her.

Ramona muttered, "I'll never forgive him."

Her mother sighed and brushed an errant curl behind Ramona's ear. "I really hope that's not the case, but it's your choice. For me, it all became too heavy. I have a good life, a good family, and that's more than many."

There was a period of childhood, sometime around third grade, when Ramona had asked about her father incessantly. Her mother's vague answers had frustrated her to no end. Eventually, she'd stopped asking even if the need to know remained all these years. The question that haunted her day and night clawed at her now.

"Why did he leave?"

Her mother pressed her lips together and closed her eyes. Wrinkles formed at the edge of her mouth, catching Ramona by surprise. When had her mother aged from the young woman in Ramona's memory?

For a drawn-out moment, Ramona thought her mother wouldn't respond.

"Many reasons. We were young and unmarried, and he was set to go to university. And while I think he loved me, he loved himself more."

Ramona gripped the counter.

"Doesn't it bother you that he has a family now? That someone else is getting what he never gave us?"

"It used to, but not anymore. Because I'm glad that your father turned out to be a good family man, even if he's not a part of our family. Life works out. There are worse things than being a single woman." Her mother winked. "Especially with a daughter whom I love more than anything in this world."

Her mother squeezed her shoulder gently as Ramona turned away to hide her tears.

"Does it bother you?" her mother asked.

Ramona nodded. It hurt more than anything else.

"Why didn't he want me?" Ramona could barely force the words out past her throat.

"Oh, sweetie." Her mother gently wrapped her in a hug. "His decisions had everything to do with him and nothing to do with you."

Her mother held her as tears ran down her cheeks. Ramona felt so safe that everything else rose to the surface.

"Mom, everything is going wrong."

She wiped at her tears with a damp dish towel and squeezed her eyes shut. She hated crying. It made her feel weak.

"Oh, sweetie," her mother repeated.

That did it. Sobs burst from Ramona as she leaned over the counter, crumpling in on herself. She had to fight her throat to take deep breaths. Now that the dam had burst, there was no stopping it. Everything that had gone wrong came to mind, until Ramona dropped to her knees on the linoleum floor and wrapped herself into a ball.

Her mother lowered to the floor beside her, rubbing a comforting hand across her back while Ramona cried. She imagined losing her job at Dusty's and getting kicked out of school for not being able to pay tuition, if she hadn't already been expelled for the *Women's Anti-Handbook*. The wide-open future she'd been building suddenly felt as if it was closing in on her like a tunnel.

She cried for a long while until the tears ran out and her breathing steadied between hiccups. When her voice felt capable, Ramona told her mother about the petition, the *Women's Anti-Handbook* and its exposure, and the tightened rules. She told her about Patsy and how their room felt like a pressure cooker. She told her about the article she'd written for *The Daily*, still tucked into her bag. She told her everything except the one thing that had caused her to wake up in a panicked sweat the past few nights. How could she tell her mother that her period was five days late? She refused to acknowledge it herself. When she finished talking, Ramona looked at her mother through glassy eyes that made her feel as though she was in a snow globe.

"Mom, I'm in so much trouble. I'm going to lose my job, and I can't afford the tuition without it. And what they're doing is wrong! It's not fair the way they treat women."

Her mother took her face between her hands and tilted it toward her own.

"Sweetie, I'm so proud of you."

"What do you mean? I failed." Tears welled again.

"You didn't fail," her mother reassured. "You're brave. You're in a tough spot, but you'll find a way through it. That's not failure, that's perseverance. You will persevere."

Ramona wiped at her raw cheeks.

"Now, you know I'm not the most conventional woman, and that hasn't been easy. For good or bad, unconventional women are noticed. You face a conventional system and want for better. That's a good thing, sweetie. Take it one step at a time, and you will find a way. Think about what the most important thing to you is and start there."

Her mother's encouragement lightened something within her that she hadn't realized weighed so heavily. Ramona wrapped her arms around her mother's shoulders. She didn't know how to move forward yet, but it didn't seem so impossible as the pair sat shoulder to shoulder on the hard floor.

CHAPTER 30

On the first day back from Thanksgiving break, they were all already gathered in the attic to discuss the stunt that Theo said would top all others. At a glance, the large sheet of parchment paper on the floor looked like a treasure map. Squares represented buildings, circles represented themselves, and 'X' marked the spot. But there was no treasure waiting for them—only the chaos that Theo counted on. Ramona and the others watched as he drew an arrow through the squares that ended at the 'X' before sitting back on his heels.

"And that's how we'll get to the construction site without being seen." Theo grinned.

As certain as he appeared, everyone else looked hesitant. Ramona grimaced. She'd done things she wouldn't have believed herself capable of a few months ago, but those were within reason. Those weren't illegal. The punishment, if caught, would surely mean expulsion. The risk was far too great. Burning down the student union building was wrong. She wouldn't do it, and she'd do her damnedest to stop Theo from making a mistake that could haunt him.

Theo looked at the seven of them, his patience thinning in the silence.

"So tell me again. What are we going to do at the construction site?" Olly asked.

Theo nodded, appearing grateful for the engagement. "We're going to climb the fence with a few liters of gasoline. Then we're going to douse the foundation of the building before lighting up the framework."

When Ramona was a child, a pot of chili had caught fire on the stove, and the resulting flames grazed the ceiling. She still remembered screaming and how terrified she'd felt being carried from the room by her mother as her grandfather put out the fire. It had been fine, nothing more serious than a ruined dinner, but the memory of flames clung to her.

"Theo," Ramona said, "this is dangerous."

They may as well have been speaking different languages. Didn't he realize this was wrong?

"I won't let anything happen to you," Theo reassured.

"That's not what I mean. Fire is dangerous … people could get hurt, and not just us."

They had discussed the risks at length, a major one being the potential of hurting others. They'd decided to scope out the construction site to make sure no one else was there before moving forward with their plan, but that wasn't very reassuring when they had little control over a fire that could spread beyond the site.

Theo didn't relent though. "We need to do something serious. If construction of the new student union building is delayed, then they'll have to delay President Johnson coming to speak on campus. It will drive Dean Redley crazy!"

The school had announced that the president of the United States was scheduled to visit campus that spring and speak to the students. A huge honor for the university and city of Seattle. While construction happened all over campus, it was rumored that the student union building was being built specifically for the president's visit.

"Theo, this is illegal," Ramona cautioned.

"Not to mention crazy," Dimitri chimed in. "We can't burn down a building. We'll get expelled, if not arrested." He crossed his arms as though that settled matters.

But Theo couldn't be so easily swayed, and everyone knew it.

Theo stood up and raised his hands as if in surrender. "First of all, it's not a building yet. It's just the wood foundation. But all right, I hear you … the plan has risks. Does anyone have any better ideas?"

When no one answered, Theo continued, "Dean Redley has left us no choice. We've protested and demonstrated peacefully for months, and he hasn't budged on removing the limitation on free speech. We tried it their way with the teach-in, but nothing changed. The war is getting worse, and we're not allowed to protest it."

"But what will burning down a wooden foundation get us?" Betsy asked.

"It will get the Free Speech Movement taken seriously," Theo said. "Besides, they won't know it's us."

"Theo," Dimitri said. "They're going to know, even if they don't have proof."

"They can't do anything without proof," Theo answered before turning to Olly and Don. "Remember when they shut us down last spring? They started this."

Olly nodded and Don actually smiled. Horror dripped through Ramona at the direction this was heading.

Theo turned to Ramona. "Think about the stricter curfew. Dean Redley did that."

True. But burning down a partially built building wouldn't change the curfew. She understood Theo's frustration and bitterness toward campus security and felt her own anger growing thinking about how all their careful planning had led them here. What Theo asked of them wasn't fair.

Sensing her lingering hesitation, Theo continued, "It's okay. You don't need to say anything now. Anyone who wants to do this should meet here at ten tomorrow night when campus is mostly empty. It will be worth it."

"Let's hope so. Otherwise, all this work will have been for nothing," Olly said.

Don grumbled. "Och, don't say that. Bad omen." His knee bounced in rhythm like a soldier's march.

"That's the spirit," Olly said, swatting at his shoulder. "Can always count on you for a positive take on things."

Don glared at him before grunting and looking away.

Suddenly, Ramona's lunch felt as if it may come back up. She had to leave. How were they taking this so lightly when she felt sick?

"I have to go to class." Ramona stood and strode toward the door.

Theo followed Ramona, catching her in the stairwell. He gripped her hand and leaned in until they were nose-to-nose.

"Hey," he whispered. "I know this isn't what you signed up for and that you have a lot going on. If you don't want to be there, you don't have to. I'm never going to ask you to do something you're not comfortable with."

It wasn't just that she didn't want to do it. She didn't want him to go either.

Theo lifted their clasped hands to his mouth. As his lips hovered over her skin, he paused.

"What happened to your fingers?"

Ramona looked down. Blood crusted in the cuticles of her fingernails. She hadn't realized that she'd picked them raw.

"That looks painful."

"It isn't," Ramona said before pulling away from him and rounding her hands into balls. "I'll see you later."

She hurried from the building. Cold wind hit Ramona, causing her to stumble back a step. She tucked her chin to her neck and kept going down the building steps and onto one of the many interwoven paths. She walked aimlessly, unsure where to go or what to do next. She had some time before class. All around her, frazzled students hustled to finish the quarter in good standing. She should be doing the same. She wished finals were her only focus.

After a while, Ramona found herself in the campus garden, a beautiful gem of a place that reminded her of *The Secret Garden*. She slowed to survey the plants, mostly sparse at this point in the season. Still, the beauty calmed her. She meandered between rows of greenery until she turned a corner and froze.

Patsy and Archer stood chest-to-chest, their faces only inches apart. Ramona shuffled back quickly, hoping that they hadn't noticed her. She settled against a bush large enough to cover her body and peered between the branches. Spying seemed like fair payback for Patsy's snooping.

"Dammit, Patsy, leave it alone." Archer gripped Patsy's shoulders as though to keep them both from blowing away in the storm. His blond hair was so wet that it looked dark.

"But—"

"No," Archer barked, cutting her off. "You already nag me like we've been married a decade, and you're not even my wife yet. I don't want to hear what you have to say."

Even from a distance, Ramona could see the glassiness in Patsy's eyes. Patsy had never so much as shed a tear in Ramona's vicinity, and witnessing this felt like an intrusion.

Patsy sucked in a heavy breath, and Archer kissed her firmly on the cheek before walking away. Ramona observed Patsy staring at Archer as he left. She couldn't understand why Patsy would let him talk to her that way. It might pain her to admit it, but Patsy was strong. And Ramona couldn't help feeling sorry for her. Especially the way Archer had said *wife* as though it was a dirty, shameful word.

Unable to stand by a second longer, Ramona stepped out into the rain.

"Are you okay?"

Patsy whipped around, and her eyes raked across Ramona.

"I'm fine."

Ramona nodded in the direction Archer had gone. "It doesn't have to be like that."

Patsy laughed without a trace of humor. "Doesn't it? It's always been this way." She blinked away a tear. "Besides, you're just jealous that no one appreciates you the way Archer appreciates me. He's right. I'm going to make a great wife."

That's not what Ramona had heard, but she didn't feel like pouring salt in a wound. Instead, she took a slow step forward as though approaching an irritable animal. She recognized the expression on Patsy's face.

"What are you so scared of?"

"I'm not scared," Patsy said vehemently.

"I think you are."

"Get away from me." Patsy strode toward her, slamming her shoulder into Ramona, hard.

Rain and wind blurred Patsy's retreating form. As hard as Ramona tried, she couldn't understand why Patsy only seemed to see herself as a wife-to-be. She wanted to hate Patsy without reservation, but now sympathy clouded her disdain. She understood the security that came from holding on to something known rather than risking the unknown.

Ramona stood in the garden for so long that her hair hung heavy with rain, and she had to rush to Public Speaking.

CHAPTER 31

A puddle formed beneath Ramona's seat during the hour-long lecture, and as class ended, her damp clothes and hair clung to her. She wanted to change immediately, so when the bell rang, Ramona stood up alongside everyone else. But she hadn't taken a step before Professor Scott called out to her.

She wasn't surprised. After their last conversation, Ramona had expected Professor Scott to ask to talk again. Still, Ramona had to fight the urge to bolt. She planted her feet to brace herself, as though preparing for battle, although whether internal or external, she didn't know. As the classroom cleared, Ramona remembered her mother's words. That made it easier to stay.

"Hi, Professor."

"Please, would you wait a moment?"

Ramona nodded and leaned against her desk.

"I've been turning over our conversation in my head, and I must apologize. That's not how I intended for it to go. I'm sorry for ambushing you with that information. It's your mother's story to tell."

Professor Scott's eyes looked so bright, so earnest, that Ramona suddenly wanted to cry for the second time in less than a week. So much pain and so, so many years of holding it. For her mother. For herself. Even for Professor Scott. Why did it have to be so hard?

"I talked to my mom this weekend. I still think that what you did was awful, but if she forgives you, that's her choice."

Professor Scott nodded. The women stood in silence until a loud thwack caught their attention as a branch hit the classroom window.

"This storm couldn't pass quickly enough," Ramona mumbled.

"This season makes me miss Arizona," Professor Scott said fondly. "If you have another minute, there's something else I've been curious about. I'll admit, I was surprised to hear Theo's idea for the program."

Cold spread through Ramona's veins.

"What?"

"Theo's idea … for the vigilante program. He came before the faculty council of student affairs and pitched it. It really doesn't seem like him, but Dean Redley was a big proponent, as you can imagine."

No. Professor Scott had it wrong. Ramona's mind raced to connect the pieces. She couldn't understand how Theo was connected to the vigilante program. It went against everything they'd been fighting for and everything Theo believed in.

"There must be a mistake."

Professor Scott must've recognized the pleading in her eyes because she sounded apologetic as she answered, "I saw it happen myself."

How could that be possible? What was Theo thinking? As Ramona stared at her professor, she couldn't stop looking at a mole on her cheek. Had that always been there? Ramona never noticed it before.

"I was sorry to see copies of your *Women's Anti-Handbook* get out too," Professor Scott continued, like a toddler knocking into things with no idea of the consequences. "Patsy presented them to the council, implying that Theo had released those as well, although that was secondhand."

Ramona's mind whirled, desperately trying to catch up. Any minute now, and a sinkhole would open beneath her feet.

"Why would you think I have anything to do with the *Women's Anti-Handbook*?" Ramona asked.

Professor Scott adjusted her glasses on the bridge of her nose. "I saw the pages on your desk when I was passing back an assignment during the beginning of the quarter. And we teachers hear things … about the *Women's Anti-Handbook*, for example. I put two and two together."

With lips pressed shut, Ramona held her professor's gaze without comment.

Eventually, Professor Scott continued, "Can I ask why you would give it to AWS?"

Fury, dark and heavy, descended upon Ramona.

"We wouldn't."

"I'm sorry." Professor Scott hesitated. "I don't understand."

"*We* wouldn't release them. I would never do that, *if* I was involved with the *Women's Anti-Handbook* at all."

"Theo claimed to have received a copy anonymously, and that's what's documented officially, so rest assured that no one will be punished for its creation. But I wanted to tell you that I myself am impressed with the act of feminism."

Ramona squeezed her nails, pressing into her palms, trying to process. It couldn't be. He would never betray her like that.

And yet, someone had made copies of the *Women's Anti-Handbook*.

"I see that I've surprised you again."

Ramona nodded, unable to get words out past her fury just yet. At the same time that Theo asked them to risk expulsion for his plan, he went behind their backs. Her back.

The tree branch scraped against the window again under force of wind, and Ramona winced at the noise. Professor Scott waited until finally, Ramona could speak. And she felt desperate.

"What would you do if your boyfriend not only went behind your back but betrayed your cause too?"

Understanding dawned in Professor Scott's eyes, still rimmed with apology.

"I would confront him," Professor Scott said. "Then I would fix what he'd done."

That's what she'd been thinking too.

Professor Scott continued, "If I may, it sounds like your boyfriend's priorities don't match your own. I'd like to give you a piece of advice."

Professor Scott paused until Ramona indicated for her to continue.

"Eighteen years ago, I made the wrong choice. I prioritized the wrong things, and that's something I've regretted ever since. If I were eighteen again, and if I were you, I would think long and hard on what my priorities are, now and in the future."

All of Ramona's priorities swirled together now, but she had no doubt which ones rose to the top. Her education. Her future.

"Thank you, Professor."

Ramona meant it. She hadn't known she'd need a fresh perspective until she had one.

A plan began to form, which she welcomed like aloe on a sunburn—anything to avoid thinking about what Theo's betrayal meant on a personal level. As much as she wanted to confront him immediately, she needed to have a plan first. If Theo was going to prioritize the Free Speech Movement, she would prioritize getting the curfew removed. She felt like a fool for letting her priorities shift at all. She tamped down the flames that raged within her, forcing her feelings to simmer like coals. She couldn't go there yet. She didn't have much time to take advantage of Theo's plan.

CHAPTER 32

The fluorescent lights overhead cast the bathroom in a dim, yellow-hued glow. Ramona wondered how a light could make a space feel dark, and yet, the campus bathrooms defied all understanding. With her reflection as a companion, Ramona gripped the white, ceramic sink. She'd spent the last few hours in the library, processing what Professor Scott had revealed. Now that she had a plan, she'd confront Theo. But first, she had to do this.

She'd held her bladder for the past hour, but couldn't any longer.

Her breaths were short, as though her lungs were filled with cement. She leaned in and stared at herself in the mirror, eye to eye. She could do this.

Nine days. Her period was now nine days late. Which wasn't unheard of in itself, but she hadn't had sex in the weeks leading up to any of her previous experiences of irregular periods. They had been careful, and yet, there was always a chance. How could she have taken such a risk?

With another shallow breath, Ramona locked herself in a stall before reaching beneath her skirt and gripping the edges of her underwear. She closed her eyes for a beat before pulling them down and sitting on the toilet in one motion. She opened her eyes and moaned.

A stain somewhere between brown and red marked her underwear.

Thank God.

The cement in her chest evaporated with each relieved breath. She clenched her hands into fists and raised them above her head as though she'd won a race. Nine days' worth of worry and fear slipped away as she sat on the cold, plastic toilet seat.

Thank God.

After a shiver shook her, Ramona peed and cleaned off. As she washed her hands, she saw her mother in her reflection this time. The sheer gravity of her relief brought guilt along with it. She'd never questioned her mother's love for her, her whole existence proof of her devotion, but it wasn't the life that either of them wanted for her.

Ramona left the bathroom in a rush and paused in the hallway when a wave of light-headedness hit her. She held on to the wall to steady herself.

From behind, a familiar voice startled her.

"What's wrong?"

Dimitri stood before her with concern clear in his eyes.

After a moment, the dizziness faded, and Ramona regained her control. But even she could hear the unsteadiness in her voice as she answered, "I'm fine."

"Ramona," Dimitri urged.

And for some reason, she felt the overwhelming urge to confide in someone safe. And someone stood before her now.

"I thought I might be pregnant," Ramona said, and when Dimitri's eyes bulged, she continued quickly. "I'm not, but I was terrified. My mother …" Ramona's voice cracked, and she was horrified to realize that she was crying now. Crying with relief and fear and responsibility. "My mother was single when she got pregnant with me, and she was only seventeen. I can't have a baby now."

Dimitri surprised her by wrapping her into a hug as tight as a corset. He held her in the empty hallway. He held her until she didn't need him any longer.

He said, "I'm here."

Her throat burned, and a fresh wave of tears bubbled. Now she felt guilty for a different reason entirely than she had a few minutes ago.

"I'm sorry," Ramona whispered.

"For what?"

Ramona let go of Dimitri and looked up to meet his eyes. "For loving your brother."

Dimitri's eyes fluttered, and his Adam's apple bobbed. Then he shrugged as though a hundred pounds rested on his shoulders. "As long as you're happy."

She couldn't tell him of Theo's betrayal, unwilling to admit her naivety. Or that she still loved someone who had betrayed her. She swallowed the lump in her throat, knowing that she didn't deserve his kindness.

"Thank you, Dimitri."

"Always."

Ramona stepped from his embrace, feeling stronger now. And the strength from one brother gave her the courage to find the other. She said goodbye to Dimitri and went in search of Theo, her anger and determination surfacing with each step. Outside, gray clouds filled the sky, and brown leaves that were yellow only weeks ago were scattered across the paths.

Fifteen minutes later, after imagining all the things she wanted to say to Theo, she found him in the attic, alone.

Theo looked up in alarm as soon as she flung the door open. Then his eyes brightened when he registered it was her. He sat on a windowsill with a book.

"Boy, am I glad to see you," Theo said.

You won't be for long.

She stood with her feet spread wide and placed her hands on her hips, yards from Theo.

"How could you?"

The book dropped from Theo's hand as he considered her. His eyebrows tugged together, an expression she usually loved because it showed his concentration. She waited. Then realization dawned as his eyes widened.

"Ramona—"

"Don't." She stomped toward him, getting in his face and pressing a finger against his chest. "I want you to tell me why you went behind my back—behind all of our backs—because I can't imagine everyone else being okay with what you did."

Until Professor Scott told her, she couldn't have imagined him being okay with it.

"I did it for the good of the group."

Ramona's eyes widened. "Oh, that's convenient."

"It's true," Theo urged. "In order to make change, we need power. And how do we get power? We need attention and support from the students. Competition drives innovation. So I came up with the idea for the program so that students would be so angry, they'd join our cause and push for student rights."

"That's crazy! That goes against everything we stand for. Think of how many students are going to get into trouble because of your plan."

At least he looked regretful as he said, "Well, that's the downside."

"The downside?" Ramona barked, incredulous. "Theo, I won't be able to sneak in from my job!"

A crow peered at them from its perch on the pine tree just outside the window. Its beady, black eyes glimmered, and Ramona could have sworn that it stared right at her as it cawed long and loud.

"Please," Ramona continued, "make me understand."

She was desperate for him to fix this. For this to be a big misunderstanding because right now, everything she held dear—her education, her job, women's rights on campus, hell, even her relationship—hung in the balance. Suddenly, Dimitri's warning came to mind, and she clenched her hands into fists.

"The administration and AWS were playing it cautiously. We needed them to do something big to give us, the students, something to react to," Theo explained.

The spit in Ramona's mouth tasted like ash.

"That's manipulation, Theo," Ramona said. "You were instigating and creating fake situations."

He had the nerve to look hurt at that. "I don't see it that way."

The usually high attic ceilings crowded in on them. She narrowed her eyes.

"What about the *Women's Anti-Handbook*?"

Guilt crawled over Theo's features. "I wanted to give us a reason to push harder. I wanted to do something the students couldn't ignore."

And that's what it all came down to. Theo couldn't get over the fact that some students simply didn't care. To him, that was unacceptable, so he would shock them into outrage. Shock them into caring.

He paced in his familiar pattern across the attic.

"You have to understand," he urged, throwing his hands into the air. "I've been working toward this for three years."

"I don't have to do anything, Theo Rhodes," Ramona snarled. "You know how hard I worked on that *Women's Anti-Handbook*, and then you go and blow it. And now I'm going to lose my job!"

She panted, her breath coming hard now.

Theo stiffened as if she'd hit him before letting out his breath like a deflating balloon. "I didn't think of that." He came toward her with open arms, but she turned her back. She didn't want to be touched by him. "I'm so sorry."

"You really didn't think of the repercussions?" Ramona whispered, stunned by his shortsightedness. She raked her hands through her hair.

"I was trying to do the right thing," Theo said. "I promise that I didn't mean to get in the way of your sneaking in."

"You can tell yourself that you were doing this for the good of the Free Speech Movement, but really, you're just selfish."

Theo's face crumpled, and silence hung heavy between them. He hovered at her side but didn't get within a couple feet of her. Good.

Finally, he said, "Please, Ramona. Just tell me what I need to do to make it up to you. Hell, I'll help pay for your tuition until you find another job."

And for some reason, his offer pushed her over the edge. She whimpered as tears spilled down her cheeks, and she wrapped her arms around her middle. Maybe that would keep her from bursting like a dam. Ever since he'd suggested arson, she'd refused to acknowledge that his intentions differed from hers. Denial tasted bitter. But now, she knew he asked for too much and went too far. As much as she loved him, she wouldn't sacrifice her values for him. She wouldn't sacrifice herself.

Behind her, Theo repeated how sorry he was, but Ramona went to the window without responding. She pressed her forehead against the glass and closed her eyes, tuning out Theo's words. After a long while, she opened her eyes to see that the crow had gone.

CHAPTER 33

While other students studied for final exams, Ramona went to speak with the university president. She had to trust that Professor Scott had been correct when she'd said that the council had no proof of who'd created the *Women's Anti-Handbook* and that she'd be safe in speaking with President Howard. She needed him in order for her plan to work.

She'd found clarity in the early hours of the morning. By midnight, the lounge had emptied of all others, and Ramona had stayed there until dawn, reflecting on all that had happened. Her world had grown so quickly, her responsibilities expanding beyond herself. She'd arrived on campus with one goal in her heart—to graduate and build her own life. While that hadn't changed, she felt herself pulled in new directions that she'd never expected. She thought of all the women she'd befriended ... Mable, Betsy, Cat, everyone at their *Women's Anti-Handbook* party ... and she wanted to help them too. As the moon sailed through the sky, Ramona plotted how to do just that.

The idea struck while she drank her third cup of steaming apple cider. Ramona grinned into her mug, feeling like the

Cheshire cat, as she imagined how she'd convince President Howard to agree to her proposal. Once satisfied with her approach, she went to bed for a few hours of much-needed sleep.

Now Ramona's heels clicked on the stones of Gauld Square, her skirt swirling around her legs with each step. She wondered how it was possible that her first quarter of college was almost over, a quarter that seemed so much longer than three months. If all this could happen in such a short amount of time, what could she do in four years?

When she reached the administration building, the metal handle chilled Ramona's hand as she heaved the front door open. She retraced her steps from that first week of the quarter toward the secretary's office, but this time, she'd go straight to the top.

When the office came into view, Ramona patted her curls before walking inside. The secretary looked up with a pleasant smile.

Good, she doesn't recognize me.

"Do you have an appointment?"

Straight to business then.

"Uh … no, I don't." And when the secretary frowned, Ramona rolled forward, "But President Howard will want to see me."

Ramona had to talk with President Howard before Theo's plan for that night. There were only a few hours left.

The secretary sighed, looking smug. "I'm sure you think so, but most things are not truly urgent. Let's schedule an appointment for next week."

The secretary turned to a booklet and lifted a pen, but Ramona held her ground. "I need to see President Howard—now."

The secretary's face pinkened, surely preparing to dig her heels in, when Ramona had a stroke of luck. President Howard appeared in the doorway.

"I'll admit I'm curious." Then he turned to the secretary and said, "It's all right, Mrs. Davis. I have a few minutes."

Satisfaction flooded Ramona as President Howard gestured for her to follow him inside his office. The furniture looked similar to Dean Redley's, and yet somehow, the room didn't feel nearly as repellent. He sat down behind his desk, and Ramona took her own seat across from him, doing her best to subtly wipe her clammy palms on her skirt in the process.

He studied her for a moment, and rather than shying away, Ramona met his gaze. She'd study him right back.

"You look familiar," he finally said. "Have you made an appointment to see me before?"

"No," Ramona answered.

"Interesting," President Howard answered, looking unconvinced. Then his eyes widened. "You were a part of that horrid human chain demonstration."

She didn't see any point in denying it, so she nodded.

"I knew it. I can't believe Dean Redley almost …"

The president stopped himself, likely remembering who he spoke to, and pivoted. "Beside the point. Now, why do I want to talk with you?"

Ramona sat forward in the chair and felt grateful for Professor Scott's class as she began her speech for an audience of one. "President Howard, I have information that you want to know. It pertains to the safety and security of this campus."

President Howard's eyes darkened. "Go on."

"I'm willing to tell you what I know so that you can put a stop to it, but I need something in return."

A bead of sweat ran from her armpit down the underside of her arm.

"Are you bargaining with me?"

Good. He finally got it.

For a moment, her tongue refused to cooperate, as though it had been glued to the bottom of her mouth. Something in her thrashed against the idea of negotiating with a person in such a position of power. All her life, she'd been taught to respect her elders and follow the rules, and if there was ever a moment that showed how far she'd come, it was this one. In another life, a different version of herself would tell President Howard everything with nothing in return. But not in this one.

At some point over the past few months, her loyalty to her friends overrode her need to follow the rules. Friends who'd welcomed her into their circle wholeheartedly. Ramona considered how she'd felt on the first day on campus—a small person in a big world—and now she felt more confident in herself than she'd ever thought possible. Her lingering conformity made her tongue rebel now, but President Howard's patience visibly drained before her eyes.

Ramona took a deep breath to steel herself. She would do the right thing by herself and by the women of this school.

Forcing her tongue into action, Ramona answered, "As a matter of fact, I am."

It was clear from the change in his facial expression that the president hadn't taken her seriously upon inviting her in, but he did now. He looked at her with something that resembled respect. President Howard tugged at his tie.

"What is it you want?"

Ramona crossed her legs and leaned forward.

"I'm glad you asked."

CHAPTER 34

While the trees were the focal point on campus during the day, the lamps stole the show at night. Gothic-style lanterns stood guard every few yards along the walkways, looking like they'd been transplanted from Europe, along with the beautiful, brick buildings.

Ramona crouched in front of Mable and behind Olly, who knelt behind Don. In front of him came Cat, then Betsy, then Dimitri, and finally, Theo in front. They had each shown up tonight. They hid within the bushes near enough to see the lamps, but not so close that they would be visible within the yellow glow. Theo had made it clear that traveling on the walkways wasn't an option. Instead, they'd stepped gingerly through the bushes in the darkness, careful not to snap twigs beneath their feet. They formed a chain, each holding on to the person in front of them. It reminded Ramona of a trust exercise they'd done at summer camp when she'd been a child.

Now, they waited for the signal. Up ahead, Theo peered through the bushes to see whether the area was clear. It was critical that they go unseen.

The deserted campus felt like an alternate universe. Ramona could hardly believe that it had come to this, that they crouched in the shadows in order to pull off the stunt of a lifetime. After what seemed like a very long time, Ramona felt Olly reach back and squeeze her arm. The signal. Ramona reached back to squeeze Mable's hand before they slowly stood as a unit and crept forward like a train slowly accelerating out of the station.

The lamps had a helping hand tonight from the silver glow of the moon. That wasn't great, as it left them more exposed. Ramona's nerves flared. So many ways for the plan to go wrong.

"Ouch, go easy," Olly whispered.

Ramona loosened her grip on Olly's hand, not realizing how tightly she'd been gripping him with her fingernails.

They walked in a single-file line and emerged from the bushes. Ramona felt oddly exposed as the wind blew her hair against the nape of her neck, and a chill shuddered through her. They'd each worn dark clothing to blend in with the night.

After a few minutes, their slow movements speeding up the closer they got, the construction site came into view. A chain-link fence sealed off the area, but they'd planned for that. They'd find a gap or jump it. They reached the fence, and the boys put down the red, gallon containers of gasoline they held. Cat held the matches. The guys scoped out the fence, looking for an opening.

Theo's voice was laced with frustration when he spoke a minute later, "The fence is shut tight. We're going to have to jump it. Dimitri and I will go first and help the girls over. Then Don and Olly will pass us the containers before jumping themselves. All right?"

The others whispered their agreement as Ramona craned her neck, peering from side to side.

"Let's go." Theo turned around and braced his hands wide on the fence, preparing to climb. He pulled himself up, and the metal groaned beneath his weight.

"Damn kid," Olly teased. "Eat much?"

"Shut up," Theo called back, taking another step up, his shoe barely finding a hold in the small openings.

As soon as Theo scaled the fence, Dimitri climbed up and quickly joined him on the other side. They held their arms out to help the rest over.

"Ramona and Mable, you go first," Betsy said, pushing them toward the fence.

The metal fence was so cold, it stung Ramona's skin. She took a deep breath before gripping it tightly and moved as slowly as possible to ascend alongside Mable. Before they made it to the top, a flash of light crossed Ramona's face and disappeared. Anticipation flooded her veins.

"What was that?" Betsy asked as they all searched for the source.

Ramona looked at Theo through the fence for some signal. Normally so certain, his nerves now troubled her. His eyes shifted wildly, searching for something before settling on the containers of gasoline.

"Change of plans," Theo said. "Toss over the containers, but stay on that side."

Shit. The gasoline needed to remain on this side of the fence.

"No way," Don said, taking a step toward the fence.

"Just do it." Theo gritted his teeth. "Ramona, Mable, jump down so that Don and Olly can throw us the gas."

"Theo," Ramona whispered as she moved to climb back down with Mable. "Maybe we should call this off."

He shook his head. "It's going to work."

Don still looked pissed, but as soon as Ramona and Mable were back on the ground, he and Olly hoisted the containers under their arms and climbed to sit on top of the fence.

"Are you sure you don't want us down there too?" Olly asked.

"Yes," Theo practically growled. "Hurry the fuck up."

Don and Olly dropped the containers into Theo and Dimitri's arms, and it was a good thing they were capped because it was a long fall, and the gasoline inside sloshed the whole way down. The edge of the building stood only a few yards away, giving them all a clear view. Theo went first, uncapping the container and splashing the gasoline across every piece of accessible wood. And seeing Theo do something so blatant, so dangerous, pulled Ramona from herself as though she were watching the whole thing from behind a television screen. Suddenly, terror filled her that he would accidentally light himself on fire.

"Theo, be careful!"

His eyes glowed in the darkness as their eyes met, and by the way his crinkled, she knew he was grinning in the way that made her heart swell. He would be fine. He had to be.

Theo continued to pour, and Dimitri uncapped his own container. Then suddenly, light illuminated the scene. The brightness blinded them after being in the darkness for so long, and Ramona covered her face. She peered through her fingers, fighting to make out what was happening.

Three figures appeared and were quickly closing in on Theo and Dimitri with flashlights raised.

"Fuuuuuck," Olly said, drawing out the word.

Theo threw his container to the ground and swatted the one that Dimitri held.

"Run!" Theo shouted to them as he shoved Dimitri toward the fence.

Well practiced, Olly and Don each jumped down and sprinted in opposite directions.

"Come on." Betsy pulled at Cat and Mable. They ran, but Betsy noticed that Ramona hadn't moved. "What are you doing?"

"Go on," Ramona said. "I'll be right there!"

She had to see what happened. Maybe she could get Theo away.

Dimitri was halfway up the fence now with Theo standing below him, shoving him higher, faster. The figures closed in on them, and a cold feeling settled in Ramona as she realized that only one of them would make it out in time. Soon, Dimitri climbed over the top of the fence, and Theo's gaze shot to Ramona with concern. Then his body slammed into the fence with the force from behind.

"Go!" Theo shouted, his voice muffled, as an officer held him against the metal wire.

No, no. This wasn't the plan. They were supposed to get away.

Ramona lunged for Theo, trying to touch him through the fence. But it didn't make a difference as Theo scuffled with the officer, who attempted to pin his arms behind his back. The pair squabbled until another officer was on them, and Theo fell to the ground. The second officer kneed Theo twice, hard, in his ribs. Theo grunted in pain and Ramona shouted.

"Don't hurt him!"

He had to stop fighting back, or they'd keep hitting him. This wasn't a part of the deal. She'd done this to save him, to save them all from doing something catastrophic.

Ramona gripped the fence and shook it, trying to get their attention.

"I don't think that's a wise idea, Miss Bronson, do you?"

Ramona froze. Shit. She recognized his voice, but he wasn't supposed to be here. Slowly, she turned around and saw Dean Redley walking toward them. Theo looked at Ramona in confusion, trying to place the voice of the man he couldn't yet see.

"I have to admit, I was skeptical when President Howard told me about the story you told him. I thought this might be another one of your pranks. But you've followed through on your word, and he'll follow through on his."

The flashlight continued shining on Theo, and the confusion on his face morphed to surprise, and then understanding, and then anger.

Dean Redley continued, "As of tomorrow, December 6, the curfew on female students will be removed."

From the ground, Theo looked up at her sharply. Understanding and then betrayal flashed across his eyes, but she could have sworn she saw a glimpse of awe as well in the moonlight. Then his body relaxed as he gave up the fight. The officers holding him down finally got Theo's arms behind his back and handcuffed him. Ramona gasped, turning toward Dean Redley.

"What are they doing?"

"You didn't really expect us to let you all go without punishment, did you? You were planning to set a fire, after all. Young Theo Rhodes is being arrested for intent to commit arson."

"No!" Ramona shouted and tried to grab Theo through the fence when another officer appeared and pinned her arms behind her back. Theo, now handcuffed, bucked against the officer holding him, trying to get to Ramona, and her throat burned at his protectiveness, even after what each of them had done to one another. The officers led Theo away, and Ramona hated that it had come to this. But as she replayed Dean Redley's statement in her mind, she didn't feel an ounce of regret.

CHAPTER 35

As usual, the lobby of Wolden Hall was packed this morning. Ramona normally resented the crowding, but she was glad for the audience now. Even though she should've been exhausted, she didn't sleep last night after seeing Theo get arrested. Adrenaline thrummed through her as she made her way through the women toward the bulletin board. She held her head high, just as she'd seen her mother do a thousand times when others stared.

Ramona reached for the giant, pink poster proclaiming the recent curfew restriction. The room hushed as she gripped the corner and pulled sharply, tearing it from the staple. She crumpled the poster into a ball, and the sound jarred the silence.

She turned toward the women of Wolden and announced, "The curfew's been removed."

Stunned silence greeted her first, with many skeptical faces.

"Really," Ramona urged. "It's true."

The women looked between one another until their skepticism morphed into wary joy. When their eyes brightened, Ramona felt it in her chest. This was their win too.

Ramona shoved the crumpled poster into her bag just as Patsy appeared before her.

"Can I talk to you?"

Surprised by the vulnerability in Patsy's tone, Ramona nodded and led the way upstairs. They didn't need an audience. While she didn't know why Patsy wanted to talk, this conversation had been a long time coming after months of tension housed in one 15' x 15' room.

As soon as they reached their room, Patsy crossed her arms.

"So you got what you wanted after all," Patsy said.

Satisfaction swirled within Ramona. She was still coming to terms with all that had happened in the last forty-eight hours.

"*We* did," Ramona said firmly. "Most female students want this. Hell, this is what a good portion of the male students want too. Not that I care much about their opinion on this particular matter."

Patsy walked to Ramona's side of the room and picked up her tube of dark lipstick. She uncapped it, and her lip curled in disgust.

"You created a *Women's Anti-Handbook* that goes against everything I've worked—" Patsy stopped, reconsidering her own words. "Everything AWS stands for."

Ramona opened her mouth but paused before the retort escaped her. She was about to say that it wasn't personal, but that wasn't entirely true. Instead she said, "AWS needs a more modern approach."

Patsy huffed and shook her head. "You ask for too much."

"How can equality be too much?" Ramona gritted her teeth. "We ask for what's rightfully ours."

Ramona's hands clenched at her sides, and her nails dug uncomfortably into her palms. Each of their chests rose and fell quickly, and the sounds of their heavy breathing filled the room.

Ramona snatched her lipstick from Patsy and leaned toward the mirror. She twisted the tube and coated her bottom lip once, then her top lip twice. She saw Patsy watching her through the mirror as she recapped the lipstick.

"Why do you care so much?" Ramona asked. "We're both women, almost the same age, and students at this school, yet we feel so differently. I wonder why that is."

"Why do I care?" Patsy said as though Ramona had accused her of cheating on a test. "This is all I have!"

Ramona stiffened, surprised by her outburst, and turned around to face her. Patsy's eyes brimmed with tears as she ripped her headband off and threw it on her bed.

"Once I get married," Patsy went on, "I'll be a wife and then a mother, and that's it. At least here, I can be the president of AWS. I'll never have this chance to lead again. And you risked taking even that away."

Ramona felt as if she'd been punched in the gut. Patsy, a twenty-one-year-old woman, may have just broken Ramona's heart. And suddenly, she saw Patsy. *Actually* saw her. In modern society, most women had a tiny window—if any window at all—to be independent. That's what Ramona was fighting to change. Maybe Patsy held on to that shard of independence rather than asking for more for fear that it could all be taken away instead.

Patsy smoothed her hair behind her ears with shaking fingers. She looked less like the enemy whom Ramona knew. She looked like a woman with little hope or control. And Ramona understood helplessness well.

Ramona sighed. She stepped forward to rest her hand softly on Patsy's arm.

"That's not true. It might not seem like it, but this is only the start. It won't be easy, but you can be more than you think. You can be more than a wife and a mother. We all can."

Patsy stared down at Ramona's hand before pulling her arm away.

"What you're saying isn't possible. At least not in our lifetime. Maybe one day, but today isn't that day."

Patsy's response sounded like shattering glass. Ramona couldn't accept a world so dire. Wouldn't.

Then Patsy whispered, "As much as I wish it could be so."

Her eyes held Ramona's for a moment before she strode from the room. As soon as Patsy had gone, Ramona tucked her arms around her waist as though holding herself together. Exhaustion, sadness, and relief swirled at finally having an honest conversation. The worst part was that Patsy felt resigned to the fate she'd spoken of. But Ramona believed in something different. Of a world where women weren't defined by their role in the family unit, but as worthy, independent humans themselves. And that glimmer of hope fueled Ramona.

Without knowing it, Patsy had given her one more reason, one more person, to keep fighting for.

Then realization struck with such force that Ramona had to sit on her bed. Being raised by a single mother had allowed her to escape the patriarchy within her own home, giving her a respite from the damaging messages that women received incessantly about their "role" in society. Ramona might absorb that message outside, but at home, she could be anything. For the first time, she felt grateful for the familial structure that she had grown up feeling ashamed of. Without it, she might be just like Patsy.

After a few moments, Ramona's breathing steadied. She unwound her arms from her body as she calmed. Then an idea struck. She went to her dresser and lifted her mother's hand mirror. The solid weight of it felt comforting in her hand. There were many times these past few months when she didn't feel like herself, when the changes felt more encompassing than the consistencies. Now, Ramona felt that distance from herself slip away, like removing a coat after coming inside from a storm. The mirror showed a new version where she was more like herself than she ever had before. She hadn't realized how much she'd been holding herself back until she put herself out there. Staring in her own eyes, where tears pooled, pride swelled at how far she'd come.

CHAPTER 36

Campus police had held Theo in jail for one night. Not long, but enough that Ramona felt bad. He'd gotten off with a citation, as it was his first serious offense, and they'd only trespassed with the intent to commit arson, rather than actually having done so. It was a good thing that the officers had arrived when they had. Ramona leaned against the counter at Dusty's now, having just switched off the "open" sign, as a lump formed in her throat upon remembering Theo's expression when they'd talked yesterday.

He'd been waiting for her on a bench outside of her last class of the day. She'd sighed, knowing that the conversation was unavoidable, and went to sit beside him.

"How could you do it?" he'd asked. Shadows as purple as squashed blackberries hung below his eyes.

"How could *you*?" Ramona had snarled back.

He'd pulled at the ends of his hair. "I thought I was doing the right thing."

"Me too," Ramona had parroted once more. "Dean Redley kept his word. The curfew is done."

"I heard. For what it's worth, I'm really glad. It was a bullshit rule."

They had sat quietly for a few minutes as Ramona thought of a hundred things to say. Finally, she'd decided on the most honest.

"I'm so mad at you, Theo. I don't know if I'll ever *not* be angry about what you did."

He had bent at the waist to rest his elbows on his knees and his face in his hands. "I know. And I'm angry too. Although, I don't know if I'm angrier about you ratting us out or angry at myself because you'll probably never want to be with me again."

Ramona had caught the hopeful way he'd included "probably."

"I don't know if I can be," she'd whispered.

Theo had sat up and leaned in close to her. His eyes shone as he'd gently, oh so gently, brushed his thumb across her cheek and cupped her chin. She leaned into his hold.

"You know where to find me. I'm sorry, Ramona."

She had no regrets about what she'd done, but she hated watching him grow smaller as he walked away. She didn't know what lie ahead for them, except that she needed time. Too much had happened too quickly.

Ramona blinked away a rogue tear and swallowed the lump. She surveyed the empty diner and its crumb-covered tables. That was enough thinking of Theo for now. She grabbed a wet rag and swayed slowly to the music coming from the kitchen. Across the diner, the clock read 12:21.

Water dripped from the rag down her arm. Grossed out, Ramona wiped her arm against her apron pocket before remembering that it held her tips. She quickly checked that the bills were safe but felt the dampened paper of the local section of *The Seattle Times* that she'd put there earlier. For the thousandth time, maybe more, she thought of Editor Grant Gruffly. She'd succeeded in getting the curfew removed without an article in his section of *The Seattle Times*. In fact, she'd lived her entire life without him.

When Ramona was a child, so young that she still believed in Santa Claus, her mother had spoken of her father. Grant Gruffly had dreamt of attending college to study journalism and nothing, or rather no one, would get in his way. Ramona's mother had assured her that they'd loved each other ever since they'd met as lifeguards at the local swimming pool, and that though it might not seem like it, he loved Ramona as well. Ramona hadn't been convinced then, and she surely wasn't now. But that didn't feel so important anymore. Maybe she'd inherited writing from him rather than love. A gift.

Throughout her life, his absence had made her chest feel hollow, as though her lungs had been replaced with an unwound spool of thread. But now she couldn't imagine where Grant Gruffly, where a father, fit into her life. She'd spent so much energy trying to resolve the absence of her father, and now she realized she didn't have to do that anymore. She knew enough to find him if she should ever want to, but for now, she didn't. She finally believed her mother when she'd said that his absence spoke of his character rather than hers.

Her mother talked of forgiveness, but that wasn't quite how Ramona would describe what she felt now. Not forgiveness, no. But acceptance. She didn't want to carry that pain with her anymore. She didn't have space for it.

Ramona crumpled the newspaper and tossed it into the trash can beneath the counter. Maybe she would no longer scan the newspaper for his name anymore.

She thought of her mother. She'd sounded good when they'd spoken on the phone earlier that day. When Ramona had told her what happened in the last week, she'd recognized the pride and worry that came hand in hand in her mother's voice.

"Oh, sweetie," her mother had said, "you did it."

She had. Never again would a female student on their university campus be limited to a curfew. Ramona could get into her car after her shift and go as far as she wanted. She could drive all night toward Portland, or even farther toward San Francisco. She could go anywhere at any time. And that was the point. The freedom to choose.

Ramona didn't know what came next, but she knew she wouldn't stop with the curfew removal. The agenda she'd written came to mind. But she'd think about that tomorrow. For now ... for tonight ... she had one more thing to do instead.

Once the counter shone, she tossed the rag back in the bucket and returned her apron to its hook beneath the counter before putting on her coat. Instead of leaving, she went to the back of the diner. Ramona flung Randy's office door open and marched in. He looked up from a magazine with wide eyes.

"May I speak with you?"

He nodded. "Sure."

Ramona squared her shoulders. "It's time that we did something about the uniforms. It's only going to get colder over the next few months, so it's a perfect time to change things up."

Randy shifted in his chair, and she cut him off as he opened his mouth.

"I've made a few inquiries and outlined the options and associated pricing here."

She pulled a packet of paper from the folder gripped under her arm and handed it over.

"The girls and I are sick of freezing most of the year, not to mention the looks that we get from the male customers. Now, it's been a few years since new uniforms were ordered, and the pricing for a new style is the same as ordering the old ones, so it makes sense to reconsider. Let me know which option you think is best."

After a moment of shocked silence, Randy found his tongue. "All right. I guess I can take a look."

"Great," Ramona nodded. "You do that."

Ramona shut the folder and was about to turn when Randy asked, "Hey Ramona?"

"Yeah?"

"I'm glad it all worked out."

Now that was a surprise. Randy wasn't one for unnecessary kindness.

"Me too. Have a good night."

Ramona strode from the office and toward the front door of Dusty's. She felt lighter than she had in months. Really, she felt lighter than she could ever remember. She pressed a palm against the metal door handle and stepped into the cold night air just as the clock overhead read half past midnight.

ACKNOWLEDGMENTS

To my family–Mom, Dad, Kate, and Sarah–and friends, thank you for your endless encouragement. There hasn't been a single instance that I've mentioned this story when you haven't lit up with excitement. You called me an author long before I did.

Thank you Kerry, Heather, Jennifer, and Devon for reading many early drafts and for rooting for Ramona all the while. How lucky am I to have found such a wonderful group of writing critique partners?

Special thanks to the team at Black Rose Writing for believing in this story, and for all of the incredible work required to publish a book.

Thank you, Joyce Mochrie, for your superb copy editing work.

Thank you, Luise Jacobs, for your creativity and artistic vision in designing a cover that so perfectly represents Ramona's story.

And finally, thank you, reader, for choosing to read this story out of so many. I'm forever grateful.

ABOUT THE AUTHOR

Author photo: Post Productions

Samantha Quamma lives in Seattle, Washington. When she's not writing about women making their place in the world, she's working in the technology industry and chipping away at her yearly reading goal.

A Future of Her Own is her first novel.

NOTE FROM SAMANTHA QUAMMA

Word-of-mouth is crucial for any author to succeed. If you enjoyed *A Future of Her Own*, please leave a review online—anywhere you are able. Even if it's just a sentence or two. It would make all the difference and would be very much appreciated.

Thanks!
Samantha Quamma

www.ingramcontent.com/pod-product-compliance
Lightning Source LLC
Jackson TN
JSHW020942030125
76403JS00003B/125

* 9 7 8 1 6 8 5 1 3 5 4 7 8 *